Books by Greg Herren

BOURBON STREET BLUES

JACKSON SQUARE JAZZ

Published by Kensington Publishing Corporation

BOURBON STREET BLUES

Greg Herren

KENSINGTON BOOKS
http://www.kensingtonbooks.com

KENSINGTON BOOKS are published by

Kensington Publishing Corp.
850 Third Avenue
New York, NY 10022

All Kensington titles, imprints and distributed lines are available at special quantity discounts for bulk purchases for sales promotion, premiums, fund-raising, educational or institutional use.

Special book excerpts or customized printings can also be created to fit specific needs. For details, write or phone the office of the Kensington Special Sales Manager: Kensington Publishing Corp., 850 Third Avenue, New York, NY 10022. Attn. Special Sales Department. Phone: 1-800-221-2647.

ISBN 0-7582-0213-X

First Hardcover Printing: April 2003
First Trade Paperback Printing: March 2004
10 9 8 7 6 5 4 3 2 1

Printed in the United States of America

This is dedicated, again, to Paul
with all my heart and soul.

ACKNOWLEDGMENTS

I would be terribly remiss if I didn't thank the people who helped me bring this book to its conclusion with their caring, belief, and support.

John Scognamiglio at Kensington Books has been an absolute dream to work with. Thanks, John, for believing in Scotty and helping me to bring him and his crazy world to life.

Julie Smith, as always, was a source of excellent advice and a great sounding board to bounce ideas off of.

My wonderful partner, Paul Willis, is a constant source of love and support and inspiration. Thanks, honey, for saying those magic words to me: "You should write a book about Decadence!"

And definitely thanks to the following people, who, either directly or indirectly, helped me in some way during the writing of this book: Jeffrey Jasper, Tom Hellenthal, Heidi Haltiner, Ken Thistlewaite, Marshall Moore, Jay Quinn, Victoria Brownworth, Katherine Forrest, Nancy Garden, Felice Picano, Mark Richards, Marika Christian, Kelly Smith, J. M. Redmann, Jim Gladstone, William J. Mann, and anyone else who I have forgotten.

I used Eden Gray's *Mastering the Tarot* for information on the tarot card deck, and the chapter headings.

And of course, the city of New Orleans, for being a constant source of joy and inspiration for me.

PROLOGUE

The name's Dansoir. Dick Dansoir.

Okay, so that really isn't my name. It's my stage name from the days when I was on the go-go-boy circuit. I started when I was in college, at Vanderbilt up in Nashville. As with almost everything that goes on in my life, I became a go-go boy on a fluke. The Goddess brings interesting experiences into my life all the time. Sometimes I don't think it's all that great, to tell the truth, but she always seems to be watching out for me.

I was working out at my gym one day when this guy came up to me and asked me if I wanted to make some easy money.

Like I hadn't heard that one before.

I was twenty-one at the time, just turned, but I wasn't some wide-eyed dopey innocent. I was raised in the French Quarter, after all, and by the time I went off to college at age eighteen I had pretty much seen everything. French Quarter kids have a lot more life experience than other kids their age. You can't really help it. The French Quarter is like Disneyland for adults, and growing up there, you get used to seeing things that other people can only imagine.

Anyway, this guy said he was booking agent and scout for this agency that booked dancers in gay bars throughout the deep South. The troupe was called Southern Knights.

"You can make a lot of money this way," he said to me above the sounds of people grunting and weights clanging. "You've got the look we like."

I looked at myself in one of the mirrors that are everywhere in gyms. I was wearing a white tank top and a pair of black nylon jogging shorts. I was pumped up from lifting, and if I did say so myself, I looked pretty good. I'm only about five-eight—nine if I have thick-soled shoes. I have curly blond hair that's darker underneath. The sun does lighten it, but that darkness always makes people think I dye it. I don't. I have big, round brown eyes. I am also one of those blonds who is lucky enough to be able to tan. I'd gotten a good tan that summer and it hadn't faded yet. The white tank top showed the tan off nicely. I also have a high metabolism and can stay lean rather easily.

But scam artists are everywhere, and I wasn't about to fall for a line from some older guy. For all I knew, it was a trick to get my phone number, or an escort service, or something else I didn't want to be involved in.

Not that I have anything against escorting. People go to escorts for all kinds of reasons—loneliness, fear of commitment, whatever—but they do fulfill a need in the gay community, and more power to them. I just never saw myself taking money from someone for having sex. I like sex. I enjoy it. So, it just never seemed right for me to take money for doing something I like.

Besides, taking money for it would make it work. I prefer to keep my status amateur.

He handed me a business card. "Give me a call, and we can get you started."

I kept the card. I put it up on the bulletin board over my desk in my tiny little one-room apartment. I originally told myself it was a souvenir, a memory of a flattering moment in the gym. Over the next couple of weeks I picked up the phone a couple of times to call, but then changed my mind and hung up. It wasn't like I was a normal, always-out-of-money college kid, anyway. My Papa Bradley had set up trust funds for each of his grandchildren when we were born, to pay all college expenses. Every month the trust sent me a check, which was more than enough money to pay my rent, bills, and living expenses. It wasn't like I was living in some huge, beautifully furnished apartment and eating steak every night, but I wasn't reduced to ramen and macaroni and cheese either.

When I went home for Halloween about a month later, I noticed in the local gay New Orleans paper that one of the bars was featuring the "Men of Southern Knights" dancing there over the weekend. Maybe it was a legit company after all, I thought to myself, so I went to check them out.

Talk about hot guys!

As I sipped my Bud Light long-neck and watched the men of Southern Knights do their thing on the bar, I became immensely flattered the guy wanted me as one of their dancers. These guys had like zero body fat, muscles on muscles, and bulges in their G-strings that definitely caught your eye. Made your mouth water. Made you want to take a dollar out of your wallet and get their attention, so they'd smile at you and let you touch them. Ah, what the hell, I thought, and got a dollar out and approached one of them.

"Do you know Barry Lawlor?" I asked him as I slipped the bill into his G-string.

"Yeah, he's our booking agent." He looked a little puzzled by the question. "Why?"

"He asked me to come to work for him."

He looked me up and down. I'd taken my shirt off and it was tucked into the back of my jeans. "Yeah, I can see why."

"You like doing this?"

He grinned at me. "Beats flipping burgers to pay the bills." He held out his hand. "My name's Mark."

I shook his hand. "Scotty."

"You should do it." Someone else was waving a five-dollar bill at him, and he winked at the guy. "It's really a lot of fun."

"Okay, thanks."

He ran his hand over my chest and pinched my left nipple. "Give Barry a call." He stood back up and walked over to the guy with the five.

When I got back to Nashville, I called him and made an appointment to see him. His office was in an old brick building in downtown Nashville. When his secretary showed me in, he got very excited. "I was hoping you'd call," he said. He had greasy-looking black hair. It was long on one side and combed over in a vain attempt to hide the receding hairline. He was a little shorter and probably about thirty pounds heavier than me. He was wearing a pink polo shirt, a pair of jeans, and a pair of Air Jordans. I figured him for about fifty. When he shook my hand, his was soft and damp and warm. His office was decorated with prints of hot guys in G-strings or bikinis or wrestling singlets. He gave me an employment application, which I filled out.

"You'll need a stage name," he said when I handed the form back to him.

"Why?"

"All dick dancers have stage names." He shrugged.

"Dick dancers?" I'd never heard the term before.

He laughed. "Yeah. When the Southern Knights are

dancing, sometimes the clubs advertise the guys by name. You can develop quite a following, but you don't want to use your own name. Psychos can track you down."

I grinned. "Well, how about Dick Dansoir?" I pronounced it den-SWAH. Being from New Orleans can come in handy sometimes. I thought I was being very clever, and he seemed to think so, too. When I wrote it down for him, he laughed.

"Smart-ass," he said. "Now I need to see you dance." He leaned back and hit "play" on a ghetto blaster. The room filled with the booming bass of a Mariah Carey dance remix.

I stood up. I am not shy about my body. Never have been. When I was in junior high school at a good New Orleans Catholic school, I got picked on a lot. I knew, even then, that I was attracted to boys rather than girls, and somehow, the bullies picked up on it. It's like they have this sixth sense that someone is different, you know? I was smaller than most kids in my class, and when they started picking on me the priests and nuns were absolutely no help. So, I went out for the wrestling team. I figured it was the best way to learn how to defend myself, and besides, I liked the idea of rolling around on a mat with my body entwined with another boy's. I was a natural. Before long my body began developing muscles. I started lifting weights. By the time I made it to high school I was kind of a minor celebrity because I was such a good wrestler. I was offered wrestling scholarships to several colleges, but I decided not to pursue it. I didn't need a scholarship, thanks to Papa Bradley, and by the time I was a senior, the thrill was gone.

I had discovered the joy of gay sex by then.

So, I pulled my shirt up over my head and starting moving my hips. I took my shoes and socks off, undid my pants, and let 'em drop. I was wearing a pair of black

Calvin Klein briefs, and danced around for him. I wiggled my butt for him; I flexed muscles when he asked me to, and when the song ended, he grinned. "You available for a gig in Atlanta in two weeks?"

And that's how it started. I went to Dallas, Houston, Atlanta, Miami, Tampa, Pensacola, Birmingham, Jackson, Memphis, Louisville, Austin, and San Antonio, among others. I went everywhere, it seemed.

But I've never been to me.

The money was really good, plus knowing I had to dance nearly naked kept me motivated with going to the gym. The only place I refused to take dancing gigs was New Orleans. My friends, even Mom and Dad, thought it pretty cool that I was doing it. My grandparents, on the other hand . . . well, let's just say it wouldn't go over well in the drawing rooms of Uptown New Orleans. Both sets of grandparents are traditional, conservative, Ronald Reagan-worshipping, Republican-voting, old-line traditionalists. Mom and Dad think Reagan was the anti-Christ, one step above Hitler on the scale of bad world leaders. Mom and Dad are the black sheep of each respective family. The Bradleys blame it on my mother. The Diderots blame it on my father. When I am at the home of either set of the grands, I just try to imagine what it was like for my parents to grow up in that stifled environment. All of my aunts and uncles and cousins are like the grandparents: overly starched, stuffy, b-o-r-i-n-g, and way too concerned about what other people say and think. Family reunions are the dullest thing you can imagine, until the liquor starts to hit and they all get drunk.

It's amazing what you can find out when an aunt or an uncle has had too much Wild Turkey.

Anyway, I avoided dancing in New Orleans to spare my grandparents.

I flunked out of Vanderbilt with about thirty credits to

go before graduating. I just lost interest. I wasn't the best student in the first place, hanging on to a C average by my fingernails, always managing to balance a D out with a B or an F out with an A. But I'd lost interest in my major completely. I'd lost interest in going to class. I'd pretty much lost interest in Nashville. So, I broke the lease on my apartment, packed up everything I owned, and headed home to New Orleans.

I kept dancing with the Southern Knights for a couple of years, but I needed something to fill my days. The money was still good, but I was getting tired of it.

I was bored, bored, bored.

"Why don't you get into personal training?" my mom said one night over tofu lasagna. "You like working out; you like going to the gym, right? So why not help other people get themselves into shape?"

So, I gave up being a Southern Knight and became a certified personal trainer. I also got certified to teach aerobics and started working at my gym, Riverview Fitness. I'm a laid-back kind of person, so I liked being able to wear workout clothes to work. Fitness is a great way to make a living. You're pretty much your own boss, you can set your own hours, if you get an obnoxious client you can't stand to be around you can fire them, and you get to spend a lot of time in the gym. I like the gym.

The problem, of course, with being self-employed is that money can be sporadic. Clients forget their checkbooks. Clients go on vacation and you don't get paid while they're gone. The summer is always a particularly bad time for business. I always find myself scraping by, getting behind on my bills, eating at Mom and Dad's a lot. I considered trying to get back on with the Southern Knights, but decided I didn't want that regular of work.

Another couple of years passed. One night I was in the Pub. It was a hot July night and I was drinking Bud Light out of a sweating long-neck bottle. The bar wasn't really crowded, still too early for the happy-hour crowd to get off work and come in. The bartender, a chubby but really sweet guy named Chet, was lazily wiping the same spot on the bar in front of me over and over again between puffs on a Marlboro. A rather harried-looking guy in a black Pub tank top walked behind the bar and poured himself a shot of tequila. Being partial to tequila myself, I watched as he poured salt on his hand, licked it, tossed back the shot, and sucked on a lime.

"Fuck," he said, tossing the shot glass into the bar sink, which was full of soapy water. It splashed water on him.

"What's up?" Chet asked him.

"One of the fucking porn stars this weekend canceled." He filled a glass with Coke. "Now what the hell am I supposed to do?"

"I used to be a Southern Knight," I said. "I can fill in, if you want."

And so it was back on the bar I went, grandparents be damned. After all, how would they find out? Only if someone they knew saw me, and even though New Orleans is a pretty small town, I figured it was pretty safe. I made almost eight hundred bucks that weekend, enough to get the phone company off my back and keep my air-conditioning running, get caught up on the rent, and buy food. They offered me a regular gig, but I decided not to take it. Dancing every once in a while is fun, but not if you do it all the time. So whenever they get in a tight spot and need a go-go boy, they give me a call. If I need the money, I drag out my G-strings and sexiest underwear and climb up on the bar.

It's not as glamorous as people think. Yes, it's really nice standing up there and being stared at, having people slip you money for kissing their cheeks or letting them pat you or stroke you, but bars are smoky places. People get drunk in bars. The bars themselves are covered with drinks and spills. Its very easy, if you aren't paying attention to what you're doing, to slip and fall.

I've fallen off of plenty of bars.

That's not fun.

I'm also one of those people who always manage to wind up having bizarre things happen to them. My friends always teasingly refer to me as "most likely to go home with a serial killer." Hey, I can't help it.

Take, for example, what happened at Southern Decadence this last year. I was minding my own business, not bothering anyone, just looking forward to having a good time and enjoying myself. I love Decadence. It's my favorite time of the year, even more so than Mardi Gras. Some call it the gay Mardi Gras, but there are differences. It's hotter, for one thing, and no parades, except for the drag parade on Sunday afternoon. Just crowds of gay men, some hot, some not, all in town to cut loose and have a great time, dance and meet kindred spirits from all over the country, have fun, and get laid.

I'd been looking forward to Decadence all summer. I was looking good, had a great tan from a couple of weekend expeditions to Pensacola with my friend David, and it hadn't been a good summer for me financially. Decadence was going to be my farewell to a lousy summer celebration.

If I'd only known . . .

Chapter One

KNIGHT OF WANDS

A light-complexioned young man with an adventurous spirit

It's not the heat—it's the stupidity.

A T-shirt bearing that slogan hangs in the window of every shop in the French Quarter that sells cheap souvenirs. The tourists, wiping the sweat off their foreheads with napkins while holding a forty-eight-ounce plastic cup filled with an exotically flavored daiquiri in their other hand, nudge each other when they spy it. They exchange knowing smiles. The slow pace unique to New Orleans has irritated them slightly ever since they got off their airplane. The endless wait at baggage claim and the longer wait in the taxi line. The check-in process at the hotel seemed endless. The line at Walgreen's that just didn't seem to move at all. The lackadaisical attitude everyone they have encountered since walking off their airplane seems to have toward efficiency has been all explained and summed up by a slogan on a T-shirt. The heat is bearable, after all. Everything is air-conditioned, for one thing, and there's those forty-eight-ounce daiquiris with names like Cajun Storm, Swamp Water, and Mind Eraser for another. Yes, the heat can be borne. It's the stupidity that is truly annoying.

What the tourists don't know is, the stupidity referred to on the shirt is theirs.

New Orleans is a whore who makes her living by dressing herself up as the City That Care Forgot. We peddle cheap gimcracks to the tourists who checked their brains at the airport along with their suitcases but apparently forgot to claim the brains again upon landing at Armstrong International. We sell them refrigerator magnets with a drunk with *X*es for eyes holding on to a Bourbon Street lamppost for support. We sell them beads they proudly wear even though Mardi Gras has been over for months. We sell them porcelain masks of white-faced harlequins made in Taiwan. We sell them forty-eight-ounce daiquiris that are flammable, or drinks in clear green plastic cups that are shaped like a hand grenade. We smile and avert our eyes as another one vomits into the gutter. We step out of the way as they stagger down our sidewalks. We plaster a smile on our faces as they drive five miles an hour through the city looking at buildings even though we have to be somewhere in three minutes and they've backed up traffic for blocks. Tourism is our biggest source of revenue, after all, and if they can't handle their liquor, oh well.

We have sold our collective soul on the altar of tourism.

In the summer, the French Quarter reeks of sour beer, vomit, and piss. At seven every morning, the hoses come out and the vomit and spilt liquor and piss is washed down off the sidewalks. By eight, Bourbon Street stinks of pine cleaner, a heavy, oily scent that cloys and hangs in the air. It hit me full force when I slipped out of the front door of the Bourbon Orleans hotel at eight-thirty in the morning. The bellman on duty winked at me. I shrugged and grinned back. I wasn't the first nonguest to slip out of the

Bourbon Orleans that morning, and I wouldn't be the last that weekend.

It was Southern Decadence, after all. Urban legend holds that Southern Decadence began in the 1980s as a bar-crawl-type party a group of gay guys had for a friend who was moving away. They had so much fun, they did it again the next year. Each year it grew and grew until it became a national event, drawing gay men from as far away as Sweden and Australia. As opposed to other circuit events, for years there was no big dance party. It was just a big block party held in what we locals call the Fruit Loop, a five-bar, four-block stretch that runs from Rawhide to Good Friends to Oz and the Pub to Café Lafitte's in Exile. All the bars have balconies, and of course, you can always take your drinks with you.

The gay boys had started arriving yesterday afternoon, with the big crush coming in today, Friday. Labor Day weekend. The end of summer, when the locals can begin to breathe a little easier. The mind-numbing heat will break in the next few weeks, and what passes for our fall season will begin. Sunny days with no humidity and the mercury hovering in the seventies and low eighties. In New Orleans, we turn off the air-conditioning when the temperature drops into the eighties and open the windows.

I headed for the corner of Orleans and Bourbon. My stomach was growling. The Clover Grill was just a few blocks up Bourbon, and one of their breakfasts was sounding damned good to my slightly swollen head. There's nothing like some scrambled eggs and greasy full-fat bacon to make you lose your hangover. The food at the Clover Grill is one of the best hangover cures in town. I shifted my gym bag to my other shoulder.

The bars at the corner of St. Ann and Bourbon still had patrons. It was probably too early for new arrivals from out of town, so these were the holdouts from the night be-fore, who still hadn't grasped the fact that the bars don't close. Tourists always have trouble pacing themselves in New Orleans. Bars that have no last call is an alien con-cept to most. The bars had been packed with tourists who had come in early for the weekend, the liquor had flowed freely, and there were very likely a lot of drugs to be had. Today the crowds would be arriving in force. By four the bars would be packed again, almost impossible to navi-gate through. I waved at Abel, the morning bartender at the Pub.

I was dancing at the Pub this weekend for extra cash. One of the porn stars, Rock Hard, who was supposed to dance this weekend, had overdosed on crystal meth on Wednesday. Condition stable. No condition to dance. Randy Westfall, the manager, had called me on Thursday afternoon to fill in. It was very good timing. I was behind on some bills. It probably wasn't very good karma to be happy that Rock Hard had overdosed, but I reasoned that it was probably a good thing. Perhaps the overdose would wake him up to the fact he had a substance-abuse prob-lem, and he would now get some help for it. The summer's heat is always a bitch on my personal training business, but this one had been particularly bad. It had been hotter than usual, which is a staggering thought. Everyone who can afford a trainer leaves town. Those who don't leave re-ally don't want to sweat any more than they already are. Can't say that I blame them. Except when the second no-tices from my utilities started arriving.

The Clover Grill was crowded. I swore under my breath. Goddamned tourists. A wave of nausea swam over me. I shouldn't have let what's-his-name last night talk me into those tequila shots. What was his name? Bill? Bob? Brett? He was from Houston and tall, with a shaved torso and a nice, round, hard ass. He'd flirted with me early in the evening, wanted to know what time I was off, and had come back. You'd think at twenty-nine I would know better than to do tequila shots at two-thirty in the morning. Dumb, dumb, dumb. Well, not that there's ever a *good* time to do tequila shots.

I headed down Dumaine Street to the Devil's Weed. The Devil's Weed is a tobacco shop specializing in fine cigars, pipe tobacco, and imported cigarettes. They also serve coffee, muffins, and bagels. Not quite the greasy scrambled eggs and sausage my hangover was demanding, but it would have to do. I walked in.

"Scotty!" Emily, the cute twenty-two-year-old lesbian who worked the morning shift, grinned at me. She wore her hair shorn close to the scalp and Coke-bottle glasses that magnified her big brown eyes. She always wore a tank top with no bra restraining her big full breasts, and a loose-fitting cotton skirt over sandals. She was from Minneapolis and had come down for Mardi Gras. New Orleans got to her and she stayed. New Orleans has that effect on people. You come for a weekend and get caught in her spell and can't leave. It just gets in your blood. I've lived here all of my life and have never wanted to live anywhere else. When I was on the stripper circuit, every weekend a different town, I never found another place I wanted to live, and I had looked. I always came back with a healthy appreciation for my home city. If a city isn't open twenty-four-seven, I don't want any part of it. Here you can drink at any time of the day without feeling any guilt. You can eat whenever you want to, because there's always someplace open. You can keep whatever hours you want. You don't have to be a part of that whole nine-to-five rat race unless you want to be. I don't. I hate waking up to an alarm.

My parents, who owned the Devil's Weed, had practically adopted Emily. She was so likable and cute, you

couldn't help but want to take care of her. She was a gen-
uinely nice person, without a mean bone in her body. She
had that good energy.

"Coffee and a bagel." I sat down on a stool. She had a
cigar burning in an ashtray.

"Liked the Day-Glo G-string." She grinned as she put
my coffee down.

I grinned back at her. "I made close to four hundred last
night."

"All right!" We high-fived. "Your mom and dad are still
asleep."

"Of course." Mom and Dad were unrepentant stoners.
They were hippies and counterculturalists who'd never
sold out, despite their successful shop. My first name isn't
Scott; it's Milton. Pretty awful, right? Coupled with my
last name, which is Bradley, and you can imagine the horror my childhood was like before my older brother started
calling me Scotty. Of course, his name is Storm, and my
sister's name is Rain. When Mom was pregnant with me,
both sets of grandparents had apparently sat Mom and
Dad down and insisted I not be named after a force of nature. I can almost see the stoner gleam in my mother's eye
when she agreed. Milton was Mom's father's name. She always claimed that she was simply honoring her parents by
naming me that. That was her cover story, and she has
stuck to it my whole life. I think both she and Dad regret-
ted it later. They're actually pretty cool parents. When I
came out to them when I was sixteen, they wanted to
throw me a coming-out party. They are both pretty active
in P-FLAG. A huge rainbow flag hangs out in front of the
store year-round. It's kind of hard to be pissed at them for
naming me after a board game company when they're so
cool. I'm sure it sounded like a good idea after a couple of
joints.

"Since you're up so early, I'm assuming you're just now on your way home?" Emily raised her eyebrows and winked.

I winked back. "I never kiss and tell." Well, I really do, but Emily was more like a little sister to me since she'd started at the shop. I would never give my sister, Rain, the details of my activities. Besides, Emily was also still a virgin. She was saving herself for the right woman, bless her heart. See what I mean about sweet? How could I corrupt her with my sordid tales?

I smeared cream cheese on my bagel and leaned over the counter to kiss her cheek. "You gonna be out tonight?"

"Yeah." She giggled. "See ya on the bar." She did a little dance for me. "I wanna pick up some of your moves."

Laughing, I walked back out into the street and headed home, chewing on my bagel and sipping the coffee. I was tired. The bagel was helping the hangover. Thank God.

My apartment was on Decatur Street in the last block before Esplanade. The coffee was hot and strong. Carrying the cup was making me sweat. I could smell my armpits and it wasn't pretty. All I wanted to do was get home, turn the air down to about sixty degrees, wash off the sweat and smell of sex, and sleep for a while.

My building has a little mom-and-pop grocery store on the first floor. It opens pretty early. I waved to Mrs. Duchesnay, who always worked the morning shift. She and her husband had started the shop years ago, when they were both very young. All six of their kids had worked there at one time or another. Her husband had been a mean old man. He was always yelling and threatening kids about shoplifting. He'd accused me of stealing a pack of gum once that I had come in with, and called my mother. I don't think he was expecting the furious harpy who stormed in and backed him up against the soda cooler and called him a fascist. He was always nice to me after that. The Quarter kids called him Mr. Douchebag. He'd disappeared about ten years ago. Quarter lore and legend believed Mrs. Duchesnay had killed him and got rid of the body. He'd been a bastard, so if she had, I always figured, more power to her. Those who believed the story didn't hold it against her. He'd been a pretty miserable person.

I unlocked the gate. There were three floors above the shop, all apartments. My landladies lived on the second floor. Velma Simpson and Millie Breen had been together for about thirty years. Velma was watering the plants in the courtyard when I got back to the staircase.

"Morning, Scotty." She nodded at me. She was nearly sixty, with steel-gray hair and wire-rimmed glasses. She was wearing a pair of tired old jean cutoff shorts and a white, sweat-stained tank top with no bra. She played tennis three times a week and jogged on the levee every day. There wasn't an ounce of fat on her anywhere. She'd been a high school gym teacher and girls' athletics coach until she'd taken early retirement a few years ago. Millie and Velma had baby-sat us when we were kids, whenever Mom and Dad had gone on a private vacation or been arrested at one of their many protests. "How'd you do?"

I opened my bag and pulled out a wad of ones, fives, and tens. "About four hundred."

She put the hose down. "Give me three hundred."

I counted out the money and handed it to her. She tucked it into her pocket. My rent was only four-fifty a month, which was a steal for the place. She and Millie could have gotten fifteen hundred for it easily. Luckily, Millie had been my mother's best friend since grade school. She was also a lawyer, so they didn't really need my rent money. I was pretty damned lucky. Anyone else would have thrown my late-rent-paying ass out on the street years earlier.

She pulled a joint out of her cleavage. "Need some help to sleep?" She and Millie always got the best pot.

"You gonna join me?"

She laughed. "Stupid boy."

I sparked the joint and took a long hit. She took it from me, took two, and handed it back to me. She waved me into a lawn chair and sat down herself. She inhaled, long and deep, then pinched it out and set it on a table. "What you gonna do today?"

"I'm gonna sleep." I felt quite pleasantly stoned.

She leaned back. "Leave your gear. I'm gonna do a load of laundry later this morning. I'll bring it up."

"Cool." I yawned.

"Does your getting home at this hour mean you got lucky?" Velma and Millie always wanted details on my sex life. I didn't mind telling them, although I did think from time to time that it was a little weird that two lesbians in their late fifties were so interested. It was a small price to pay, though, for them being so cool about the rent.

I smiled at her. "Guy from Houston."

"You like them cowboys."

"He had the nicest ass." I winked at her and then launched into the gory details.

I'd been dancing for about an hour when he came up to the bar. I'd seen him in a corner, sipping on a Bud Light long-neck. He was good-looking, all right. Short black hair, blue eyes, dark tan. He had a red tank top tucked into his belt, and a torso shaved smooth. Big pecs, melon-sized, abs you could do your laundry on, and a pair of tight jean shorts rolled up at the knee. He grinned up at me. Nice, even white teeth. He stroked my calf. I knelt down with him in between my legs.

"You're pretty," he said, pulling a five out of his pocket.

"You ain't bad either." I put my hand on his chest. Solid as a rock. Skin smooth as a baby's butt. Definitely shaved.

"What time you getting off?"

"Two in the morning."

"I'll be here." And he was. Simple as that. At 2:10 we were downing tequila shots. Half an hour later we were in his room at the Bourbon Orleans with our tongues down each other's throats. He did have the nicest, tightest, hardest ass I've come across in a long time.

I'd left his five on the nightstand when I left.

Velma sighed. "Ah, to be young again."

I yawned. "Can I go to bed now, Aunt Velma?"

She handed me the roach. "Take this for later."

I kissed her cheek. "Thanks, doll."

I was so tired by the time I got upstairs that I decided not to shower but to go straight to bed. I collapsed on my bed and closed my eyes.

I was asleep in a matter of seconds.

Chapter Two

THE TOWER

Conflict, change, unforeseen catastrophe

I dream in living color.

My dreams are vivid, alive. I can smell and taste and feel in my dreams, as well as see and hear and talk. All of my senses are awakened and made more vivid by my slumber. This can be a really good thing when the dream is pleasant. When I have happy dreams, I wake up all blissful with a sense of joy that I rarely find otherwise. When I have erotic dreams, I have the most amazing sex with the most amazing people. I love sleeping as a result. My dream life is so incredible that I always look forward to it.

On the other hand, my bad dreams are extremely intense.

The one I woke up from around noon was one of the worst. I woke up drenched in sweat and panting. I could hear my heart's rapid beating in my ears. I sat up in bed, trying to calm my breathing and slow my heart down to a normal pace. The dream, so vivid and intense, was fading away. I tried to hold on to its memory. It continued to fade, though, in the bright glare of the sun. Soon all I could remember were the screams of the multitudes dying.

Yuck.

I shivered and got out of bed. I walked naked into the kitchen and started a pot of coffee. I turned the thermostat up to eighty-five. I brushed my teeth and put on my red satin robe. I poured some coffee into a cup and walked into the living room and retrieved my deck of tarot cards.

The deck is worn. I've had it since I was eight years old. One of my parents' friends had given it to me. Madame Xena. She fascinated me when I was a child. She professed to be a psychic. Her clients numbered high-society wives, politicians, everyday people. She held seances and read the tarot. She always wore flowing robes and a turban. Tall and reed-thin, with sharp cheekbones and a prominent nose, she was prone to histrionic gestures and declarations. She came to dinner one night and sat next to me. I couldn't take my eyes off of her. Her robes and turban were a deep purple. Just before dessert, she grasped me by the chin and stared into my eyes for several minutes. Her eyes were hazel with flecks of gold. She turned to my mother. "Isabelle, this child has the gift!" she proclaimed.

I didn't know what she was talking about, but both of my parents were tremendously excited. Storm and Rain just glared at me. The next day, a package was delivered to me by messenger. It was a deck of tarot cards and a book on interpreting them. There was a single note: *"Use the cards wisely and fairly, boy."*

The cards fascinated me with their pictures and many different meanings. I started playing with them, learning the different ways to lay them out and read them. I got to be pretty good at it. I used to make Storm and Rain let me read for them all the time, and later their friends. My friends thought it was weird, and of course the priests and nuns at Jesuit High School considered it Satanic. That was fine with me. Both sides of my family were Catholic, but my parents believed in the Goddess and raised all three of us to do the same. In high school, right around the time she started calling herself Rhonda, my sister entered the Catholic Church. Storm never talked about religion. But I remained true to the Goddess. It just made sense to me, more than what the priests and nuns taught.

I always drew comfort from the cards. My gift, such as it was, had not come from Jesus, after all, but from the Goddess. I wasn't quite sure how it worked. I couldn't read minds, couldn't communicate with others telepathically, and couldn't pick the lottery numbers. The only thing I could do was read the cards. They almost always told me something whenever I did.

And sometimes my dreams warned me about the future. They were never really explicit, but I could almost always get the cards out and learn more about the dream once I woke up.

It was something I pretty much kept to myself. Obviously, my family knew about it, but I didn't tell my friends. I'm pretty unconventional as it is, without telling people I was sort of psychic on top of it all.

I shuffled the cards and laid them out in the Celtic method. I put a Stevie Nicks CD on before trying to read them. For some reason, Stevie's beautiful, hoarse voice always seems to help me channel the Goddess through the cards. I love Stevie. I have all of her recordings. If I ever did drag, I would do Stevie. Alas, I would make a really ugly woman.

As I flipped the cards, Stevie was wailing about rooms being on fire. The last remnants of the dream were fading, but the song seemed eerily appropriate.

The phone rang. Just as well. The reading was inconclusive. They couldn't seem to make up their minds about what to say. Danger warnings mixed in with pleasures of the flesh.

"Hello?"

"Hey, dude, how'd you do last night?" It was David, my best friend and workout partner. David was ten years older than me. He taught music in a Catholic junior high school. He was also the band director and drill team coach. He's pretty good at putting together halftime shows. I always say, if you've got to have a show, hire a gay man to put it together. I went to a drill team competition once to be supportive. You really can tell the difference between the drill teams run by the gay men and ones run by straight men or women. It's very telling.

We'd met, ironically, in the bathhouse on Toulouse Street. It was the usual thing. Exchanging glances in the gloom. A smile and a nod. He walked up, put his hand on my chest, and I'd invited him to my room. Once there, we dropped our towels and started making out. He was a pretty good kisser, and we were about the same size. I was more muscular than him. He was leaner, well defined, with a nice shape to him. It was only about five minutes later when we realized that we were sexually incompatible. That's one of the nice things about a bathhouse. When you meet someone and you wind up being incompatible that way, it isn't a big deal. There are plenty of other guys wandering around in a towel looking for what you have to offer. It's much more practical on that level than picking someone up in a bar and not finding out until you're back home. Then you have to make do. But we were in the baths, so we smoked a joint, laughed about the absurdity of it all, and then began prowling the floors and mazes together for some hot-bottom boys.

From such humble beginnings great friendships are born.

"I made almost four hundred." I wrapped my arms around me and took the phone out onto the balcony. My balcony is the best thing about my apartment. It looks out directly onto the lush green lawn of the Mint, and I could see the big ships passing up and down the river on the other side of the levee. A cruise ship was going by upriver. I'd heard that one of the big gay cruise companies was making a three-day stop for Decadence. More tanned muscle boys turned loose on the city. In my opinion, you can never have enough tanned muscle boys on the prowl in the Quarter with their shirts off. The river level was actually higher than my balcony, and I was on the third floor. That was pretty high. The level of the river was getting dangerously high. The summer had brought a lot of rain to the Ohio and Missouri Rivers and lots of flooding throughout the Midwest. That water had to wind up somewhere, and it winds up coming through New Orleans on its way to the Gulf. Kind of creepy.

Thank God for the levee. We'd be underwater if it weren't there.

I have lots of plants out on my balcony. Ficus trees, a huge philodendron, and some massive elephant ferns. I also have a real nice little white plastic table with matching chairs, so I can go out and watch the ships go by. I can also watch pedestrians, the tourists browsing through the antique shops that line Decatur Street. They aren't nearly as entertaining as watching the tourists on Bourbon Street, of course, but I have wasted a lot of time out there relaxing.

I sat down. The change from cold to oppressive heat had the desired effect. Within minutes I was sweating and went back inside.

"Cool. We still on for the gym?"

David couldn't afford to pay me to train him. He was one of those people who can't gain weight. When we met he weighed 125, all lean, wiry muscle. After a couple of years of free advice and listening to his complaints about not getting bigger, I caved and asked him to be my workout partner. I had always worked out alone, and didn't really like the thought of having someone there with me. Oddly, I enjoyed it. In the seven months he'd been working out with me he'd gained fifteen pounds of muscle. Every time he looked in the mirror at the gym he'd turn to me and say, "Thanks, Scotty." He also said that anytime we were in a bar and some hot guy would give him a once-over.

I am damned good at my job, if I do say so myself.

"Yeah. I need to pump up for tonight." The gym would be a zoo. All the tourist boys would be trying to get a pump on for tonight, to get the blood flowing through their muscles so they would look bigger than the guy dancing next to him. If I weren't dancing, I'd have just avoided the whole mess. The last-minute need for a pump before going out always struck me as dumb. It's kind of late to be worrying about how big you are, anyway. You look like what you look like, and there would be so many guys on drugs looking to get laid, there really didn't seem much point in hoping that you'd gain a quarter-inch pump. But when you're dancing for dollars, and one of the other guys was probably some porn star, every little bit helped.

"You off at two again tonight?"

I knew where this was going. "Yeah."

"Do you want me to score some X for you?"

Yes, I know Ecstasy is bad for you. Cigarettes are bad for you. Pot is bad for you. Fat is bad. Anything to excess is bad for you. You can become addicted to exercise as well. Moderation is the key. I see nothing wrong in occasionally taking a hit of X and dancing all night, but never, ever when I am working on the bar. Some dancers do it, or crystal meth or coke or something to make them less inhibited, more flirtatious, or just to deaden themselves to being an object of desire. Not me. When I'm on the bar I want to have a clear head. It's safer that way. I don't have any problems with showing my dick to someone for a five

or a ten. Hell, I show it to enough people for free. I don't
need drugs to lower my inhibitions. What can I say? I like
getting the attention. It may not be politically correct to
say it, but I like looking good. I like being desired. I like
being irresistible. It's a real rush, standing up on the bar
and shaking your ass and knowing that people are staring
at you with lust in their eyes and hope in their hearts.
"No, I don't think so. I don't want to be out till seven in
the morning."

"Let me know if you change your mind."

"See ya at five." I hung up the phone. I looked at the
cards on the coffee table. I shuffled them and tried again.
This time made even less sense than the last time. What the
hell? I tried a third time before giving up.

Fucking cards, I thought, picking them up and wrap-
ping them again in their blue silk wrap. Immediately I
apologized to the Goddess. I lit a white candle for purity
and closed my eyes.

If she chose not to speak to me, who was I to question
her?

I went back into the bathroom and looked at myself in
the mirror. I'd shaved my entire body yesterday before
dancing, except for a small patch of pubic hair, which I
had trimmed down. I don't have a lot of body hair on my
torso usually. There's just a small patch in the center of my
chest with a small trail of dark hairs leading down to my
pubis area. But even that little bit, if not shaved, could
make a difference of about a hundred dollars in tips. Gay
men like their strippers smooth. I checked for the razor
stubble and telltale red bumps that come from shaving. I
had used a hair-removal cream on my legs. There were a
couple of red bumps on my chest. I got an astringent scrub
and lathered them up. Got to look pretty.

After getting cleaned up, I made myself some lunch and
turned on *General Hospital.* Just as I was getting worked

up about a pretty heroine who just found out she was not only pregnant but dying of leukemia, the phone rang again. Saved by the bell! I was starting to tear up. "Hello?"

"Scotty, honey, are you busy?"

It was my sister, Rain. "Never too busy for you, Rain." Besides Mom and Dad, I was the only one who still called her Rain.

I heard her breathe in. She was counting to ten. She always did when I called her by her birth name. "Can you read the cards for me?"

I always suspected that Rain's conversion to Catholicism was merely a way of rebelling against our parents. Mom and Dad rebelled against their strict, uptight Uptown society parents by becoming pot-smoking, free-love hippies. Rain rebelled by becoming a strict, uptight Uptown doctor's wife who didn't have a job. She shopped, got massages and facials, and did charity work. She threw massive dinner parties for her husband's coworkers, trying to help out his career. She belonged to the Mystic Krewe of Iris. Never had a hair out of place. Mom still lit candles hoping she would wake up and become a feminist.

My brother, Storm, wasn't quite as extreme as Rain. He went to law school and was now a partner in a big firm. He was still pretty freewheeling, but he belonged to the right Mardi Gras krewes and played the corporate lawyer game. Mom and Dad still gave him lectures on the evils of corporate America, but rather than getting mad the way Rain did, he just laughed. Our grandparents adored both of them and didn't know quite what to make of me. They pretended not to know I was gay, even though Mom and Dad sent them P-FLAG flyers and once tried to hang a rainbow flag on their houses.

"What's up, girlfriend?"

Rain giggled. She liked it when I talked gay to her. "I

was just wondering something, and the cards always seem to help."

Yeah. She was a good Catholic. I retrieved the cards, shuffled, said a silent prayer to the Goddess, and laid them out. I flipped them and frowned. "Whatever it is, Rain, it's probably not a good idea. It'll be hard to pull off, very difficult, and the reward won't be worth the effort."

She exhaled. "Damn."

I waited. Rain couldn't keep things in for long.

"I just met this really nice gay surgeon last night, new in town, and he seemed so right for you. . . ."

One of her major problems was her constant need for closure. She used to always fix Storm up with women, and any gay man she met was a possible life partner for me. Storm had good-naturedly gone along with all of her matchmaking schemes until he finally got married. Unfortunately for me, he married one of the girls she set him up with, and she was convinced she would find the right man for me. I stopped going along after a steady stream of eligible upwardly mobile gay men bored me to tears. "Rain—"

"I know, I know, but I wish you would just find someone nice and settle down." She went on in this vein for another five minutes, and I listened. You couldn't stop her, anyway. Storm said she was like a bulldozer once she got started and the best thing to do was to get out of the way. "Even Storm likes him and agrees with me."

I made a mental note to have a chat with Storm. It was my turn to count to ten. As I counted, I started feeling bad. She meant well, after all. She worried. How lucky was I to have a sister who loved me? "Okay. Pick a night and have us both to dinner, okay?" Hell, what would it hurt? She was a damned good cook, and she was a master of wine selection. She had the doctor's-wife thing down to a science.

"You mean it?" She squealed. "Next Thursday night good for you? Around eight?"

I agreed and hung up. It really took so little to make her happy.

And six days was plenty of time to wiggle out of it.

Chapter Three

THE SEVEN OF CUPS

An imagination that has been working overtime

The gym was packed.

"Looks like a casting call for a porn movie in here," I said to Svetlana Volchkova as she handed me a towel and a locker key. Svetlana was the assistant manager of Riverview Fitness. She was very beautiful, with long thick black hair she'd inherited from her Lebanese mother, and a Queen Nefertiti profile. Despite her dark coloring, she'd inherited blue eyes from her Russian father. She'd been working at Riverview almost as long as I had. She was in her late twenties, and loved to have fun. She also had a great sense of humor and was a big flirt. She and her fiancé, a great big former football player for the Saints, could often be spotted in the gay bars dancing. He was pretty cool and didn't mind the boys flirting with him. They were both great dancers. "Gay bars play the best music," she would always say.

She rolled her big round eyes. "Decadence." She shrugged. She winked at me. "Shame all these pretty genes are out of the pool, though."

I made my way back to the locker room. Riverview

Fitness was in the mall at 1 Canal Place, next to the food court. Only in New Orleans would a health club be located next to a series of cafeteria-style food places that cooked with grease. It was weird to walk past the smell of the grease and the smell of the popcorn from the movie theater just beyond the food court on your way to work out. I'd given in to the temptation of a big bag of popcorn on my way out more than once. It was an okay gym, kind of on the small size, but very convenient for Quarter residents, and not nearly as expensive as the snobby one up on Rampart Street with the indoor pool. The clientele working out at any given time was generally about ninety percent gay, with the stray straights thrown in for good measure. I nodded at some guys I knew. A heavyset black woman who was a regular at my aerobics classes waved at me. She was one of my favorites. She might not be able to keep up with the routine, but she always kept moving and loved my class. Those are my favorites—the ones who really get into it. I don't use those overpriced tapes you order from the aerobics companies, either. I always get my tapes made by deejays in the gay bars.

I threw my bag into a locker. The locker room was filled with gay men in various stages of undress. Generic gay party boys, really. Big muscles, veins bulging, the obligatory tattoos on the biceps and the occasional one on the back. Expensive underwear that cost twenty bucks a pair, if not more. Workout clothes that cost more than I make in a month that strategically display the bodies to best effect. Some were coming and going from the sauna, steam room, and showers, with white fluffy towels wrapped tightly around their waists. It was always like this on party weekends. Usually, the regulars don't shower here. They show up in their workout clothes, work out, and then head home to shower and change. Not much point in getting cleaned up when you're going to start sweating again when you get outside.

There was probably some good action going on in the steam room. Riverview's steam room had been listed on a Web site (cruisingforsex.com? Something like that) as one of the Top Ten Cruising Places in North America. I'd wondered about that. Nothing has ever happened to me in the steam room, although David swears by it.

Maybe I'm just doing something wrong.

If the straight owners knew about the Web site listing, I am sure they would be horrified. They were both nice guys, pretty mellow, and cool with the fact their clientele was mostly gay. But I can guarantee they wouldn't be cool with sexual activity going on in the steam room. It was surely some kind of health code violation.

David was changing and trying not to look like he was staring. I smothered a laugh. David is about an inch shorter than me and cuts his hair short, close to the scalp. He was a natural redhead before it started going white on him. I call him the "whitest man in North America." He doesn't tan easily and turns red rather than brown. He slouches in the shoulders a bit but has a pretty nice body. Working with me and putting on that fifteen pounds was a major improvement. He had a nice lean, muscled body before, but now he's definitely a hottie. He pulled on a battered and paint-spattered T-shirt he'd cut the sleeves off of with the MGM studios logo on it. He always wore that damned shirt, along with the cutoff nylon blue sweatpants with the white stripes up the side.

He didn't dress to impress at the gym.

"I love Decadence," he said as I walked up to him.

"What's not to love?" I shrugged. "Just try not to drool on the equipment, okay? I don't want to have to sic Svetlana on you."

We headed out to the gym floor and started working out. Usually we talk a lot and camp it up a bit. David likes to think he is butch, but he can be really nelly when he puts his mind to it. He can sing the entire score of *West Side Story,* for example, and has done it while waiting for a machine. He has been known to launch into "I'm Gonna Wash That Man Right Out of My Hair" while I am doing bench presses. I call him Broadway David. But with all these muscled out-of-town boys around, the chances of him revealing his Broadway show-tune side were slim. We started on a chest machine. When it was his turn, I spotted someone.

"Isn't that Jeremy Fontaine?" I pointed.

David looked. "Yeah, it is. Haven't seen him in a while."

Jeremy used to be a waiter at the Clover Grill. He was a cute little guy, about five-four with reddish-blond hair and freckles. He'd waited on me more times at the crack of dawn than I cared to remember. He was from Mississippi originally and had lived in a small studio apartment near the corner of Burgundy and Ursulines. He'd had a long, ugly relationship with a crack addict. When that ended, he decided he wanted to attact a higher quality of boyfriend and he started training with me. He had a bit of a crush on me, and one night when he was drunk he'd confessed his all-consuming desire for me. It could have been awkward. Don't get me wrong; Jeremy is cute as a button, but he was a client. I don't have sex with my clients. There's something kind of sleazy about sleeping with someone who pays you for other services. Plus, he was still in that incredibly needy postbreakup stage. Definitely not a good idea. I had rejected him gently, and when he showed up for his next appointment he was very embarrassed. I made a joke about it to break the tension. I grinned at him. "You can't help it if I'm completely irresistible," I'd told him, and then we both laughed. We never mentioned it again.

Then one weekend morning on my way home from the bars, I stopped in for an omelette at the Clover and he was gone, no one knew where. He'd called the night before and quit over the phone, come in and picked up his last paycheck, and that was that. No one had the slightest idea of where he'd gone or why. He was just gone. That had been maybe a year ago. I didn't think too much of it. I was a little hurt that he hadn't called to cancel his next appointment. I didn't schedule anyone else into that time, but sure enough, he no longer showed. I just sighed and never thought about it again. New Orleans is a transient city. People come and go all the time.

He looked different. He'd shaved his head and had a barbed-wire tattoo around his right biceps. He was wearing long shorts and a tank top. He'd kept working out, it looked like. It was a good look for him, more butch and masculine. I wondered if he still collected Disney dolls. He'd been very proud of his doll collection. When he saw me looking, he looked away.

"Oh, but no," I said under my breath. "You're not playing that game with me, missy. You don't just disappear for a year without a word and then pretend you don't recognize me, uh-uh, no way." When we finished with the machine, I walked over to him. He was doing crunches on a mat.

"Hey, Jeremy, where've you been?"

He stopped doing his crunches and squinted up at me. "Do I know you?"

He *was* going to play that game. "Yes, you know me. Scotty Bradley. For God's sake, Jeremy, I was your trainer for about a couple of months."

"Oh, yeah, hi." He seemed nervous. His eyes kept darting around the gym. He wouldn't look directly at me. "I, uh, got a job and moved to Shreveport."

"Oh. In town for Decadence?"

"Um, no. I forgot it was Decadence."

Yeah, right. Whatever. You could *not* forget that Labor Day was Decadence weekend. Not unless you had amnesia, or a stroke or something. Especially when you'd lived here and worked as a waiter. It was one of those things you don't forget, like Mardi Gras and Jazz Fest.

Well, I certainly wasn't about to waste my time pulling his teeth out to get him to talk to me. "Nice seeing you." I turned to walk away, and stopped dead in my tracks.

There was a guy using the pullover machine staring at us. Now, I can appreciate a good-looking man just as much as the next, but it is very rare when one can stop me dead in my tracks. This guy was, well, can you say *hot daddy?*

He was balding, with short-cropped blondish-gray hair on the sides. There was a long scar on his cheek. He was wearing a pair of black-and-yellow striped spandex bike shorts that showed a rather ample endowment between his thickly muscled hairy legs. He was wearing a black strap tank top that showed blond hair on his chest. Thick, veined, muscles all over his body. The type of body you see in muscle magazines that you cut out and hang on your refrigerator. Steely gray eyes. The outline of dimples in both cheeks, if he ever smiled. He didn't look like he did smile very much. I could picture him in leather easy, with the harness, leather pants, and leather cap. He had that total masculine energy thing going for him.

I smiled at him. He scowled back.

Guess he was interested in Jeremy. Then again, he could be straight. Straight guys were more and more appropriating the gay look, which could explain the spandex shorts. It's hell on the gaydar. Oh, well. I made my way back to where David was doing military presses. "What's up with Jeremy?"

"He acted like he didn't know me, the asshole." I sat

down and started my set. "Did you see the hot daddy in the spandex?"

"Oh, yeah." David grinned. "I'd let him fuck me."

I just laughed. "Well, I made eye contact and smiled, and all I got was a scowl. Maybe he's straight."

"He seems to like Jeremy."

I finished my set and turned around. Sure enough, he was doing biceps curls with a pair of forty-pound dumbbells and watching Jeremy. David was right. Daddy must like them young. Or he could just be a chicken hawk. Jeremy could pass for a teenager, even with the shaved head.

After that, I stopped watching people and focused on getting my workout done. David kept a running prattle of commentary about the other guys in the gym, and I would occasionally say something to give the illusion of conversation. David was good with that. Put him in a room with a lot of muscle boys and he could go nonstop. Sometimes he'd lower his voice and say something like, "I could eat that ass with a spoon," or "Oh, yeah, Daddy, I'd let him fuck me." He was toying with the idea of being a bottom, but he kept chickening out, or not being able to find a top. Sometimes I got the feeling that he wanted me to initiate him into the world of the bottom, but we were too-good friends now. I'd probably start laughing.

One of the major disappointments in David's life was that he didn't get laid enough. He liked to say he was too choosy. At first, this kind of bothered me. The implication was that I wasn't choosy. I pointed that out to him once, more than a little annoyed. "No, you're just lucky," he'd responded. "Hotter guys hit on you than me." He frequently told me he hated me when I hooked up with a hot guy.

It was a weird friendship.

After we finished, David went home. He never showered or anything at the gym when he worked out with me.

Before we started working out together, he used to always talk about all the activity he got in the steam room. I've never understood why he stopped, and he's never really explained. It's not like we haven't gone to the bathhouse together on occasion. Maybe having me there weirded him out. Who knows? I got undressed amongst the hordes and decided to sit in the steam room for a while. I like the steam. It feels good. The muscles, all tensed up from the workout, relax in the wet heat. It also clears out your sinuses. I wrapped a towel around my waist and headed back there. I opened the door and stepped inside.

The swirling steam made me a little dizzy at first. *It was like this in the dream,* flashed through my head. "That's crazy," I told myself. For just a moment I could hear the screams of hundreds of people dying again, and then it was gone. "Yeah, hundreds of people being scalded to death in a steam room is what I dreamed about." The room was empty. I sat down in one of the white plastic chairs and closed my eyes, stretching my legs out and letting the steam do its magic. I let my mind relax and start to wander.

Relax, I told myself. Think good thoughts.

A swamp. I saw a swamp. I could hear the crickets chirping, the tree frogs croaking, the rustle of birds in the trees. Water—murky, smelly, dirty water. Danger. There was danger. I was splashing through the water. I stopped. Can't make noise they'll find me and they'll kill me if they find me have to get away have to warn people have to stop them hundreds of people will DIE—

The door opened. I jumped and opened my eyes.

"Sorry," said Hot Daddy. His towel was draped over his shoulder. Wow. His workout clothes had really left nothing to the imagination, but seeing it in the flesh, unclothed was, well, something else entirely.

"It's okay," I croaked out. "Must've dozed off."

He sat down in the chair next to mine and closed his eyes.

I closed mine again and tried to relax again. I pictured the swamp again, but nothing would come. No smells, no sounds. Damn it all to hell.

My imagination was definitely working overtime.

I sighed. The gift, such as it was, was not an exact science. Sometimes messages came to me in dreams. Sometimes I could meditate and see things. But it was hard to tell the difference between real visions and my overactive imagination. That's why I used the cards. The Goddess would speak, if willing, to me through the cards. Maybe the pictures on them helped me to focus. But me trudging through a swamp? Hundreds of people dying? Hardly. That was my imagination; it had to be. Some movie I must have watched in a stoner fog sometime coming back to haunt my—

A hand brushed my leg.

I opened my eyes and glanced over at Hot Daddy. His hands were draped over the arms of his chair. His eyes were closed.

Imagination again?

I closed my eyes again. Damn it, I was starting to get a hard-on. Thank God I had worn the towel. Wishful thinking was all it was. I wanted him to be interested in me. I wanted him to go back to my apartment and . . .

I opened my eyes. Yep, Hot Daddy's eyes were open and he was looking at me. Still no smile. The scar on his cheek looked even more intense with sweat running down it. I looked at his hand, then met his eyes again.

Make a move, damn it, I thought, concentrating, trying

to send my thoughts to him. Damn, I wish I was tele-pathic!

He smiled at me and then closed his eyes again.

I thought about touching him. I thought about reaching over and putting my hand on his hard, muscular leg. I thought about removing my towel and holding on to my hard-on until he opened his eyes again and I could show it to him. I thought about all kinds of things—the kinds of things I would like to do to his body, the kinds of things I wanted him to do to mine. *Come on, open your eyes, look at me, damn you; look at me!*

He sat there, doing nothing. His breathing was even.

I watched, waiting, ready to react to any sign of interest.

His mouth opened.

He snored.

The hell with this. I got up and went to the showers.

Chapter Four

EIGHT OF PENTACLES, REVERSED

Intrigue and sharp dealing

My stalker was waiting outside when I left to go to the bar.

I call Kenny Chandler my stalker, but he is basically harmless. He's not a stalker in the sense of leaving fifty messages on my voice mail every day, or rabbit-boiling, or following me around. He's actually a very sweet guy. In his mid-thirties, he had recently started working out. He's only about five-seven and reed-thin, but his workouts were starting to show. His arms, which once were just skin and bone, were now showing defined muscle. He wore a scraggly brown mustache, had greenish-brown eyes, and was starting to lose his hair a little bit. He was from Chalmette, one of the outer suburbs of this city. Locals jokingly refer to people like Kenny as Chalmatians. The typical Chalmatian might have a GED rather than a diploma, some tattoos, be missing a couple of teeth, and not be particularly bright. They also have an odd accent; a kind of mixture of Cajun and Brooklynese. No one ever gets that right in movies or TV shows.

I slept with him one night in the spring when I'd had too

much to drink (tequila shots again) and was feeling a bit down on myself. He'd introduced himself to me at Oz and offered to buy me another drink. He was nice; he was sweet; he was sort of cute; so a few hours later I invited him back to my apartment and fucked him.

That, apparently, was all it took for him to fall in love with me.

Don't get me wrong. I would like nothing more than to be in love and in a relationship, but Kenny was all wrong for me. I don't want a man who is going to wait on me hand and foot. I don't want a man who is going to agree with everything I say, do whatever I want him to do. Kenny's insecurities about his appearance and his slavish devotion to me were turn-offs. I like a guy to have a mind of his own. (Okay, I did kind of like the slavish-devotion thing, but only to a point.) He had taken to hanging around outside my front door on Decatur Street on weekend nights, waiting for me to come out, smoking cigarette after cigarette and drinking a bottle of Bud Light out of a brown paper bag. I wasn't sure if he did this every weekend, but he was always there every time I went out. It bugged Millie and Velma. Millie thought we should call the cops on him. I always talked her out of it, and he was always real nice and respectful to both of them whenever they came out and found him there.

He was kind of like a puppy.

"Hey, handsome," he said, smiling when I walked out with my gym bag.

"Happy Decadence, darlin'." I gave him a hug and a kiss. "What're you up to?"

He shrugged. "I scored some X and a little K, so I am gonna party it up tonight, maybe get lucky with some pretty tourist." He sighed. "If I'm lucky. Those boys don't really notice me."

We started walking up Decatur Street. Sometimes I

wondered if Kenny was really that down on himself or if he was just fishing for compliments. There were two ways to respond to this statement. I could either be complimentary: "Kenny, with that hot body you're getting from going to the gym, you'll be the hit of the party," or I could be sympathetic: "Now, Kenny, how you gonna get lucky with that bad attitude? You gotta believe you look good or no one else will." I opted for the former.

It was the right choice. His face lit up. "You really think so, Scotty?"

I smiled at him. "Of course I do, Kenny. I don't say things I don't mean. You're turning into quite the little hottie."

I hoped I wasn't giving him false hope. His confidence was so fragile, all it would take was some muscle boy to be rude or mean to him to shatter it. I've never understood why muscle boys can be so mean. But of course, the chances of that happening this weekend were slim. They'd all be drunk or drugged out of their minds. Usually that meant they'd be nicer.

Usually, but not always. I hoped Kenny would find one of the ones who got nicer when in an altered state, rather than one of the ones who became even bitchier. But to me, Decadence always brought out the nicer side of people.

We headed up Ursulines. Decatur Street was annoying to walk up. Like Bourbon, it was always crowded with tourists stopping to gawk in windows or trying to figure out where they were. It never occurs to them, apparently, that other people also need to use the sidewalk. It's not the heat—it's the stupidity. The shops on Decatur are a curious mix. There's the antique shops, and then the little grocery stores that cater to tourists. They're the ones that have the postcards of the president's and first lady's heads superimposed onto bodies dressed in leather bondage gear, or naked women who weigh about five hundred pounds plastered on their windows. Talk about your eyesores. They make a lot of money selling cigarettes, sodas, and beer at jacked-up prices. All the groceries on their shelves have a thin layer of dust on them.

The lower Quarter off of Decatur was very quiet. Fewer bars, fewer restaurants, fewer reasons for people to be down there. It was more residential, with high fences littered with either broken glass embedded in cement or razor wire. We got to Bourbon and turned left. We passed some groups of guys heading away from the bars, weaving a bit. On one stoop sat a guy in Lycra shorts with his eyes half closed. Sober, he was probably really pretty. Whatever state he was in was definitely unattractive. Drool coming out of his mouth, eyes glassy and unfocused, a couple of other guys similarly attired were talking to him, trying to get him oriented. An early SDC (Southern Decadence Casualty). It was a typical grouping. One of the guys was terribly concerned, wanting to take care of the casualty. The others looked annoyed. They wanted to have fun and didn't want to be saddled with a fucked-up friend. Nice.

As my mother says, "if you can't handle your drugs, don't do them."

"Hey." I nodded to them as we passed them. One of them looked me up and down and smiled. I laughed to myself as we kept walking.

Gay guys can always cruise.

We turned onto Bourbon Street. It started getting more and more crowded as we headed up. There was a big crowd in the street in front of Lafitte's. Guys on the balcony were throwing beads down to guys in the street. Jeans and shorts were being pulled down and dicks waving. I shook my head. Guys with cameras were everywhere. If these guys only knew . . . those pictures of their dicks would be on the Internet within 24 hours. But then again, they'd probably never know.

The corner at St. Ann and Bourbon was a mob scene. Guys of all shapes and sizes and colors were talking, drinking, dancing, cruising. Oh, yes, I would make a lot of money tonight if this crowd was any indication. It would only get more crowded later. I smiled at a couple of guys obviously cruising me. I kissed Kenny on the cheek. "You have fun tonight, okay? Don't let the bitchy ones make you feel bad, all right?"

He smiled back at me. "Thanks, Scotty. You give 'em a good show."

I watched him disappear into the crowd, and pushed my way into the bar and headed back for the office, where I would shed my sweats, oil up my body, and get ready for work. On my way through the crowd, my ass got grabbed a couple of times. Well, why wouldn't it? I do have a nice one. I've been told enough times that I had to believe it.

Ah, Decadence. I grinned. I should make lots of money tonight.

I knocked on the office door. Joey, the night manager, let me in. Joey was a nice enough guy. He was missing a tooth in the bottom row. He had dark hair and a goatee. His Bourbon Pub T-shirt fit tightly. He was wearing khaki shorts. He was always really cool to me. His boyfriend was an emergency room nurse, and just as nice as Joey. They lived in Uptown and had a pool. I'd been to parties at their house. He wiped sweat off his forehead. "Thanks for filling in again, Scotty."

I shrugged. "No problem."

I stashed my bag in a corner. Two other guys, the ones I'd be dancing with, were already back there. I recognized the tall blond immediately. Cody Dallas, flavor of the season in porn movies. He was tall for a porn star, about six-two. I'd rented one of his movies on David's recommendation. He had a huge cock, which was his stock in trade. His hair was white-blond and darker underneath. He was wearing a pink Day-Glo thong. His body was darkly tanned and solid as a rock. His skin was smooth all over. Big pecs and arms and shoulders and thickly muscled legs. He looked like he'd been a football player or something. He had a cool kind of aura. He was immensely likable on video. Some people just have that kind of charisma. I've danced with porn stars before. Some of them were cool, some were divas, and some were just a mess. His eyes weren't dilated. He nodded to me and smiled. Beautiful smile. It lit up his entire face. Definitely not a diva, which would make life easier.

The other guy was the one who really caught my eye. About five-six, he weighed at least 180 pounds and it was all muscle. His hair was cut short in a military style but was blue-black. His skin was olive, and the shadow of his beard gave it a bluish tint. His eyes were a bright blue. He was wearing a black thong that emphasized his round, hard ass. He was loosening up, twisting his torso from side to side. Every movement caused muscles to ripple throughout his body. "Hey," he said and smiled at me. Perfectly aligned white teeth. He stuck out his hand. "I'm Colin."

"Scotty." His grip was hard and strong. His hand was moist. There was a thin sheen of sweat on him. He winked at me and glanced over at Cody. I followed his eyes. Cody had his thong down and was using a pump on his dick. I rolled my eyes at Colin, who laughed.

"I don't use the pump," he whispered to me.

"Me, either," I said, dropping my sweats and pulling on my American-flag thong. I got a bottle of baby oil out and rubbed it into my chest, arms, and legs. Not too much; it wouldn't do to be touched by a spender and be oily. Just enough so that my skin would shine in the dim bar light. Colin took the bottle from me and squirted some into his hands. He rubbed them together and started massaging some onto my ass.

He was good.

I felt myself getting hard.

He smacked my ass, hard enough to sting. "We should get out there, I guess."

The office door opened and the earlier shift, drenched in sweat, came in.

I finished lacing up my boots. "Let's go, then."

Cody was obviously the star attraction of the night. They'd been advertising his appearance for weeks, both him and Rock Hard. Most dancers and porn stars tended to be on the small side, like me and Colin. Cody was big in every way. Once on the bar, his physical presence demanded attention from the party-goers. Too bad, I thought as I hoisted myself up on the bar. He'll get most of the money tonight, but I should still do okay.

The deejay was playing a remix of "Absolutely Not," by Deborah Cox. A great song. I maneuvered myself into a space where there weren't any glasses or bottles on the bar and started dancing. You have to be careful on the bar, always keeping your eyes out for bottles, glasses, and spills. Like I said, I've fallen off of more bars than I care to remember. I love to dance, especially to a hot song. Rain always says we should have known I was gay because even as a kid I loved to dance. I may not be the sexiest or prettiest go-go boy on the bar, but I knew I was the best dancer. I glanced over at Cody and smiled to myself. No rhythm whatsoever. Colin was moving okay, nothing special. I closed my eyes and listened to the beat. I didn't move my feet, just started moving my hips from side to side. My shoulders and arms started to move as well. When the chorus came, I was in full, fluid motion. Every muscle in my body was moving to the music. I felt a hand stroking my calf. I opened my eyes and looked down. A spender. Moving my hips from side to side, I crouched down to him.

Let the games begin.

At eleven-thirty we took a break. The music was still going strong, and the crowd was growing in size—as well as more fucked up. The air was thick and heavy and the bar was starting to smell like sweat. The office was air-conditioned. I wiped myself down with a towel and started pulling damp, crumpled bills out of my socks and boots.

"Nice crowd," Colin said. He was doing the same.

"Never been to Decadence before?" I asked. Cody was lining up a white powder on a picture frame. Too bad. I was hoping he wasn't into that.

"First time." Colin pulled off his black thong and pulled on another. It was red.

"It gets pretty wild." I pulled off my own and dug through my bag for the white one. The flag thong was soaked through. I pulled up the white one.

"You guys want some?" Cody asked as he finished the line.

"What is that?" I asked.

"Tina." He grinned at me. His big brown eyes were starting to glaze over.

"No, thanks." Okay, I smoke pot. I have been known to take Ecstasy from time to time. But I don't mess with anything that goes up your nose. Coke, K, Tina—I just don't see the thrill in inhaling something up your nose that is habit-forming.

Cody shrugged and walked back out to the bar.

"She's a mess." Colin shrugged his big shoulders. "I worked with him at Hotlanta a couple of weeks ago. She didn't sleep the entire weekend. Won't last long at this rate. Dumb as a post, too."

"Where are you from?" I took a swing from my bottle of water.

"Philly." He sat down on the couch with his legs spread. He grinned at me. "Have a seat."

Tempting, oh, so tempting. "We'd better get back out there."

He reached up and smacked my ass again. "Sure?"

I grinned. "I need to pay my rent."

He laughed. "Okay."

It was about a half hour later that I saw the man with the scar.

I was kneeling down with my thong pulled down. An older, overweight, hairy guy with no shirt had offered me ten bucks to show him my dick, so I did. He touched it and gave me another five. I stood up and readjusted myself in the thong. I glanced over into the corner of the bar and he was there. He wasn't wearing a shirt. He had a bottle of water in his hand. He was wearing jeans that hung low off his hips, and no underwear. When he saw me look over, he looked away quickly. He looked great.

So we're gonna play that game, huh? I thought to myself. I walked down the bar to where he was standing in the corner, and started pumping my hips in his direction. He kept scanning the crowd, ignoring me. I kept moving and looking at him.

Someone touched my leg.

I lost focus.

The room filled with fog. I couldn't see anything. I could hear screaming, lots of screaming. Sirens in the distance, crowds fighting, explosions; death was everywhere, death and its foul smell; everyone was going to die—

And then it was gone.

Someone was still touching my leg.

Automatically I crouched down on the bar.

It was Jeremy.

"Hey," I said, trying to shake off whatever it was. I shivered despite the heat.

"Hey, Scotty." His eyes were darting around the crowd.

Oh, sure, now you remember me, I thought. *Now that you're all hopped up on something.* He wasn't wearing a shirt. He was wearing a long pair of khaki shorts that reached his knees. A black T-shirt was tucked into his waistband. "You okay, guy?"

"They're after me, Scotty."

Great. Whatever it was, it induced paranoia. "Who?"

"I need a place to hide. Can I hide out at your place? It'll just be for a couple of hours, I swear."

Exactly what I need. Some spaced-out kid coming down in my apartment. "I don't think so, Jeremy."

"Please?"

I shook my head. "Uh-uh."

He hung his head. "I'll meet you back here at two and when I explain, you'll understand, okay?"

"Sure, Jeremy, sure." I glanced at my watch. It was almost midnight. *Surely by then he'll have come down,* I reasoned. I stood back up.

I watched him push his way through the crowd and out the doors onto St. Ann. I glanced back over into the corner. The scarred man was pushing his way out onto St. Ann as well.

He walked off in the same direction that Jeremy had gone.

Definitely a chicken hawk, I thought to myself. Too damned bad.

Another guy waved a dollar at me.

I went back to work.

Chapter Five

TWO OF CUPS

The beginning of a new romance

Two in the morning came at last.

My legs felt like they were going to fall off. Dancing in boots for four hours is not as easy as it looks. My feet ached. My calves felt like they were on fire. My socks and boots were filled with crumpled bills. My socks and thong were soaked through with sweat. My hips and knees creaked as I climbed down off the bar. It wasn't as crowded as it had been earlier. Most of the party boys were upstairs on the dance floor by now, drugs hitting, dancing with their shirts off. I felt like I had lost five pounds of water through sweat.

I had some blisters on my feet, too. I was going to have to get new boots. They'd even rubbed my skin a little raw at the top. A couple of guys stopped me so they could touch my chest, butt, and abs. I smiled and wished them "Happy Decadence." My lower back ached as well. All those hip movements. I needed to stretch everything out.

Joey answered when I knocked on the office door. A Camel nonfilter was dangling from a corner of his mouth. "You wanna keen dancing?"

I shrugged. "Up to you."

I collapsed in a heap on the couch. Fuck, I was tired. I sat there for a minute, then reached over and dragged my bag to me.

"You giving up for the night?" Colin asked as he came in.

"I'm beat."

"Yeah, I'm pretty over it." He straddled a chair. "I think Cody's gonna keep going, though."

Big surprise there. He was doing everything but hanging from the ceiling. Once, on my way to the bathroom, I walked past him. His thong was down and someone was licking whipped cream off of his dick.

I wondered what the fee for that was.

I yawned as I untied my boots. It would feel good to have them off. They really were designed for look rather than comfort of wear. I eased my aching feet out of them. Crumpled-up dollars fell on the floor. I swept them all up into my hands and shoved them into my bag. I picked up the boots and dumped the damned things into the bag. There were bills in there, too, but I'd wait till I got home to count it. It could even wait until tomorrow morning. It had been a good night, even with the competition from Cody. I slipped my soaked socks off and emptied them of bills into my bag. I tossed them into the garbage. I didn't ever want to touch them again. They were soaked with sweat. I probably had lost at least ten pounds of water on the bar. I leaned back onto the couch.

"You hungry?" Colin asked. He had slipped his thong off and was pulling on a pair of tight black underwear.

My stomach growled. I hadn't eaten since before going to the gym. "Yeah."

"Wanna grab a bite to eat?"

"Everything'll be packed," I replied. I looked him over.

He was pretty hot. What the hell. "We can go back to my place and I could heat up something."

His thick black eyebrows went up. "You live here? Cool."

I had half of a vegetarian lasagna in my refrigerator that Aunt Velma had dropped off earlier in the week. I sat on the floor, straightened my legs out, and leaned forward to stretch out the tightness. It felt good. "Yeah, I'm a native." I reached into the bag and pulled out my trusty cutoff white sweatpants. I stood up with a groan. I peeled the soaking-wet G-string off and slid the cutoffs on with a groan. Colin's arms came around from behind as he pressed up against me. He squeezed me. It felt good. "Mmmmm."

He wasn't just hungry for food.

What can I say? I'm just irresistible.

I usually don't sleep with other dancers. It's not a hard-and-fast rule, something I have embroidered on a sampler hanging in my living room. It's usually because I am too tired and just want to go home to bed and sleep. Usually the other dancers are hopped up on something, and I don't want to be bothered. There's nothing worse than taking someone home, expecting some good, hot, sweaty sex, and they can't get hard or sit still long enough for any fun. No, thanks.

But Colin seemed to be sober. His pupils weren't dilated. He did have a great body. I could feel his hard chest up against my back. I could also feel another telling hardness through his underwear. Nice. I turned and we kissed. Even nicer. He had just sucked on a breath mint or something, because his breath was all sweet and pepperminty. His lips were full, firm yet soft. I slid my arms around him and squeezed his butt. It was hard as a rock.

I pulled back and grinned at him. "We'd better stop. I

don't want Joey to come in here and catch us doing what I wanna be doing."

I'm never too tired to get laid.

Colin laughed. "Okay." He pulled on a pair of cutoff sweatpants and a white tank top. "Let's go."

I put on my T-shirt and picked up my bag, slinging it over a shoulder. I opened the office door. A Whitney Houston remix was blaring. "My Love is Your Love." We walked past the stairs that lead up to the dance floor and past where the partiers pay cover to get in. The Pub was still packed. Cody was up on the bar, a towel dangling off his big erection. He saw us and winked, turning and wiggling his tanned ass at us. I grinned. It was easy to see why he was a big star. He sure knew how to work a crowd.

Well, having the body of death probably didn't hurt much, either.

We pushed through the crowd and out into the street. There was a huge crowd of people on both St. Ann and Bourbon Streets. The music from Oz was blaring. Scantily clad guys were dancing in the street. The air was thick and heavy. The sky was full of clouds. It hadn't cooled off much after the sun set. If anything, the air had gotten thicker and heavier. Hopefully, it would rain during the night, cool everything down for a little while. On the opposite side of St. Ann, a smaller crowd was picketing.

JESUS DIED FOR YOUR SINS.
REPENT AND BE WASHED IN THE BLOOD OF THE LAMB
THE LORD PUNISHED SODOM AND GOMORRAH
GAYS WILL BURN IN HELL
AIDS IS A JUDGMENT FROM GOD

And other charming sayings like that.

I shivered in spite of the heat.

Most Christians are good people. I accept that. They do

their best and try to lead positive, healthy lives. But as with any group of people, there's that lunatic fringe that likes to point fingers and be holier than thou. Those people scare the shit out of me. Their whole religion is built on tolerance and love. How they can twist that into intolerance and hate is beyond me. They are always out picketing during Southern Decadence, Mardi Gras—anytime there's crowds of revelers out in the Quarter. The Decadence crowd usually ignores them and has a good time in spite of their efforts. Mardi Gras, on the other hand, can get ugly. They usually pull up to the corner of St. Ann and Bourbon in a flatbed truck with loudspeakers and try to preach the gospel, to save souls. They usually get pelted with beads and empty cups. The Quarter horse cops get between this group and the gay boys, keeping an eye on things, making sure things don't get out of hand.

Tourist dollars, after all, were at risk here.

I glanced over at the picketing Christians. I had to admire their tenacity. It was pretty late at night.

Colin took my hand and squeezed it. "You okay?"

Everything went out of focus again.

The fog.

The screams.

I staggered and stepped off the curb into the garbage accumulated there. My foot turned and I fell into a group of shirtless guys. One of them caught me. "Hey, buddy, you okay?"

I shook my head. Everything swam back into focus. I looked at him. His pupils were as big as quarters, and if his eyes were open any bigger, the top of his head would pop open. He was huge. About six-five, maybe 220 of hard muscle. His left nipple was pierced. There was a sun tattoo around his navel. A thin line of hair ran up from the tattoo to a patch between his massive pecs.

He was smiling at me.

He was also holding my ass in both big hands.

Being irresistible is a curse sometimes, I'm telling you.

"I'm fine." I took some deep breaths. That was scary.

Colin took my hand and pulled me through the crowd. I saw empty steps leading to the front door of one of the houses. I sank down onto them and waited for my goose bumps to go down. Colin stood in front of me. "Scotty? Are you okay?"

I forced a smile. "Yeah. Just got dizzy all of a sudden. The heat. Hungry, too, I guess." I couldn't tell him I'd had a vision. He'd think I was crazy.

The gift, as Madame Xena had called it, wasn't easy to explain. People either thought I was completely insane or wanted me to pick Lotto numbers for them. If it only worked that way! It came and went as it pleased. Reading the cards helped me focus and made it work in some ways. Sometimes I got a sense from people, but from most people, nothing. From Cody I'd sensed good energy, a really nice guy. I got nothing from Colin. There was no sense of whether he was healthy or sick or unhappy or even a good person—nothing, which was just as well. Usually, if I sense someone's aural vibrations I don't sleep with him. I don't think it's fair to the guy, really. It gives me an unfair advantage, if that makes any sense.

So I just keep it to myself. There's no sense in spreading it around. Outside of my family, which is pretty wacky anyway, I don't let people know about the gift. It's just easier that way.

I also don't know what triggers it, or why.

Sometimes I think it's just some cosmic joke the Goddess plays with me.

"Stay here; I'm gonna get you some water." Colin disappeared back into the crowd.

What was she trying to tell me? First there was the dream I couldn't really remember. This was the third time

I had sensed the fog and heard the screams. I sent a silent plea to her: *Please tell me what this is all about. Please.*

No answer.

Big surprise.

Colin came back with a plastic bottle of water. I took it from him and drank. My heartbeat had slowed down and I was starting to feel somewhat normal again. The water was good. I was pretty dehydrated.

"Still want me to come over?" He shifted from one foot to the other.

"Yeah." I grinned at him. "Why wouldn't I?"

He smiled. "Well, I'd hardly let you walk home alone now anyway."

Great. He probably thought I was nuts or something. How erotic. I stood up. "Let's go. I probably just need some food. I didn't have dinner. Dehydrated, too."

He took my hand as we walked up Bourbon Street. "This is sure a pretty city."

"You've never been here before?"

He shook his head. "First time."

"Where are you from?"

"I live in San Francisco now, in the Castro." He shrugged. "We moved all over when I was growing up, so I really don't have a place I call home."

"Isn't San Francisco home now?"

"Not really. Just another way station." He laughed. "Although I do like it here. What's it like to live here?"

"I've always lived here." We reached the corner of Barracks and turned right. "I can't imagine living any-where else. Whenever I've gone to another place, like on vacation, it's not too great. I mean, everyone and every-thing is so uptight. New Orleans isn't like that at all."

"I see that." He squeezed my hand. "Seems like a great place."

"It is."

Barracks was completely deserted and dark except for the soft glow cast by the streetlights. A few blocks up, cars were passing by on Decatur, and there were plenty of people milling about on the sidewalk. The silence seemed a little weird after the noise and crowds on Bourbon Street. My ears were ringing a little from the loud music I'd been hearing all night long.

I heard footsteps behind us.

Footsteps on a deserted street. Not a good omen.

I started walking a little faster.

A voice screamed in my head: *Run, Scotty!*

It happened so fast, I didn't have time to react. Something grabbed the strap of my gym bag and yanked just as I set my foot down on one of the major cracks in the sidewalk. I stumbled, and the sudden pressure on my shoulder strap yanked me sideways. I started to fall. Out of the corner of my eye I saw Colin turn to grab me as I fell, and the concerned look on his face switched to anger in a split second. As I was falling, the pressure on my shoulder strap increased. I saw Colin start to swing his bag around just as I hit the ground. There was a loud "Oof!" as Colin's bag connected. My shoulder strap broke at the same time, and I grabbed for it.

Colin swung again.

I looked up.

I saw a face. His head was shaved clean. His nose was hooked, with a pronounced bump in the middle, like it had been broken once. Small, beady eyes beneath bushy eyebrows that met in the center. He wasn't wearing a shirt and had a flat stomach and muscular shoulders and arms. There was a black swastika tattoo on his left chest, and another one of razor wire around his right biceps. The expression on his face . . .

Then Colin's bag connected with it and the face was gone.

There was a crash as a body hit the street.

I scrambled to my feet, holding on to the bag, just as Colin was stepping over me. We went back down.

I heard running footsteps in the street, heading away from us, back toward Bourbon Street.

"Are you okay?" Colin stood up and reached down for me.

I took his hand and he pulled me up. I started shaking.

Okay, so it wasn't the most butch reaction. New Orleans is not a crime-free city. Pockets get picked; tourists get mugged; women get raped; cars get stolen. But it's never happened to me. No one I knew had ever been mugged. That only happened to people I didn't know. But there I was, within two blocks of my home, and someone had tried to take my bag and who knows what else. If I'd been by myself . . .

But I hadn't been. Thank the Goddess.

Colin put his arms around me and squeezed. I held on to him for a few minutes.

Colin had saved me, had saved the more than four hundred dollars in soggy bills in my bag.

My bag.

I looked down at it. I had the broken strap in a death grip. Over four hundred dollars, not to mention what Colin had in his.

"We'd better get to my place quick," I said, breaking the hug.

He nodded. "I don't think he'll come back, but it's a good idea."

My hands were shaking so bad, I couldn't fit the key in the lock. Colin took the keys out of my hand and opened it. I led him down the passage after making sure that the gate had locked. Okay, I checked it twice. We went up to my apartment. This time I could get the key in the lock and opened the door. I switched on the lights and dropped my bag. Colin shut the door and I dead-bolted it.

"Nice place," he said, and then I shut him up by putting my mouth over his. I pushed him back against the door and slid my hands down till they were cupping his hard ass. He put his arms around me and lifted me off the floor. I wrapped my legs around his waist.

"Bedroom?" he asked.

I nodded to the open door.

He carried me in and set me down on the bed. He pulled his shirt over his head while I did the same. He grabbed my sweatpants and yanked them down. In movies, of course, they always come off easy and quickly. Real life is a different story. They tangled on my sneakers. I finally had to reach down and untie my shoes and kick them off. While I was doing that, he took off his shorts and under-wear and stood there watching. I struggled out of my underwear, and then he lay down beside me. I rolled over on top of him and started kissing his ears, his throat, his mouth. He rolled me over and was back on top of me, and I spread my legs. Our crotches ground together as our hands explored, as our tongues explored each other's mouths.

"Fuck me," he whispered into my ear.

I grinned at him. "Love to." I rolled him back over onto his back and climbed off the bed. "I just need to light some candles."

"Okay." He sat up. His muscles rippled. Wow.

I lit the white candles I had scattered around the bed-room. White is for purity. Sex is a sacred rite to the Goddess, a way of praying.

Sometimes, I really love praying.

I got some condoms and lube out of my dresser and walked back over to the bed.

"You are so hot," Colin whispered.

I grinned. I love being irresistible.

Chapter Six

QUEEN OF PENTACLES, REVERSED

A suspicious and mistrustful nature

I couldn't sleep.

I'd wiped the results of our coupling off of his chest and stomach with a towel and went into the bathroom to get rid of the condom. When I got back, Colin was sound asleep. I stood there for a moment and looked at him. He was gorgeous, absolutely gorgeous. The light from the moon was drifting through the slats on my shutters, streaking lines across his smooth torso. One arm was draped casually over his forehead, revealing the dark patch of hair in his armpit. His face was utterly peaceful. For a moment, I wished I had a decent camera. The way he was lying there was such an amazing pose, it should be captured on film.

I climbed back into the bed. My silk sheets felt wonderful against my skin. I cuddled up to him. His skin was so soft and smooth, it was almost as silky as the sheets. I wondered briefly how he kept his skin so soft. It was an amazing contrast. His muscles were so well developed, but his skin . . .

I closed my eyes and spooned up next to him. I could feel his soft, even breathing.

I opened my eyes.

I couldn't sleep.

My stomach growled again. Okay, okay, I told myself. Food first, cuddling second.

I walked into my little kitchenette and pulled the vegetarian lasagna out. I spooned a big helping onto a plate and set the microwave for three minutes. I went back into the hall and grabbed my gym bag. Might as well count and straighten out the money while I waited. It certainly wasn't going to do it on its own.

I set the bag on the counter. I unzipped it and dumped everything out. Soaked G-strings, damp money, big, clunky, totally uncomfortable boots. I picked up the wet G-strings and tossed them into the sink. They made a wet, splooshing sound. *Yuck.* I picked one up and rung about a liter of water out of it. Nice. Well, that could wait until morning.

I started straightening the bills out and making little piles. Most of the bills were ones, but there was the occasional five or ten. They were all wet. I spread them out on the counter to dry. I felt sorry for the teller at the bank who would take my deposit on Tuesday morning. The smell of sweat would be on them no matter how dry they were. *Blech.* There weren't any twenties. I was idly wondering how much Cody got for the whipped cream on the dick trick when I turned my boots upside down to empty them out.

A black, unmarked computer disk rattled onto the counter.

"What the fuck?" I said aloud just as the microwave dinged. I grabbed my plate of lasagna, a fork, and the disk and walked into the living room. I turned on the television, muted the sound, and sat down. A rerun of *The Brady Bunch.* Was there anyone anywhere on the planet who hadn't seen every single episode of that show a hundred times already? The lasagna was extremely hot. I had to blow on it to try to cool every mouthful down before putting it in my mouth. On the television, Jan was having a nervous breakdown for some reason or another. I didn't like the Jan episodes much. My favorite was the one where Marcia got hit in the nose with a football right before a big date. "Oh, my nose!" I smiled at the memory. My eyes kept coming back to the computer disk, though. Where the hell had that come from?

I didn't have a very good feeling about it, and that wasn't the gift talking. Why the hell would someone put a computer disk in my boot? Who had done it, and why? It could have been anyone, really. I just paid attention to the money in their hands, nothing else. And of course, someone could have slipped it into my boot while I was working money out of someone else.

I tried to remember as I ate. *Think, Scotty, think. Anything out of the ordinary?* No. I hadn't paid much attention. Dancing doesn't require a lot of thought, and it sure doesn't require a lot of observation other than to see who's looking at you. I was moving around the bar pretty much all night. I tried to respond when someone touched me, giving them a big smile that would make them part with some cash. It wasn't always possible. When I'd kneel down, for example, with someone in between my legs, people on either side of me would run their hands down my legs or touch my ass. It would have been easy for someone to slide the disk into my boot then and I wouldn't notice. And my calves and feet were pretty much numb with fatigue after the first hour. I wouldn't have felt the disk in there, with all the crumpled-up bills shoved in there and in my socks.

I put the plate down and picked up the disk. I held it in both hands and closed my eyes. I emptied my mind of thought and focused on the disk, trying to pick up anything, any vibrations, anything that would tell me who put it there.

And why.

I was drawing a blank.

I was about to put it down on the table when everything swam out of focus again.

Fog swirled, blurring my vision.

I heard a loud noise, an explosion of some sort.

Water, running water, cascading, loud.

Screams.

Horns honking.

Sirens.

Screams.

The disk fell out of my shaking hands.

I believe in evil. I always have. Maybe not in the Christian sense, with Satan and his horns and forked tail egging humans on to commit unspeakable acts, but it is there, always lurking. I believe that we all have choices to make, a choice between being good and doing evil. I've always believed that evil is a human creation, that nature in and of itself is good, that the power of the universe is positive rather than negative. Only humans have the ability to do evil, to make evil and give it strength and power.

But the disk itself was evil.

Yeah, right, jackass, I told myself. Inanimate objects can't be evil. An inanimate object can only pick up the evil vibrations from the people who handle it. Someone had handled it who was evil, or who committed evil acts.

But maybe what was on the disk was evil.

I got out my cards and started shuffling absently. I spread them out and looked at them: Danger. Destruction. Terrible change brought about by violence. Indecision.

I looked at the disk again.

I don't own a computer. I don't like technology much. Sure, I have a cell phone and a beeper, but half the time they aren't turned on. They're just gadgets, tools of my trade as a personal trainer. Maybe it's because of the conspiracy theories my parents have always drilled into my head since I was a kid. I don't know. Mom and Dad don't have a computer with Internet access. They have a computer to do inventory and bookkeeping for the store, but no Internet. One night at dinner, Storm had been extolling the joys of the Internet, and how they should get a Web site for the store, and on and on. "Think about it," he'd said. "People from all over the country could order cigars from you. Or any of your merchandise. They'd pay for shipping and handling. Think of the money you could rake in!" Totally the wrong approach for Storm to make to them, I thought at the time. It was amazing how little he knew our parents. Mom and Dad just listened, very politely. That should have tipped him off. When he had finished making his case, and had me half-convinced to go out and buy a computer, Mom lit a joint and said, "But how do we know the government isn't monitoring the Internet?"

"They aren't," Storm replied.

"Do you know that?" Mom blew out the smoke and closed her eyes. "How do you know that they aren't watching everyone? Monitoring their conversations and E-mails? Seeing what Web sites they visit? Keeping track of what they buy and who they talk to? It would be really easy, wouldn't it? And then couldn't the government be able to tap into your computer and see everything that's in it? Orwell didn't even have the imagination and vision to see the world of computers. And isn't the government involved? Weren't they involved in the forming and creation of the Internet? Do you really think they just stepped back and said, 'Here, have at it; knock yourselves out; have a great time with this?' A government that was capable of producing a Richard Nixon? A government that could bomb innocent women and children at will without a second thought? A government who could let thousands of its citizens die from AIDS and pretend it wasn't happening? Why wouldn't they monitor activity on the Internet and track everything in the interests of national security? Of course they would, honey, of course they would. I'm afraid one day in the not-so-distant future we are all going to wake up and find out that Big Brother is a reality. I'm sorry, dear, but I for one am not willing to sacrifice my personal freedoms for the 'convenience' of the Internet."

Needless to say, I didn't get a computer.

But David had one.

David spent hours on the Internet looking for sex, cruising Web sites, sending messages to possible tricks. David couldn't believe that I was so stupid as not to have a computer. I'd gone over to his house a couple of times and played on the Internet with him. It was truly amazing to me the way people would send, proudly, pictures of their naked bodies and their erect penises and their spread asscheeks to a total stranger. He showed me his own listing on a site called Hotgaysex.com or something like that. His picture was a torso shot, a pretty flattering one that emphasized his lean body. "People coming to New Orleans check these sites out," he'd enthused, "and if they like your picture and what you have listed on your profile, they send you an E-mail and their own picture. I've made a lot of dates this way—and have wound up with a lot of really hot guys. You really need to get on the Internet, Scotty. You could even have your own Web site for your training business. People who want to work out can do a search for trainers, and you'd come up. Think about all the business you could get!"

When I first became a trainer, I'd run an ad in the local gay paper, along with a picture of me flexing my biceps. I'd gotten exactly two clients from it in two years. Most of the calls I'd gotten had been people looking for escorts. Apparently, they thought *personal trainer* was merely a new euphemism for *escort*. I'd gotten to where I could identify the escort calls pretty easily. They might actually talk about training for a little while, and then it would always go in a different direction. "Would you be willing to train me just wearing a jock?"

Somehow, I didn't think the staff at Riverview Fitness would be too thrilled by that.

I'd used David's computer a couple of times to make flyers for my training business. I was sort of able to understand how to work it. How hard could it be, really? One of the reasons that I always used to not buy one was that I couldn't understand how to work one, and he always insisted that it was easy, that a child could do it. "In fact," he said, "children do use computers every single day. They're better at it than I am."

Yeah, whatever. Both David and I both knew the real reason he had a computer was to help him get laid.

I looked at the clock. Three-thirty. David wouldn't be home yet. He had probably taken a hit of Ecstasy a little before midnight and right now was dancing onstage at either the Parade or Oz with his shirt off with a big dopey grin on his face and touching the sweaty torsos of the guys dancing around him. He would only just now be starting to come down from the high a bit and trying to decide whether to go to the bathhouse or go home.

Of course, David didn't have to be home for me to use his computer. I have a key to his house to feed Gershwin, his cat, when he goes out of town from time to time. It was only a few blocks away. I could take the disk, walk over there, check it out, and be gone before David even got home. If he went to the bathhouse, he'd be there till at least six.

I walked into the bathroom and brushed my teeth. I

pulled on a pair of shorts and a tank top. I walked into the bedroom to get my shoes.

Colin. What the hell was I going to do about Colin?

He had rolled over onto his stomach in his sleep, turning up his perfectly round butt. There was a mole on the back of his neck I hadn't noticed earlier. He was snoring slightly.

I should, if I was smart, just crawl in there and curl up with him.

I couldn't very well just leave Colin alone in my house. Fuck. He seemed like a nice guy, but I didn't even know his last name. He could very easily just wake up, find me gone, and help himself to all my money, my television, and my VCR and be long gone before I got back. I could wake him and send him on his way. I could wake him and bring him along.

I put on my shoes and walked back into the kitchen. I swept all the money back into my bag. I grabbed the disk and my keys. I closed the back door without a sound and headed down to the second floor. I got out the key to Millie and Velma's apartment, unlocked their door, slid my bag inside, and shut and locked it. There. The money was safe. If he was a thief and wanted the TV and VCR, he could have them. I never used them much for anything besides porn, anyway.

I opened the gate. Decatur Street was silent. There were people blocks away milling about in front of one of the bars, but everything seemed okay. No muggers to be seen anywhere. I headed down Decatur to the Marigny.

The Marigny is just on the other side of Esplanade from the Quarter. Some people call it the "poor man's Quarter." Up until a few years ago, it was a derelict neighborhood. The houses looked ready to fall down, businesses had closed, and no one with half a grain of sense walked through there alone at night. David had bought his double-shotgun house there for a song and then had to sink a hell of a lot of money into making it livable. He wasn't the only one with the bright idea of buying a wrecked house there and redoing it. Over the last few years, the neighborhood had made an incredible comeback. People who couldn't afford the rents in the Quarter bought houses and renovated. Businesses, bars, and restaurants started opening up again. Frenchmen Street, just on the other side of Esplanade from Decatur, was turning into a mini-Bourbon Street without the pickpockets, strippers, whores, and neon. That was the route I took. There were plenty of people out on the street even at this late hour, which made me feel somewhat safer. David's house was on Pauger, which ran into Frenchmen.

All the lights were off when I got there. I thanked the Goddess for my luck. I was slipping the key into the lock when I heard David say, "Scotty? What the hell?"

He was wearing a pair of khaki shorts that were soaked through with sweat. He had his arm around a Hispanic guy who was about five-four and all muscle. Mentally I swore to myself. Well, at least I had gotten there now instead of letting myself in later and walking in on them.

"Hey."

They climbed the steps. David's eyes were wide open and dilated. So were his companion's. David stared at me. "What's up, dude?"

"I need to use your computer."

David shuffled from one foot to the other. "Not a good time, dude." He always overused the word "dude" when he was rolling. "This is Ramón, from Dallas. Why do you need my computer?"

"I need to see what's on a disk." I pulled it out of my sock. "Nice to meet you, Ramón." Ramón nodded. He was bouncing on the balls of his feet. They were both flying.

He took it from me. "Can't it wait till the morning?"
I sighed. "Yeah."

David unlocked the door and opened it. "Give me a call in the morning. We'll talk about it then."

I stood there for a minute. I didn't like the idea of leaving the evil disk in David's possession, but then again couldn't think of a reason not to. And I could hardly tell him that I thought the disk was evil.

Not with Ramón standing there.

David didn't know about the gift, and now wasn't the time to tell him.

I sighed. "Okay I'll call you in the morning, but it'll be really early."

"Okay. Good night, Scotty." He winked at me. "I'm probably not going to get a lot of sleep, if you know what I mean."

The door closed behind them.

Chapter Seven

THE MOON

Bad luck for an acquaintance

I sat down on the steps for a minute to think. Patience wasn't one of my virtues. I didn't watch miniseries on television, because I hated to wait to see what happened. *Of all nights for David to get lucky,* I thought to myself, and then shrugged. Who was I to begrudge David sex? I'd already gotten laid tonight. Maybe this was the Goddess's way of telling me it was better to wait till morning to find out whatever was on the disk. It probably wasn't anything important, nothing major. My curiosity had just gotten the best of me.

Again.

I stood up. How incredibly stupid and impulsive I'd been to run out of the house that way. I'd left a total stranger alone in my apartment. Granted, I'd made sure my money was safe, but at the very least it was rude. How would I feel if I woke up in a trick's apartment and the trick had left me alone? It would be very weird, to say the least. I'd wonder if I should stay or go. What would I do? Probably get dressed, leave a note on the nightstand, and get the hell out of there. I didn't want Colin to leave just yet. I'd really been looking forward to sleeping next to him. He'd been sleeping pretty soundly when I left, but . . .

I imagined Colin waking up and finding me gone, wandering around the apartment, calling my name.

Waking up Millie and Velma.

Now *that* was a terrifying thought. Millie and Velma on the warpath is not a pretty picture.

Okay, rein in the imagination. At the very least, he'd be weirded out. Not cool, Scotty.

I started walking back home. The Marigny was quiet and still. No sound, no wind, no nothing. The air hung heavy and damp, like a hot, wet towel. I felt the sweat starting to form and run down from my armpits. My socks were already damp. I was thirsty. My internal water level probably was too low. My feet and calves hurt. I yawned when I reached the corner of Frenchmen Street. I was exhausted. I could almost hear my bed calling me. All I wanted was to get home, climb into bed next to Colin, and sleep for a month. That thought kept me going, even though I could have curled up on the sidewalk and gone to sleep right there. My soft bed, my silk sheets that felt so good on my skin, and Colin's muscular body, his amazingly soft skin that would feel even better than the sheets. My eyes started to half close. My mouth was completely dry. My tongue felt like it was made out of cotton. I needed water badly. I was walking slower. It was taking tremendous effort to take every step. My back was starting to ache again.

In other words, I was a mess.

I paused at the corner of Frenchmen and Esplanade to reach down and grab my toes. The stretch felt great on my back, but my feet were still screaming at me to get home. I sighed and straightened back up. No cars were coming, so I crossed against the light.

As I crossed Esplanade, I could see someone was sitting

in front of my gate. Great. Probably some homeless kid wanting a cigarette or a dollar for something to eat. I hadn't brought any money with me. I'm not one of those people who can just walk past someone spare-changing and pretend they don't exist. A lot of these kids in the Quarter are runaways, from abusive parents or bad situations of some sort. They head to the anonymity of the Quarter and they disappear. They walk around spare-changing, carrying their backpacks with their hair dyed vibrant colors like blue and bright red and yellow. Nobody will ever find them in the Quarter, which is the point. The saddest thing is that for the most part, nobody is even looking for them. Their parents are glad they're gone. Some people, as my mom would say, shouldn't have children.

Whenever I see one, they remind me how lucky I was to have my parents. I just can't ignore them. I don't know how anyone can. Human beings can be horrible sometimes.

I wish I could feed all of them.

As I got closer, I realized that it wasn't one of the lost kids. For one thing, he was dressed all wrong. The kids usually wore pants cut off below the knees, and Keds, and black T-shirts that showed their midriffs. The ubiquitous backpack wasn't there, and the hair was cut too short. It was probably just some passed-out drunk.

I'd rather deal with one of the kids.

As I got closer, I sighed.

"Kenny?" It was Kenny. What the hell was he doing here? I knelt down. His eyes were closed. I shook him gently. "Kenny?"

His head lolled off to one side limply.

"Kenny!" I shouted, shaking him harder. His entire body slumped over to one side. My hand, my right hand where I'd touched him, was wet and sticky.

I looked at it.

Red and sticky.

Blood.

My breath started coming faster and faster.

I stood back up and took a step back.

My vision began to blur.

The fog.

The screams.

The explosions again.

Danger.

Evil.

Oh, sweet Goddess, no.

I kept backing up, not even sure what I was doing or where I was going. I couldn't take my eyes off of Kenny's limp form. I saw that a pool of red was spreading beneath him—blood, a puddle of it.

Who knew he had so much blood in him? I thought wildly. I backed into one of the poles that held up the balcony and slid around it.

Death.

Evil.

Screams.

An explosion.

I was in the presence of evil.

I had to get away.

I had to.

I stepped back off the curb. I lost my balance, stumbled, and fell backward onto Decatur Street just as a car crossed Esplanade. Vaguely I was aware of the headlights coming. My head hit the pavement. My head exploded with pain. *I'm going to die,* I thought as my eyes closed; I am going to die. . . .

"He's coming around," someone said. It sounded like he was talking a million miles away in the distance. My head hurt. I opened my eyes. I was looking at the clouds.

They were pinkish-colored. Flashing red lights blinded me momentarily.

"Have some water, son," a deep voice said. I turned my head in that direction and saw a shiny bald head. Black. As my senses started to come back, I saw that he was wearing a cop's uniform. I sat up a bit, took the bottled water I was being offered, and drank. It was a sip of heaven. I kept gulping it down until the plastic crinkled.

"I'm Officer Washington," the deep voice said softly. "I almost hit you when you fell into the street. How are you feeling?"

"My head hurts." I closed my eyes. Kenny. "Kenny . . ."

"Easy, now. Have some more water."

I obliged, finishing off the rest of the bottle. I heard a siren approaching. "But Kenny—is he—oh."

"Is Kenny his name?" He gestured over toward the gate.

"Yes. Kenny Chandler. Is he—"

"I'm sorry, he's dead." He squatted down beside me. "Do you want to tell me what happened?"

"I came home and he was just lying there. I thought maybe he'd just passed out or something, so I tried to wake him up, but . . ." I closed my eyes and saw his head loll again to the side. Lifeless. Dead. I started to cry. "Who would do this? Kenny wouldn't hurt anyone!"

"What's your name, son?"

"Scotty. Scotty Bradley. I live here." I wrapped my arms around myself. I was shivering in spite of the heat. I bit my lower lip in an effort to get control of myself. Never cry in front of a cop, as my mom always said; never lose control. Of course, she meant when arrested for protesting something, but hey, it sounded like damned good advice to me now.

"And Kenny was a friend of yours?"

"Sort of." I thought about it. "I knew him." He wasn't

really a friend, not someone I would ever go out to a movie with or just hang out with. I didn't know him well enough for that. I'd just slept with him once. The irony struck me as almost funny. I'd been intimate with him but didn't know him well enough to call him a friend. Nice life you've got there, Scotty. "He was, um . . ." The hell with it, just say it. "I slept with him once. We met in a bar a couple of months ago. But I didn't know him that well. I don't know where he lives or his phone number or anything like that."

Officer Washington's eyebrows went up as he wrote down what I said, but he didn't say anything.

He didn't have to. The eyebrows said it all.

I felt like a whore.

"Did you see him tonight? Before you got home?"

I nodded and swallowed. "When I went out around nine-thirty, he was waiting for me down here. He did that sometimes. I mean, I'd come out to go out at night and he'd be waiting for me."

"He was stalking you?"

"No, I mean, I guess he was. I mean, I wouldn't call it stalking—I mean, I wasn't afraid of him or anything. But it was all harmless. I teased him about it." It sounded stupid to me.

He scribbled some more. He had an odd expression on his face. Hell, it sounded strange to me, now that I was putting it all into words for the first time. "He was a nice guy, not dangerous or anything. He was just lonely, I guess, and I was nice to him." I'd never thought about it before. He must have been lonely. Of course he was lonely. It never occurred to me even to think about it. Why hadn't I ever thought about it? Where were his friends? Didn't he have any? How terribly, sadly lonely Kenny must have been. Why else would he have hung out around my front gate every Friday and Saturday night, waiting for me to come out? He never rang my buzzer to see if I was home. He never called me on the telephone. He just came by, stood around out here, smoking cigarettes and drinking Cokes out of a plastic bottle or a beer out of a brown paper sack until I came out.

What did he do on the nights when I stayed in? Okay, granted, there weren't many of those. I usually went out every weekend on both nights, and sometimes on Sundays for tea dance as well. How long did he wait there for me when I did stay home? Did he wait for an hour and then give up, go along on his lonely way down to the bars? I didn't even know what time he showed up to start his vigil every week.

And I never gave it a second thought. To me, Kenny had just been a part of the scenery, like the old Mint across the street or the levee.

And now he was dead. *Goddess, what a horrible, horrible person I am. Oh, Kenny, I am so sorry.*

I looked over and saw them zipping him into a bag. I felt the lasagna churning in my stomach. I took a couple of deep breaths.

Another car drove up while I was trying to keep the vomit down. Officer Washington got up. "Stay here, Mr. Bradley," he said as he walked away. I could hear him talking in low tones to someone else. Someone walked over to Kenny.

"Mr. Bradley?"

I looked up at a statuesque black woman. She was wearing cream-colored slacks and a matching blouse. Her hair was cut close to the scalp. Her features were strong, with defined cheekbones and full lips. I stood up. She was taller than me, a little over six feet. Her forearms were strong and muscular. She obviously spent a lot of time in the gym. She pulled a pad and pen out of her purse. She flashed a badge at me as well. "Venus Casanova. I'm the police detective in charge now. I need to ask you a few questions."

"Scotty Bradley." I nodded at her. Beads of sweat were appearing on her forehead. I couldn't tell how old she was, but there appeared to be some gray strands in her hair. I repeated what I had told Officer Washington.

"Where were you this evening?" she asked.

"I danced at the Pub tonight."

"Out having a good time?"

I felt myself blush. "Well, no, I was working. As a go-go boy."

Her left eyebrow went up, but she smiled. "What time did you get off work?"

"Around two."

"And you were just getting home around four-thirty? Where did you go after you were finished dancing?"

Never tell the police everything without talking to a lawyer first, my mother's voice echoed in my head. Of course, my mother thought the police were the tools of an oppressive fascist state, just waiting to railroad anyone and everyone. "I actually came straight home."

"Alone?"

"No, with one of the other dancers."

"And you went back out?"

"Yes, I walked over to a friend's to see if I could borrow his computer." Well, that *was* true. I wondered if I should say anything about the disk to her. Yet I kept hearing my mother's voice, and besides, it did sound kind of stupid. If I were a cop and someone told me that they left their house around four in the morning to go see what was on a disk that someone slipped into their boots while dancing on a bar, I would think it very strange. I saw myself going down to police headquarters on Royal Street, being grilled for hours under a hot light. "I couldn't sleep, and sometimes when I can't I go over to David's and play on the Internet until I get sleepy."

"But you didn't stay there?"

"Well, no, I was just about to use my key when David came home with someone. Obviously I'd just be in the way, so I came back here." I shivered again. "And found Kenny."

"What is your friend's name and address?"

They were going to check to see if I'd gone over there. Made sense, I guess. I hoped David had the presence of mind to make it sound like I went over there to play on the Net at four in the morning fairly regularly. I had gone over there. That was true.

I gave them David's name and address.

I was now lying to the police. Well, not really lying. Just not telling them the whole truth.

Probably not a smart thing to do.

I'd talk to Storm in the morning. It was very convenient to have a lawyer for a brother. He'd tell me what to do, how to handle it, and if I was in any trouble, he'd get me out of it.

"So you didn't see Kenny at any time between when you came home the first time and when you came back?"

I shook my head. "No."

She handed me a business card. "If you think of anything else, give me a call. Even if it seems like nothing, okay? Anything could help."

"I will do that, Ms. Casanova."

She turned as though to walk away and then stopped. "Oh, what happened to your friend that you were dancing with? The one you brought home with you?"

"He's still upstairs."

"A good friend?"

Lord, here we go again. "No, I just met him tonight for the first time."

"You left a stranger alone in your apartment?"

I nodded. God, what she must be thinking! Oh, well, get over it, sister. "He was asleep and I was bored."

"Do you make a habit of leaving strangers alone in your apartment?"

"Well, no, not really."

"Then why this time?"

I shrugged. "I know it sounds stupid, but I don't know. At the time it seemed okay, you know? He was asleep and I figured I'd be back in about an hour."

"And what's his name?"

"Colin."

"Last name?"

I didn't need the gift to know she was going to ask that. "I don't know." I decided not to add that I didn't even know if Colin was his real first name.

"Maybe I should come up and ask him a few questions." She bit her lip.

Oh, Goddess.

I tried to imagine what it would be like to be woken up out of a deep sleep by the police in someone else's apartment to be questioned about a murder. I probably wouldn't like it much. "Do you really have to?" I asked, knowing the answer. Ah, well, poor Colin. There was no way around it.

It was definitely a one-night stand Colin would never forget. Hopefully, he would remember the sex part fondly.

If nothing else, it would make for a great story: "Yeah, I was dancing in New Orleans and went home with this guy. The sex was really great, I had a great time, and then I went to sleep. Next thing I knew I was being woken up by a police detective and questioned about the murder of some guy I'd never even seen before or heard of. Weird town, New Orleans, but kind of fun."

I sighed.

"Yes." She smiled. "Since you don't know his last name, I'd better."

"Okay."

They were loading Kenny's body into a van with *CITY MORGUE* written on the side. I stepped over the chalk outline and the blood. I felt my gag reflex engage and I struggled not to throw up. I took some deep breaths. "Are you okay?" Detective Casanova took my arm.

The wave of nausea passed. "Yeah." I shook my head. My eyes were tearing up again.

Poor, poor Kenny, I thought, and unlocked the gate with Detective Casanova right behind me.

Would this night ever end?

Chapter Eight

THE HEIROPHANT, REVERSED

Unconventionality, nonconformism

The passageway that leads from the gate to the court-yard behind my building isn't as narrow and claustro-phobic as many in the Quarter. It's wide enough to bring a pretty big sofa through, for example. The sidewalk is bro-ken in places and definitely tilted, and there's no light. On either side is a brick walk, but there's no cover. You look up and on a clear night you can see the stars. This, of course, can prove to be a royal pain in the ass when it's raining, since water pouring off the roofs on either side drains off the side into it. It fills up with water and your feet get completely soaked up to the ankles. Millie and Velma keep saying that they're going to put some kind of cover on it to keep people dry. They usually say this after one or both of them have gotten completely drenched. Once they dry off, they don't bother with it. They find it amusing when it happens to me.

On this night there were no stars to be seen. Puffy white clouds were reflecting the lights of the Quarter back down. The reflected light was enough to see by, which is a good thing. Millie and Velma have never bothered to light it, either. I heard Detective Casanova swear under her breath when she stubbed her toe on a particularly bent part of the sidewalk. Give her credit though, she didn't fall down.

The stairs behind the building are steep. Each floor has sixteen-foot ceilings, so to get up to my apartment you have to climb up thirty-two feet. I turned on the stair light, hoping we wouldn't wake up Millie and Velma. After years of living in the Quarter, Millie and Velma can sleep through almost anything. The police sirens out front wouldn't wake them.

But they sure can hear someone climbing the creaky steps at five in the morning.

"Try to be as quiet as possible," I whispered to Detective Casanova. "The ladies who own the building live on the second floor, and I don't want to wake them up, especially since I have a cop with me."

"I'll have to wake them eventually," she replied. "We'll need to ask them if they heard or saw anything."

Great, I thought to myself. At this point, I was still hoping that my parents wouldn't find out anything about all of this. They might be stoned all the time, but they still worried. Fortunately, they don't read the papers, which they consider a tool of the corrupt city government, and all the news it reports hopelessly biased, if not completely fabricated. But if Millie and Velma had to talk to the police . . . *Sheesh.* I could hear my mother now, insisting that I move back in with them over the Devil's Weed.

Then my heart sank. Mom and Dad might not read the papers, but both sets of grandparents do. I was going to be hearing from both sets at seven in the morning, after their breakfasts and coffee. All four of them considered the Quarter an evil place, rife with crime and sin, and were always, *always* begging me to move out of there to Uptown.

Like Uptown was any safer than the Quarter.

I climbed the steps with Detective Casanova on my heels. My calves were screaming with pain. I was going to have to soak my feet, maybe even get a massage. At this rate, by the end of the weekend I wouldn't be able to move. Hopefully, I had some Ben-Gay or something in the bathroom.

I didn't hear any signs of movement from behind Millie and Velma's door, so I thanked the Goddess silently and headed up to my landing. I slipped the key in the lock and switched on the hall light, holding the door open for the detective.

They might be hippies, but Mom and Dad raised me right.

I showed her into the living room and headed back for the bedroom. I opened the door and switched on the light.

The bed was empty.

I looked into the bathroom. Also empty.

I came back into the hallway and looked at the chair just inside the door, where Colin had thrown his bag. It was gone.

I walked back into the living room. "He's gone."

Her plucked eyebrows arched up to her scalp line. "Oh?"

I didn't like the sound of that "oh." It sounded like she didn't believe me. Well, not that she didn't believe the apartment was empty, but that he had been there in the first place.

"You can go ahead and check if you don't believe me." I made a gesture around the apartment. I dropped down into a chair. "I guess he woke up and left while I was gone."

"What did you say his last name was?"

"I don't know what his last name is." I sighed. "I said that already."

"Do you know where he lives?"

"He's from San Francisco." I shrugged. "They brought him in to dance this weekend. If I had to guess, I would imagine he went back to where the Pub puts up the dancers, that B and B on St. Ann."

She wrote that down and asked for my phone number. I gave it to her. I showed her to the door. "Don't leave town. I may need to talk to you some more."

"All I want to do is go to bed." I yawned to illustrate my point.

She nodded, and I shut the door behind her. I listened to her footsteps on the stairs. She'd be waking up Millie and Velma next. And as soon as she was done with them, two lesbian furies would be flying up the steps and pounding on my door.

I just wanted to go to sleep.

I got a bottled water out of the refrigerator and walked back into the bedroom. I felt like total shit. My legs hurt, my head hurt, someone had killed Kenny . . . and where the hell had Colin gotten off to? What was all that about?

I couldn't blame him, I guess. I wouldn't feel too comfortable if I woke up in someone else's house and that someone else wasn't there. But he'd made such a big deal about wanting to spend the night. And to be honest, I was kind of looking forward to having sex with him again in the morning.

But should I be even thinking things like that since Kenny was dead?

I decided to take a shower to wash the sweat and slime off of me. I took a big slug of the water and turned on the shower. I stripped down and climbed into the water. Damn, it felt good. I soaped every inch of my body and used my loofah sponge. I swear by my loofah sponge. It keeps my skin exfoliated and feeling soft to the touch. When I dance, the spenders like the way my skin is firm but soft as crushed velvet. I get compliments from my tricks about how good I feel when they hold or touch me.

It may be vain, but I kind of like that.

The bathroom was filled with steam when I climbed out and grabbed a towel. I rubbed myself dry and brushed my teeth. I rubbed some moisturizing cream into my face. There weren't any wrinkles yet, but I was starting to think that I might need to do something about the dark circles that were starting under my eyes. Rain swears by vitamin E cream. Whatever. I found the Ben-Gay in the medicine cabinet and spread some liberally on my calves. My back was still sore, so I did some more stretches to loosen it up. Some Ben-Gay back there would probably help. I'm pretty limber, but not limber enough to reach back there.

I walked back into the bedroom and had an immediate heart attack.

"Didn't mean to scare you." Colin grinned at me. He was stark naked and lying on top of the covers. His hands were behind his head, his big lats fanned out. Damn, he was gorgeous. He had thrown his bag into a corner.

"Where the hell were you?" I managed to gasp out as I did relaxation exercises to slow my heart rate down.

He shrugged. "I heard the sirens and went out onto the balcony to see what was going on. I saw you talking to that cop. I got dressed and grabbed my bag, and when I heard you coming up the stairs I went and hid on the balcony."

The balcony. Of course. I never even thought about looking for him out there. My heart was now beating at a seminormal rate. Now that I knew I wasn't going to have a myocardial infarction, I wanted to slug him. "Why the hell did you do that?"

He shrugged. "I have my own reasons for not wanting to talk to the police."

"You're gonna have to." I sat down on the edge of the bed. "You have to confirm my story."

"All I can confirm is, we came back here, you fucked me, then when I woke up, you were gone."

"Listen, dumb shit." I was starting to get really mad. "A friend of mine was killed. When I came back here I found his body against the gate. I didn't kill him, and they seem to believe that I didn't. At least for now. If you don't say you were here all the time, which I can confirm, they're going to think you might have seen something, or maybe, just maybe you killed him yourself."

Even as I said it, I felt the hackles raise on the back of my neck.

What if he *had* killed Kenny?

Whoops! I could be alone with a killer. I sent a silent, quick prayer to the Goddess.

Nothing. No sign of danger. It might not stand up in a court of law, but I was pretty sure he was okay. At the very least, I was safe with him, unless the Goddess was playing some kind of cosmic joke with me.

You never can be sure with her.

"I didn't kill him." He sat up, his stomach rippling. "I didn't even know someone was killed until you just told me that. That's horrible. You poor baby." He patted the bed beside him. "Come, lay down with me."

"The sirens woke you up?"

"Uh-huh."

My mind was working, tired as it was. "You didn't hear a shot?"

He shook his head. "No."

That was weird, but apparently Velma and Millie hadn't heard it either. I sat down on the edge of the bed and yawned. "So why don't you want to talk to the cops, guy?"

He shrugged. "I just don't."

"What is your last name, anyway?"

He laughed and reached for me. He grabbed my arm and pulled me across the bed. Damn, he was strong. I didn't resist, but even if I had tried, I probably wouldn't have been able to keep him from dragging me over to him. "My name isn't Colin, it's Bill. Bill Palladino." He put his arms around me and started kissing my neck.

I tried to pull away from him. "Would you have told me that ever?"

"Probably not."

He was kissing my shoulders now. "Colin—Bill—don't."

"Why not?"

"A friend of mine was killed." I pulled away harder, and he let me go. "It doesn't seem right."

"I'm sorry." He crossed his arms. "Someone you were close to?"

"Well, no." I felt bad having to say it, but it was true. I stood up and walked over to my full-length mirror. I watched him over my shoulder and told him about Kenny.

I'd seen Kenny around before. New Orleans is a very small town, and the gay community even smaller. He always stood by himself in the bars, a cigarette in one hand and a drink in the other. He always wore jeans and a T-shirt, even in the hottest part of the summer. I always smiled at him and said, "hey," but for the most part never gave him much thought. The night I slept with him, I'd drunk too much for sure. Tequila again. Someday I'll learn that José Cuervo is not a friend of mine, but that night I was in a mood. I'd been on the dance floor at Oz working this cute guy. He'd been alone, moving to the music, in his own little world. I gave him the eye and he gave it right back to me with a big grin. We started dancing together, and I eventually got him to take his shirt off. His body was just okay, but there was something about him. The way he danced was really sensual, the kind of dancer that you just know would be a great time in bed. We danced together, letting the tribal, incessant beat of the music move our hips, bringing our crotches together, rubbing our hard-ons together through our jeans. I grabbed his butt and danced with him close. We kissed a few times. He was a great kisser, the kind that makes goose bumps come up on your arms. I can't stand guys who can't kiss for shit. After about an hour of this, just when I was starting to get to the point where I was going to ask for his name and then ask him to come home with me, some older guy came up to us, glaring. He pushed me away and grabbed the cute guy. I was just about to say something when the older guy said to me, "Keep your fucking hands off my boyfriend."

Boyfriend?

Damn it.

I was pissed.

Why do guys pull that shit? They have a boyfriend and still flirt, lead other guys on, and then pull back when things start heating up. "Oh, I can't; I have a boyfriend." This was even worse. This boy sure seemed all fired up to go home with me until the boyfriend showed up.

Fuck, fuck, fuck.

It's just not cool. He should have told me there was a boyfriend in the picture.

Fucking tease.

I stormed off the dance floor and ordered me a shot of tequila and downed it, fast. I'd wasted an hour or two on some jackass with a boyfriend. It was three in the morning already, and most all the available guys in the bar who weren't flying high on some drug had already hooked up with their trick of the night. I ordered another shot and downed it. I glanced around the dance floor. I was all worked up from dancing with the tease. I didn't want to go home and pop a video in to jack off. I wanted a body next to me.

"Slow down, there, stud," someone said next to me. I turned and looked at him. The flush of tequila was starting to make itself felt in my head. It was Kenny, even though I didn't know his name at the time. I ordered another shot. "What's it to you?" I asked. I'm usually not that rude, but like I said, I was in a mood.

He shrugged. "Nothing, I guess."

I downed the shot. "Sorry," I said. "I'm just pissed."

He laughed. "I could have warned you about an hour or two ago, that guy is a tease."

"Why didn't you?"

"Would you have listened?"

I thought about that for a minute. The tequila was softening my edges a little. I know some people say tequila makes them crazy, puts them in a fightin' mood, but all it does for me is make me relax. It gets me all warm and fuzzy. I grinned at him. "No, probably not. My name's Scotty."

"Kenny." We shook hands.

We stood there and talked and bought each other tequila shots. He made me laugh. I don't really remember what we talked about (tequila is not good for short-term memory), but I remember relaxing and having a good time. Finally, at about four-thirty in the morning I invited him back to my place. Why the hell not? So he wasn't the kind of guy I normally tricked with, and maybe I was viewing him through tequila-colored glasses, but by four-thirty he was looking kind of cute to me. Even after we got back to my place and he was undressed with his pale skin and his bones sticking through the skin in places, I still managed to have a good time with him. He'd been a good kisser. He kept telling me over and over again how beautiful I was as he touched me, wonder in his voice.

And now he was dead.

I started to cry. "I'm a horrible person," I sobbed as

Colin pulled me in closer and held me tight. "I never bothered to even get to know him. He was just always there, waiting for me every weekend night, ready to walk me down to the bars and talk to me, and I never cared enough to find out anything about him. Isn't that awful? Of course Kenny would be down there waiting for me; he was always there, and I just took it all for granted, you know what I mean? Like I am so pretty and wonderful and . . ." I couldn't talk anymore.

"Shhhhh," Colin whispered in my ear. "You go ahead and cry." His big, strong arms felt wonderful around me. He gently kissed the top of my head.

It seemed like a couple of hours, but it was probably just a few minutes before I was finally able to get control of myself.

"You okay?"

I nodded. "I'm tired."

He got up and turned off the light. "Let's get some sleep, okay, baby?"

I stretched out on the bed. It creaked a bit as he climbed in beside me. I curled up and put my head on his chest.

His heartbeat and even breathing lulled me, and finally I fell asleep.

Chapter Nine

TEN OF CUPS, REVERSED

Chance of Betrayal

I hope Alexander Graham Bell is roasting in hell. The shrill, annoying, demanding, insistent ringing of the telephone woke me out of my sleep. Apparently, I thought as I opened my eyes, sleep was not in the cards for me this weekend. I slipped out from under Colin's arm and walked out to answer the damned thing. He was snoring softly, the big chest rising and falling. I glanced at him as I walked out. His hair was matted all over his head. There was a little bit of drool on the corner of his mouth. I grinned to myself until I started to walk out of the room. My calves were screaming. The Ben-Gay had not helped at all.

The green numbers on the microwave clock said 8:17. I'd gotten two whole hours of sleep. I looked at the caller ID before picking up the phone. It was Storm.

"Why," I said into the phone, "are you calling me at this ungodly hour of the morning, you sadistic bastard?"

Storm chuckled. "Baby bro, I've been up since seven."

"You need a therapist. A good one. Nobody sane gets up at that hour on Saturday."

"Well, I thought I should call and make sure you're okay."

"I was until the phone woke me up."

"Sorry to disturb you, my Queen." Storm always called me that. My Queen. I suppose I should be offended by it. If a gay activist ever heard him call me that, they'd boycott his law practice and parade around in front of his office with picket signs. But he'd been calling me that ever since I came out. One year on my birthday, he'd bought me a tiny little rhinestone crown.

Storm always teased me. Some of my earliest memories are of Storm teasing me and tickling me until I screamed. That didn't change as we grew up. Okay, he doesn't hold me down and tickle me until I wet myself anymore. Storm could aggravate a saint. But it's all good-natured in his mind, and a guy couldn't ask for a better big brother than Storm. Storm was the one who realized how mean the other kids were being to me and started calling me Scotty. When I came out to the family, Storm was right there at the P-FLAG meetings with Mom and Dad. He donates money all the time to gay causes. He participates in the AIDS Walk. He does pro bono work for gay legal cases. Storm's wife, Marguerite, doesn't quite know what to make of me and of Storm's gay activism. She's a proper Uptown lady, having gone to the right schools, pledged the right sorority in college, and married herself a lawyer. She always looks a little lost and confused at family get-togethers. She always has this look on her face like she's thinking, *I did everything right, so how did I end up in this family of lunatics?* Of course, her first Thanksgiving dinner at Mom and Dad's, Storm "forgot" to warn her not to eat the brownies. To this day he swears it was an honest mistake, but having grown up with him, I tend to doubt it.

To this day, Marguerite will not eat anything my mother bakes. Can't say as I blame her.

"Storm, I'm really tired. I had a long night—"

"That's why I'm calling. My sources tell me that you had an encounter with New Orleans's finest last night, and you just might need a lawyer."

"Oh." I rubbed my eyes. Storm was nothing if not persistent. If I tried to get out of talking to him about this, he'd be pounding on the back door in a matter of minutes. It was one of the reasons he was such a great lawyer. I wasn't going to get back to bed anytime soon. With a sigh, I started filling my coffeemaker with water. Maybe I could get a nap in the afternoon. If I didn't, I was going to fall asleep in midpelvic thrust on the bar that night. I would fall headfirst off the bar into the crowd. Stage dives aren't real popular with the gay crowd.

It wouldn't be pretty. "Yeah, a friend of mine was killed last night. I found the body."

"Are you okay, my Queen?"

"Yeah. If I wasn't so damned tired I'd probably be having a nervous breakdown or something, but I am just too damned tired. I freaked pretty good last night, though." I laughed. "Well, two hours ago. And how do you know about all of this, anyway?"

He laughed. "I see all, my Queen. It's in the cards."

I was too tired to be irritated. Storm loved to tease me about my psychic gift. Well, he actually called it my "psycho gift." "Yeah, well, I had to talk to the police, and they kept me up way past my bedtime." I yawned.

"Your story seemed kind of weird to me."

"Who the hell told you about all of this?"

"I have a friend in the department. Baby bro, you wouldn't have been lying to the police, would you? That's not a good idea, especially with Venus Casanova. She's a tough bitch."

"Well, I didn't tell them the *whole* truth." My coffeemaker is one of those great ones that will stop brewing if you take the pot off. You don't have to wait till the whole pot is brewed to have a cup. Ah, modern technology. I filled up a mug and sweetened it. "I mean, it had nothing to do with Kenny's being killed, and I didn't really know how to explain why I went over to David's at four in the morning."

"Yeah, that was the part I thought was funny. The police aren't too thrilled with it, either, just to let you know. You should have called me."

"Wouldn't the police have thought it odd that I wanted to confer with my brilliant legal-genius brother before talking to them? Wouldn't that have looked like I had something to hide?" The coffee was good and strong but it really wasn't going to help much. Every fiber of my body was tired.

"Talk to me, my Queen."

So I told Storm about the disk. I told him about Colin (Bill? Whatever) and how he'd hidden on the balcony from the cops.

Storm whistled. "What's up with that? The cops find out he was there all along and you're both going to look really bad."

"He didn't kill Kenny."

"How can you be so sure?"

"I am, Storm."

"Ah, yes, your amazing psycho powers. I don't suppose your amazing psycho powers chose to reveal to you who, exactly, did kill this guy?" When I didn't answer, he went on, "I thought not. But it's not good that he is avoiding the cops. You need to call this detective and get him to talk to her. And you should come clean about this disk thing, too."

"Yeah, I guess. But can't I at least wait until I know what's on it first? I mean, what if it's just porn or something?"

"Why would someone slip a computer disk of porn in your boot?"

"Why would anyone slip a computer disk of any kind in my boot?" I finished the mug and refilled it. "None of it makes any sense to me."

He whistled. "How do you manage to get into these situations, anyway? You need to call her. And that's the most brilliant legal mind in Louisiana talking. Come clean to the police, and if they give you any trouble, beep me. I'm leaving here in a few minutes but should be home around eleven."

"Where are you off to on a Saturday morning so early?"

"A fund-raising breakfast for the Sonnier campaign."

I whistled. "Have you told Mom and Dad you're working for him?"

Jack Sonnier was running for governor. He had been governor once before. He hadn't been popular. Like most politicians, he broke all of his campaign promises once he was in the governor's mansion. One of the major promises he'd made was cleaning up the environment. Louisiana had sold its soul to the petrochemical companies in the 1970s, and the quality of our air and water was an absolute joke. The EPA tried to get Louisiana cleaned up, but the massive corruption in Baton Rouge stymied them at every turn. Once in office, he started ramming major tax breaks through for the petrochemical companies and making insane offers to others to get them to put plants in Louisiana. Mom and Dad despised him with every fiber of their being. When his term was up, he was convicted of several charges of misconduct and spent a couple of years in jail. Sonnier had always claimed it was a conspiracy put together by his political enemies, a setup, but he *had* been to jail. Now he had paid his debt to society and was running for governor again. Only in Louisiana could a man convicted of bribery and extortion while in office run again.

Mom and Dad considered him on a par with Nixon. "Only," Mom sneered, "not as charming or as good-looking."

"Yes, I have, and they are behind me on this one."

I almost choked on my coffee. "They are?"

"Don't you ever read the newspaper? Or watch the news?"

"As little as possible." Considering who my parents were, I considered my complete and total political apathy a badge of honor. I eat dinner at Mom and Dad's enough to have a working knowledge of what's going on in the world.

"You don't know anything about Willy Perkins?"

"No."

"He's the handpicked candidate of the religious right. He's pro-life, antigay, racist, you name it. He wants to put prayer back in the schools. He wants abortion limited to rape and incest victims. He has actually called New Orleans a 'city of sin.' He showed up at a debate with Jack Sonnier with a plastic fetus pinned to his lapel and called Jack a baby-killer."

"Wow. Yeah, I guess I can see why Mom and Dad would vote for Sonnier."

Storm laughed. "They even contributed to his campaign fund. I think they both had to do a ritual cleansing afterwards though. It's great, you know? I'm getting a lot of mileage out of them supporting Sonnier."

"I'll bet you are." He really was incorrigible.

"You beep me if you need me, okay?"

I hung up the phone and walked into the living room. I turned on the television with the sound down. No sense in waking up Colin/Bill/whoever.

Okay, I was procrastinating. I didn't want to call Venus Casanova. I didn't want to tell her I hadn't told her the

whole truth and that unbeknownst to me, Colin/Bill/who-
ever had been hiding out on the balcony. Like she'd believe
anything I said after I'd already lied. I wouldn't believe me
if I were her. I mean, I hadn't really lied to her; I just hadn't
told her the whole truth. There was some wiggle room
there, but still . . . I'd better just wait and see what was on
the disk. If it was nothing, which it most likely was, then
I'd call her and just tell her that Colin/Bill/whatever was
sleeping in my bed and to get over here quick. If by some
long stretch of the imagination it actually was important
and might have something to do with Kenny's murder,
then I'd have something to tell her. She'd be pissed, but I
could deal with it. I could always beep Storm if things
looked like they were going to get ugly.

My eyes ached from being so tired, and my legs were
aching as well. I put the coffee down on the table and
stretched out on the sofa. Maybe I could just take a little
nap out here for a few hours. David wouldn't be awake
for hours, anyway. . . .

Just as I drifted off, the phone rang again.

I should have prayed to the Goddess for uninterrupted
sleep. Maybe this was her way of punishing me for not
lighting a candle yet this morning. Whatever.

The Goddess can be a bit of a bitch sometimes.

Caller ID identified David as my caller. "So how was the
jalapeño?"

"Quite tasty." I knew he was grinning from ear to ear.
He really liked Hispanic boys. "He's sleeping now. When I
get off the phone I may just go ravage him some more."

I started to ask him why he was still awake, but then remembered the dilated eyes from the night before. Ecstasy
keeps him awake. He'd take a nap in the afternoon, maybe
after the little Hispanic boy (what was his name?) went
back to wherever he was staying. Then he'd get up, smoke

some pot he'd bought from my dad, play online for a while, then head on back out to get some more Ecstasy and hopefully another little Hispanic boy. "So, did you see what was on the disk?"

"About that . . ." David hesitated. "Now, don't get me wrong, Scotty; you're my friend, and every time I look in the mirror and see my body I say 'Thank you, Scotty,' but I have to tell you this: I really don't think it was cool of you to go into my house without me knowing it."

"I know." It had been a shitty thing to do. "But I didn't."

"Only 'cause I came home."

"It kinda seemed important at the time."

"Have you ever done it before?"

"Only to feed Gershwin."

"You swear?"

"I swear. If I'm lying, may I never get laid ever again."

That satisfied him, as I'd known it would. "Well, it wouldn't have done you any good, anyway. The disk is written in a program that I don't have in my computer, and none of the translation programs I have can make it readable."

"Oh." When it comes to computers, I am a complete Luddite. I just assumed because it was a computer disk a computer could read it. "So there's no way of telling what's on it?"

"You could take it down to a Kinko's or a cyber-café and see if they have the program it's written in."

"I guess it's not important." I shrugged.

"Want me to bring it back over? Where did you get it, anyway?"

"Someone put it in my boot last night."

"Really?"

"Yeah." I thought about it for a minute. I almost told him to keep it, but something spoke to me as my mouth started to form the words. *Get the disk back. The police would probably want it, and it wouldn't be cool to send them over to David's.* "Yeah, I guess you should give it back. Later's cool, though."

He yawned. "Well, dude, I am going back to bed."

I hung up the phone. I looked at it in my hands.

Storm wanted me to call the cops and tip them off about Colin/Bill/whoever.

I couldn't do it.

I knew it was wrong.

But he didn't kill Kenny. I knew that.

The cards. I'd ask the cards to be on the safe side.

I heard him in the bathroom as I spread the cards out. I lit a white candle for purity. I just hoped he wouldn't come out until I was finished.

I turned over the last card.

He didn't kill Kenny.

But he's lying about something.

He walked into the living room stark naked, still rubbing his eyes. Drops of water glistened in the morning sun on his chin. "You weren't there in the bed with me."

"The phone." I shrugged. "My brother called. He heard about what happened last night."

"Oh." He looked at the candle, the cards. "You read the tarot?"

I nodded. "I have a gift for it." I started picking up the cards. I started shuffling them. "There's coffee in the kitchen."

"Okay." He kept watching as I shuffled, cut the deck, re-shuffled. "Do you just ask questions?"

"Yes. I'm doing a reading for myself now." I started to spread the cards again. I closed my eyes and focused.

The fog.

Screams.

He will be important to you.

I opened my eyes. He was staring at me, his face a little pale beneath the tan. I looked at the cards I had laid out.

"Who are you, really?" I asked him. I pointed at one card. "This tells me your past, and it's unclear, except for some pain and possible criminal activity. This tells me your present, which is more of the same. Your future shows choices to be made—perhaps you aren't happy with the course of your life. This one tells me you are afraid of the choice you must make. This one tells me that you're basically a good person but prone to making mistakes by taking the easy way out."

He swallowed. "Um, I don't—"

"You know I speak the truth." My voice didn't even sound like my own. It was firm, clear, almost imperious. "My brother is a lawyer, Colin/Bill/whoever-you-are. And he told me that I have no choice but to call that police detective and tell her how to find you, that you hid out on the balcony while she was here, and she may not believe that I didn't know you were out there. I could be in trouble here, Colin/Bill/whoever, and this card"—I pointed to another one of the cards in the layout—"tells me that you really don't like to cause trouble for people. Particularly those who are undeserving of such trouble."

"Okay." He sat down and leaned back in a chair. "There is a reason I didn't want to talk to the police last night, why I still don't want to this morning. Please don't call them, okay? It's not a great idea."

"And?"

"I'm probably wanted. I'm a thief." He smiled at me. Damn, he was pretty. "A cat burglar."

Chapter Ten

KING OF WANDS

A man firm in friendship or enmity

So how does one react when one's trick of the night before tells one he is a cat burglar?

I don't know if anyone has ever posed such a question to Emily Post, but I feel quite certain that the answer would not be to goggle at them stupidly, open and close your mouth a couple of times, and then burst into laughter.

It isn't, I know, very nice to laugh at people. I certainly don't like being laughed at. It's the main reason I don't tell people about the gift, after all. So I try to refrain from laughing at other people whenever possible. Oh, I tease my friends (Storm taught me well), and I joke with them about things, but laugh at someone? That's just something a fine Southern gentleman simply does not do. My parents may be French Quarter hippies who spend most of their waking hours smoking pot, but they raised me right. Laughing at someone shows poor manners and reflects badly on your mama, as either of my fine Uptown grandmothers might say.

You especially don't laugh at someone when they are being dead serious.

To his credit, Colin/Bill/whoever just sat there calmly, waiting for my hysterics to stop.

In my own defense, I have to say it was pretty funny. How could I not laugh? I'm not sure what I was expecting him to say, but "I'm a cat burglar" wasn't it. "I'm a cat burglar" was along the same lines as "I'm really a super-hero and Colin is my secret identity," or "I'm from Alpha Centauri here on a mission of peace," or "I'm a secret agent with the FBI." And given everything that happened in the last twenty-four hours, why couldn't he be a cat burglar? It was just too, too perfect. My life had, finally, turned into a Fellini film. Goddess knew it had been threatening to for years.

I finally stopped laughing and apologized. "I'm sorry, but when you said that, it made me think of—oh, I don't know—cartoons or something; and then I got this mental image of you dressed all in black, climbing up the side of a building and—" Damn it, the laughter was coming back again. I took a couple of deep breaths and fought to hold it in.

"It's true, though, and I would really prefer not to talk to the police." He folded his arms, making the muscles flex and bulge even more. He almost looked like he was pouting. This was getting way too insane.

"Okay. I'm sorry I laughed." I reached for my coffee. "So how does one become a cat burglar, anyway?"

"Looking for a new career option?"

"Well, no." I remembered an old Cary Grant movie with Grace Kelly. *To Catch a Thief*—that had been the name of it. I'd seen it when I was a kid, and remembered thinking that the life of an international society thief looked awfully glamorous. "Don't get me wrong: I'm not exactly the biggest fan of law enforcement, but the

Goddess wouldn't like it." I gestured at the cards and the candle. "And I serve Her. Have you heard of the rule of three? Where whatever you put out into the universe comes back threefold?"

He smiled at me. "You tell me all this New Age stuff, and that you have a 'gift' for reading tarot cards, but it's funny that I'm a cat burglar?"

He had me there, damn him. "I said I was sorry I laughed. So what do you burgle?"

"Some things are better that you don't know, Scotty." That smile again.

"Then why are you stripping?"

"Contacts." He shrugged. "Besides, a lot of these people who come to circuit events are richer than you'd think. Rolex watches, laptop computers, rings, bracelets—you name it, these guys leave 'em scattered all over their hotel rooms. And they get so wasted all weekend, they can't remember if they actually brought the stuff with 'em or just planned to, you know? And it's not like they can call the police with all the drugs they've got scattered all over their rooms. Plus, it's kind of fun. It's a rush, better than any drug I've ever tried." His eyes lit up. "Come on, Scotty, admit it. You've hustled before, haven't you?"

"No." I was easy with my favors, but I never charged for it. I was a slut, not a whore. "Why?"

"Really? Okay." He shrugged again. "That's how I got started, you know. I was turning tricks for an escort service in West Hollywood. All these closeted people in the entertainment industry—movie stars, TV stars, musicians—they can't go to bars, so they order hustlers to come in and satisfy them. I was at some movie star's house one night, and after he got what he wanted from me, he told me to let myself out and fell asleep. He had this gorgeous ring just sitting there on the nightstand. It was the biggest diamond I'd ever seen. I put it in my pocket and walked out. I thought for sure he'd call the service or the cops, but nothing ever happened. I mean, he really couldn't, because then they'd want to know why I was there in the first place, you know?" He laughed. "I asked around and found one of the other escorts knew a guy who bought stuff like that, so I sold it to him for a couple of grand."

"But that's stealing." I almost bit my tongue off as soon as I heard the words. Well, *duh.* I was tempted to ask who the movie star was, but held my curiosity in check. I always read the tabloids when I am in line at the supermarket. Well, not the ones with the headlines about Satan appearing in the clouds or alien babies, but I like the ones with outrageous gossip about celebrities.

Hey, I want to know.

"I was just a piece of meat, a hard-on attached to some muscle to these guys." He stood up and walked over to the balcony doors. I watched his ass flex as he walked. "It was pretty soul-destroying, being a whore. I felt like I was always leaving a small piece of my soul behind with those trolls. But stealing that ring, Scotty, it made me feel *alive,* like I was really doing something. You know what I mean? I wasn't letting them treat me like a possession, something they could buy and play with for a while and then dismiss, send along when they'd had their fill. Okay, maybe, just maybe it's all just a way of justifying it all to myself, to give me an excuse to steal, but I started enjoying it. I'd been trained as a gymnast, and I never really stopped doing that, so it was really just a matter of schooling myself, learning about security systems, learning to climb walls—"

"You really do climb walls?"

He grinned at me. "Yes, Scotty, I can really climb walls if I have the right equipment. And yes, I dress all in black when I am doing it. I even put some of that eye-black stuff on my face."

"Okay." I shook my head. Surely this was all a dream

that I would wake up from sometime soon. I wasn't really hearing all of this, was I?

"So, you can see, I would really rather not talk to that nice Detective Casanova."

I shook my head. "Okay, but you have to. I know you didn't kill Kenny; the cards told me so, but . . ."

I stopped because he was laughing, laughing so hard that tears were starting to roll out of his eyes. "What's so funny?"

"You." He wiped his eyes. He mimicked me, and I'll be damned if he didn't sound just like me, the rat bastard. He was better at it than Storm. " 'I know you didn't kill Kenny because the cards told me so.' Aren't we a pair? The burglar and the psychic."

I'd been right. Being laughed at isn't much fun. I felt my cheeks start to burn. "Yeah, well."

"Now, what's this about a computer disk?"

My jaw dropped. "How did you—"

He waved his hand. "Know about that? I listened to you while you were on the phone; I'm not psychic. I'm not in jail, Scotty, because I pay attention to what's going on around me and I don't take unnecessary risks. That's a sure trip to the state pen, thank you very much."

"Oh." Made sense, but it kind of bothered me to know he'd been listening to my calls. "It's over at my friend David's house."

"And someone slipped it into your boot last night at the Pub?"

I nodded. "But David's computer can't read it."

"Okay." He walked back over and put his hand on my leg. "Do you really think this disk is important?"

"I don't know." I didn't. "But someone slipped it to me last night, and then Kenny turns up dead on my doorstep later the same night. Maybe it's all just a weird coincidence, but . . ."

"Don't forget, someone tried to mug us last night."

I had forgotten. "Oh, yeah." I felt a little ill. "So if—"

"You're sure you have no idea who could have put it there?"

I closed my eyes and thought for a minute. I'd had a moment on the bar, when the vision had come to me again, and when it had passed, I'd looked down and saw . . . "Jeremy."

"Jeremy?"

"This guy I used to train." I decided not to get into the whole vision thing with him. I'd already been laughed at once. I closed my eyes again. Hot Daddy had been there, too, and had followed Jeremy out. I could hear Jeremy's voice: *"They're after me; can I hide out at your place? What time do you get off? I'll meet you back here then."*

I'd thought he was on something and forgotten about it. He'd never shown up.

"Are you willing to do some cloak-and-dagger stuff?"

"What do you mean?" I needed to call Venus.

"I have a laptop back at the B and B. A really good laptop. I have an encryption program that will decode pretty much anything, and we can find out what's on this disk."

"You think this disk is important?" I wasn't really paying much attention to what he was saying. All I could think of was Jeremy. I was trying to remember if his eyes had been dilated. I didn't think they were, but I couldn't remember for sure.

"You know it is." He ran his fingers up my inner thigh. "That's why you didn't tell the police about it, which most people would have done—and you should have. Think about it: someone slipped you a disk, and then later that night a dead body shows up at your front door. You were kind of suspecting there was a connection between the two already, weren't you?"

I pushed Jeremy out of my mind. "No, I just thought it sounded stupid. That's why I didn't tell the police. They'd have thought I was nuts. And they would have wanted to see it, and I knew David was going to . . ." I shrugged. "I didn't want to bother him again."

You didn't tell the police about it because it wouldn't have done any good, a voice said inside my head. *The police cannot be completely trusted in this.*

Oh, Goddess.

"So, what about this cloak-and-dagger stuff?" I asked.

"We need my laptop, but I can't risk going back to the B and B in case the police are looking for me." He kissed my cheek. "They may not be, but I don't want to take that risk. You'll need to go down there with my key and get my laptop."

"But if the police are looking for you, won't they think it funny when I show up and grab your laptop?"

"Nah." He smiled. "You're one of the dancers, and chances are the cops watching the B and B, if there are any, won't know that you're a local, anyway. It probably won't be the same people who were here last night, right? If they do stop you, just pretend that you're returning to your room, you tricked last night, and you have no idea where I am. Go in, grab the laptop, and bring it back here. Swing by David's on the way there and pick up the disk."

"And what will you do?"

He leaned back onto the sofa, his arms behind his head. "I'm going to sit here and wait for you to come back with everything we need, and then we'll get to the bottom of this disk thing."

"What if the police are watching me?"

"You live here. They have no reason to watch you, and even if they are—if they follow you to the B and B—it makes sense for you to go there, since the other dancers are staying there. If they question you about that, you can say you're going there to look for me, to tell me to contact them about last night." He smiled lazily at me. He seemed to have it all figured out.

Okay, maybe it wasn't the brightest thing in the world to agree to. Maybe it was one of those times when I should have listened to Storm and done exactly what he told me to do. But the Goddess seemed to be pushing me on this path. Why else would she have put Bill/Colin/whatever in my path, had me be attracted to him and bring him back with me? Somehow, there was a pattern in all of this, and who am I to question the Goddess?

I called David. He was still awake, fortunately. I told him I was coming over in a bit to pick up the disk. If he wondered about the change in plans, he didn't say anything. I wondered if his trick was still there. I hoped not. I got myself another cup of coffee. I decided to at least make myself look somewhat presentable. I washed my face, wet my hair, and dried it. Bill/Colin/whatever had lain back down on the bed and closed his eyes, but when I came out of the bathroom trying to work a brush through the thick tangle of curls on my head, his big brown eyes were open.

"You've never hustled?" he asked again.

"No." I pulled on a pair of white Calvin Klein underwear, readjusting myself. I dug through a drawer for a pair of shorts. "Why?"

"You'd make good money in West Hollywood."

"Well, of course I would." I wiggled my ass at him. "No one can resist me." I buttoned the fly of my khaki shorts. "But then I'd have to live in West Hollywood." I grinned at him. "And besides, I don't want to wind up becoming a cat burglar to save my soul."

He threw a pillow at me. I caught it and flung it back at him. I pulled on an old Halloween Ball T-shirt and slipped

into my sandals. I put on a Saints ball cap and my sunglasses. "How do I look?" He gave me a thumbs-up. "I'll
be back in a flash." I leaned over and kissed him on the
cheek. Some stubble was starting to come up.

I managed to escape the building without running into
Millie and Velma, which wasn't something I particularly
wanted to do. Then again, Millie and Velma had my bag
and my money. I stopped on the steps just past their door.
The odds weren't good that I'd be able to get my bag out
of there without their knowing it. They were most likely
awake already and having breakfast. They always rose
early, and it wasn't a chance I was willing to take. As soon
as they thought I was awake, they'd be climbing the steps
and pounding on the door. I sent a silent prayer to the
Goddess that Venus hadn't woken them up. I kept on
going, avoiding the places where the stairs creaked. I made
it to the front gate, opened it, and checked both ways before stepping out onto the sidewalk.

The only people in sight were an overweight couple in
their mid-fifties walking past. They were wearing hid-
eously garish matching outfits, a weird mixture of reds
and oranges and yellows in polyester. Both were wearing
straw hats. Their skin was white as paper, varicose veins
on their legs. They looked at me as though I were insane.

They're dressed like that and they have the nerve to
think I'm acting weird?

It's not the heat; it's the stupidity.

I shrugged and headed over to the Marigny. The morning was hot, the air practically steam. There were people
out and about on Frenchmen Street. Sidewalks getting
hosed down, a couple of dogs sniffing garbage cans. The
sky was clear and blue. It was going to be hellishly hot
later in the day. My armpits were starting to get wet. I
wiped my forehead. I turned up Pauger Street. The street

was completely deserted. I glanced around, making sure there wasn't anyone around, watching. No one in sight. I felt foolish. But hey, better safe than sorry, right?

When I got to David's, there was an envelope with my name on it taped to his black metal mailbox. I opened it. The disk was there, and a note reading, "Went to bed. Talk later." I sighed in relief. I wasn't in the mood to get into any of this with David, and he would want to tell me all the gory details of his romp with Ramón or whatever his name was, and I wanted to get this over and done with as quickly as I could.

I slipped the disk into the gym bag I'd brought with me and headed into the Quarter.

Chapter Eleven

EIGHT OF WANDS

Approach to a goal

The air was so thick, it was like wading through Jell-O. The wet, heavy air just clings to you. I wiped my face with my shirt again. I crossed Esplanade back into the Quarter. I reminded myself to keep my eyes open. If the cops or anyone were following me, they were too good for me to spot them. That was a relief. Now it was just a matter of whether someone was watching the B & B for Colin to come home.

I was feeling pretty damned crabby by the time I reached the corner of Bourbon and Governor Nicholls. The neighborhood was pretty quiet—nobody really out and about except some joggers and people walking their dogs. I could see some people farther up the street hosing off their sidewalks. Other than that, it was almost like a ghost town. All the gay-boy tourists were most likely out cold in their hotel rooms, resting up for tonight. Of course, they'd also probably just gotten in. Which, I reflected, was exactly where I should be. In bed, sound asleep, instead of doing some covert operation for Colin.

Recovering his laptop right from under the noses of the cops.

What had seemed a little thrilling back in the air-conditioned cool of my apartment seemed pretty stupid in the heat of the morning. He was, I realized with a sudden cold fury, most likely fucking with me. And if he was indeed a professional thief, how stupid was I to leave him alone in my apartment with my television, stereo, and VCR? And on top of that, who knew? Maybe by retrieving his laptop I was becoming an accessory to some crime he was planning on committing this weekend. Great, exactly what I needed. Hadn't he said that circuit weekends were great places to find people to rob? But then again, I reasoned as I stopped into the Nelly Deli for a bottle of soda, my stuff was probably safe. No matter how good of shape he was in, there was no way he was going to lug all of that down the stairs and manage to get out of the building without Velma and Millie noticing.

And hell hath no fury like my lesbian aunts.

I wouldn't wish *that* on someone I hated.

"Hey, Scotty." The woman working the register was a friend of Velma's. She was short and heavy, with graying hair that she was always pushing out of her face. I couldn't remember her name. She was wearing a shapeless muu-muu and had dark spots of perspiration under both arms. She smiled at me. She looked tired. The air-conditioning was going pretty strong in there, but the smell of frying eggs and the heat from the grill in the back of the place was fighting it pretty hard. The air felt heavy with the grease I felt settling on my arms. "How's Velma and Millie doin'?"

"Fine." I paid for my Coke and headed back out, feeling a little bit better about things.

"Tell 'em to stop in. Haven't seen 'em in a while," she called after me.

I stepped out into the heat and took a big swig of the Coke.

"Hey, sexy man!"

Well, of course I turned around. "Oh, hey." It was my Texas cowboy from Thursday night. That, of course, now seemed like it was a million years ago.

He walked up to me. He still looked good, although I suspected he hadn't been to sleep yet. He was wearing a pair of khaki shorts that hung down low off his hips. The shorts looked damp and soggy, which couldn't have been too comfortable. Some razor stubble was starting to appear on his once-smooth chest. A black tank top was stuffed into his backside on the right, which helped pull the shorts down low. He wasn't wearing underwear. The shorts hung low enough so I could see his tan line and the crack of his butt. It was a sexy look, which he was obviously very aware of. He lit a cigarette with a shaking hand. "Didn't see ya last night, Scotty."

I shrugged. "I was dancing from ten till two; if you came into the Pub you had to see me."

He weaved a little bit as he stood there, puffing on his cigarette. "Oh, we went to Oz last night."

Which could explain, dumb ass, why you didn't see me last night, I thought. The heat was getting to me. I took another swig out of my Coke. "That's cool. Was it fun?"

He grinned at me. "Yeah, it was. Didn't find anyone as hot as you, though."

"Of course not." I grinned back at him. Who was I to argue? I started across the street, stopping briefly to let a United cab speed by. Cabs in the Quarter can be fatal if you're not paying attention.

"Where ya heading?"

"Running an errand for a friend." He followed me across the street. Great. A puppy dog. Just what I needed.

"Mind if I walk with you a ways?"

I was sorely tempted to say no, just to see what he would say. That was the kind of mood I was in, but my normal self won out before I could be mean. "I'm heading up to Bourbon and St. Ann." The B & B was on St. Ann, between Bourbon and Dauphine. I'd have to figure out a way to ditch him in the next few blocks.

"I'm heading that way, too, back to the hotel." Oh, yeah, he was staying at the Bourbon Orleans. He grinned at me. "Wanna come with?"

I needed to change the subject. "Where've ya been?" Better to ignore the come-on. Besides, he was in no shape for a tête-à-tête, even if I'd been in the mood for one.

"Some guys I met last night invited me to a hot-tub party." He laughed a bit. "Hot guys, not as hot as you, of course, but there was a group of them and I thought it sounded kinda fun, so I went. We all got naked, but no one could get hard."

"Drugs'll do that." I never understood the mentality of these guys. Everyone knows that gay party drugs inhibit erections, so why try to get laid when you're on something? Some of the guys had started taking Viagra to get past that. Now, I ask you, does that make sense? Take one drug to make you horny, and then another to get you hard because the first one made you limper than a noodle? No, thanks; that's not for me. But then I've never had an erectile dysfunction problem, I am proud to say. My Mr. Happy doesn't take much to get going, no matter what. Just another hot body and some heavy petting and *boing!* He's ready to go.

" 'Course, had you been there, we'd have all been hard." He touched my arm and squeezed it. "Damn, you are such a hottie."

"You're too sweet."

"I mean it." He leered at me. "Sure I can't talk ya into coming back to the hotel with me?" He squeezed my ass.

Ugh. You just told me you couldn't get hard, so what was the point? I wanted to scream at him, but I didn't. His mind was still frying from whatever he had taken. Okay, so I wasn't being my most patient. I just ignored the hand on my ass. I couldn't blame him for wanting me again. The sex had been pretty hot, and to be fair, if I weren't on a covert operation I'd probably go see if I could get him up. It would be a challenge. But the thought that the police might be watching Colin's B & B, that someone might have killed Kenny because of this disk I was carrying in my bag . . .

I stopped walking.

Texas Boy might, just might be the perfect cover.

I grinned. "Hey, buddy, would you mind doing something for me?"

He grinned back at me, and I noticed his overly dilated pupils for the first time. Oh, yeah, Texas Boy's brain was frying hard. This is your brain on drugs. Maybe this wasn't a good idea, after all. "I'd do anything you wanted me to, Scotty."

"I need to pick something up at a friend's room," I said, starting to walk again. "He's staying at a B and B, and needs his laptop out of his room." With any luck, his mind was just addled enough not to wonder why my friend needed me to pick it up instead of getting it himself. "But the owner of the B and B is someone I'd rather not run into, if you know what I mean." I winked at him. "Would you mind running in and getting it for me?"

He slipped his arm around my waist. "I'd do anything for you, Scotty." He squeezed. The implication was there. *Maybe you'd do something for me in return, right?*

"Aren't you sweet?" I leaned into him as we got closer to St. Ann. "I knew when we hooked up the other night that you were the kind of guy I could depend on."

There were people still out at the corner of St. Ann and

Bourbon when we got there. Not really a big surprise. The music was still blaring from both bars. People were drinking already. I just figured they hadn't been to bed yet. Some of them were definitely looking sloppy or at the very least, frayed around the edges. Pace yourself, people, I thought to myself. Why don't they ever learn? The straight end of Bourbon was pretty much people-free. The Christian protestors had decamped. I stood on the corner in front of the Pub, hoping to lose myself in the small crowd if anyone was watching. I gave Texas Boy the keys and pointed out to him where the B & B was. I stood there watching him walk up to the front door and go in. No one seemed to be paying any attention to him, which was good. Nobody sitting in a car. The coast, apparently, was clear.

I guess maybe I was being a little paranoid. This wasn't a James Bond movie, after all. This was more than a little crazy. What the hell was I doing, getting poor Texas Boy involved in something that could get him into a lot of trouble? I shook my head. This was all just nuts.

"Scotty!" someone shouted from behind me.

Great, I thought. *Is everyone in this fucking city who knows me out this morning?* I turned around just in time to be enveloped in a huge bear hug. I was lifted and swung around. My feet brushed against some guy wearing a leather thong and boots, who just smiled at me and moved out of the way as I came around again. The guy was kissing on my neck. "Put me down!" Who the hell was this?

He obliged, and when I could see his face I breathed a sigh of relief. "Have you been to bed yet, Cody?"

Porn superstar Cody Dallas grinned down at me. I could smell stale liquor on him. He was still wearing his G-string, a red one, completely drenched in sweat and leaving absolutely nothing to the imagination. It was easy to see why he was a porn star. Other guys were ogling him.

Who wouldn't? If his endowment and porn-stardom didn't make it clear that he was a top, I'd be ogling him myself. His body was a work of art. No telltale signs of steroid abuse, either. "Nah, I just stopped dancing a couple of hours ago on the bar, and then went over across the street to see what was going on. God*damn*, there are some hot guys in this town. I could get used to this."

"They're mostly tourists." I grinned back at him. There was just something about him that being around him put you into a better place. That indefinable thing that some movie stars have, you know what I mean? Cody had the kind of face and body that should—and probably did—intimidate the hell out of anyone, but there was just something about him that was, oh, I don't know, work-of-art-like that you didn't think of anything else. You wouldn't get intimidated standing next to Michelangelo's *David*, right? Cody was that same way. You just appreciated the perfection and couldn't really take it personally. He just made you feel good to be around him. "Aren't you tired, baby?" I certainly was. I looked over at the B & B. No sign of Texas Boy yet. I glanced at my watch. It had been ten minutes since he'd gone inside. How the hell long would this take? Should this take? How hard could it be to find a fucking laptop computer? Then again, he was on something. With the way my luck was going, he might walk into Colin's room and then completely forget why he was even there.

What if he passed out in there? Christ. That's all I'd need. He had the keys. I couldn't very well go to the manager and ask him to let me into Colin's room.

"I can go days without sleep." Cody shrugged. "But when I do crash, I crash hard."

"Really?" I turned back to him. His pupils were normal-sized. Last night I'd seen him snorting something. Maybe it had worn off. Maybe he wasn't one of those people who snorted stuff to keep him going. Maybe he needed it to shed inhibitions so he could dance. Yeah, right; he fucked people on film for a living. Like he had any inhibitions.

"Yeah, I just have a lot of energy." He started dancing again. Someone reached out and caressed his ass. He spun around and blew them a kiss, with a big smile. "How was Colin?"

I grinned at him. "We had a good time."

"Great." He draped a tree-trunk-like arm across my shoulders. "You two make a pretty hot couple." He winked at me. "I'd have liked to watch you two."

I looked back up the street. Texas Boy was coming out the front door with a laptop carrier in his hand. He grinned and waved at me.

Idiot! I glanced around to see if anyone had noticed, if anyone was watching, but I couldn't tell. Of course, I was so damned tired, I probably couldn't have noticed anyway. It didn't look like anyone was watching. Maybe the police weren't onto Colin's status as a cat burglar yet.

Or maybe he was just fucking with me.

"You hungry?" Cody asked. "I'm starving."

"No, I already ate." Texas Boy was fast approaching. I looked over at him again and was kind of annoyed to see that he was staring at Cody. *I thought I was the hottest thing ever, you ass. Get your ego under control, idiot,* I told myself. This was a good thing. Maybe I could pawn off Texas Boy on Cody.

What a great plan! Sometimes I even amaze myself.

Texas Boy handed me the laptop carrier with hardly a glance at me. He only had eyes for Cody. Okay, I could understand it, but still. "Here ya go. Who's this?"

I tried to hide a grin as I introduced them to each other. My grin faded as I realized I didn't remember Texas Boy's name. Not to worry. Texas Boy leaped into the breach admirably.

"My name's Byron," he said as he stuck out his hand.

Byron? I would never have remembered that in a million years.

"Happy Decadence." Cody reached down and gave him a bear hug and a peck on the cheek.

"You hungry, Byron?" I asked.

"Starved." He and Cody were staring into each other's eyes, that unmistakable gay-mating-ritual expression on both their faces.

"Let's go grab something to eat," Cody growled.

"I can think of lots of things I'd like to eat," Texas Boy replied, reaching out and tweaking one of Cody's nipples.

"I got something you can feast on," Cody growled at him, returning the favor.

Byron stepped closer until their chests were almost touching.

Cody grabbed him and pulled him close, and they started kissing.

"Hey, guys, get a room!" I said.

They stopped kissing. "Great idea," Cody said.

"I got a room right over there," Byron replied.

"All right, then, catch you guys later," I said. They barely even nodded to me as they walked across the street toward the hotel.

I was pretty proud of myself for pulling that off. *Damn,* I thought to myself, *I'm good.* I watched them as they walked up Bourbon Street. . . . Texas Boy was now holding on to Cody's ass. Cody's arms were around him, his mouth on Texas Boy's neck.

The crowd was watching them go. Some cameras were out and taking pictures.

It's not called Decadence because it's a cute name, after all.

Now to get back home and find out what was on the disk.

And maybe get back to some semblance of what passed for normality in my life.

Yeah, right.

Fuck normality.

I wanted sleep, and lots of it. Let Colin play with the disk and the laptop. I was going to get in the shower, wash off all this nasty sweat and stink, and go lie down on the bed.

And sleep till Monday.

Somehow, though, I didn't think it was in the cards for me.

I finished my Coke and tossed it into a full garbage can.

I headed back up Bourbon Street.

A car slowed down beside me.

Nervously I glanced over at the driver.

It was a woman. "Which way to Esplanade?"

"You're going the right way." I smiled at her. "Just a few more blocks."

"Thanks." She floored it and the car sped down Bourbon Street.

Really, Scotty, I said to myself. *You are getting way too paranoid.*

Chapter Twelve

FIVE OF CUPS, REVERSED

Return of an old friend

The last thing I expected was to see Jeremy Fontaine standing in front of my gate when I got home.

I groaned to myself. Will this never end? So much for sleep.

"Scotty!" He sighed in relief when he saw me. "I've been ringing your buzzer."

"I wasn't home."

He glanced up and down the street. Decatur was still fairly deserted but was starting to come to life again. In another couple of hours it would be clogged with cars and tourists. The guy who owned the antique shop across the street was smoking a cigarette and drinking a cup of coffee. He waved. I waved back. The door to the Duchesnays' shop was open, and I could see Mrs. Duchesnay putting price tags on a box of Campbell's soup cans. She didn't look up, her forehead furrowed in concentration.

Jeremy looked like he hadn't slept either. He was still wearing the same clothes he'd had on the night before, best I could tell. Beads of sweat dotted his forehead. Some were trailing down the side of his face. He smelled of sour sweat, like he hadn't bathed in a couple of days.

The 82 Desire bus roared by in a cloud of smelly, gag-inducing exhaust.

Clean air isn't much of a priority in New Orleans.

"Um, I was wondering if I could come up and talk to you for a bit." Jeremy kept looking up and down the street. I followed his eyes. There were small groups of window-shoppers a couple of blocks away, but no one else in the immediate area. It was kind of annoying. If anyone should be looking out it should be me, after everything that had transpired in the past twenty-four hours.

"This isn't a good time for me." I got my keys out and started to unlock the gate.

He grabbed my arm. *"Please,* Scotty. It's a matter of life and death."

I turned and looked into his eyes. They were bloodshot, frantic. He had my forearm in a death lock that was starting to hurt a little bit. I tried to pull free, but he wouldn't let go. "Jeremy, let go of my arm."

He released it. "Please, Scotty."

"You put that damned disk in my boot, didn't you?" I stared at him. I was too tired to be pissed off at him. "Why the hell did you do that?"

"I can explain."

"What the hell is going on, Jeremy?" I opened the gate. "What the hell have you gotten yourself involved in?" *And me, you rat bastard,* I added mentally.

"Can we talk inside, please?"

I nodded and stood aside to let him pass. He glanced up and down the street again and walked past me. He was limping a little bit. I shut the gate behind us and made sure the lock caught. He followed me down the passage to the stairs and started up. We had just made it past the first-floor landing when the door opened. Millie stepped out with a look on her face. I knew that look.

I was in *big* trouble. That was the "you are so lucky I haven't boiled you in oil, young man" look.

Damn it.

"Scotty, can you come in here for a moment, please?" She smiled. It wasn't a pleasant smile.

Jeremy stopped climbing. "Um, Aunt Millie, I'm kind of in a hurry."

"This won't take long." Her voice was steel wrapped in velvet. Not a good sign.

"Jeremy, would you mind waiting for me upstairs?" He nodded and went on up the steps.

I followed Millie into her apartment. It was an exact replica of mine, only better furnished. People who think lesbians missed out on the gay decorating gene have never seen the inside of Millie and Velma's apartment. Their hardwood floors were dust-free and shone, reflecting the light shining from the wrought-iron chandeliers. The side tables in the hallway were made of dark mahogany polished with beeswax with white marble tops. The walls were painted a deep, soothing emerald green. All the fixtures were gold. Black-and-white prints of swamps and bayous hung on the walls, framed in gold. A photographer they knew, whose depictions of the harsh, stark, untamed beauty of the swamps drew you in, had done all the prints. A large antique gold mirror hung on one wall. Their drapes matched the walls perfectly. The balcony windows were open, the sheer drapes moving in the slight breeze from off the river. It was warm, despite the air from the ceiling fans. Millie and Velma tried not to run the air-conditioning. The living room was filled with classy yet comfortable sofas and love seats. The tables matched the ones in the hallway.

Sitting on top of the marble-topped mahogany coffee table, on top of issues of *Architectural Digest, Vanity Fair, Curve,* and *Southern Living,* was my gym bag.

I sat down in a wing-back chair, facing them across the coffee table. I leaned back and folded my arms. Velma was wearing a pair of paint-spattered blue cotton sweatpants and white T-shirt reading *NEW ORLEANS: PROUD TO CALL IT HOME.* Her feet were bare and she glanced momentarily at the coffee table, as if trying to decide if she could get away with putting her feet up. She apparently decided not to try it.

Millie was a terror in the courtroom. Her specialty was criminal law, but her true passion was environmental law. She took on many pro bono cases against corporations and the state, had testified in both Baton Rouge and Washington, and was known to strike terror in the heart of the corporate CEOs. Millie was slight and delicate, while Velma was sturdier and taller. This morning she had on all her makeup and was wearing white linen slacks and a red silk blouse. Her feet were bare. Her fingernails and toenails had French manicures, the little white half-moons glittering in the light from the chandelier. A gold chain hung around her neck, and a gold heart with a half-carat diamond dangled from it. Velma had given that to her on their twentieth anniversary. Her graying black hair was pulled back into a severe bun, and her gold glasses perched on the end of her nose as she looked at me above them. Her dark-brown eyes were unforgiving. She sipped out of a coffee cup, her lipstick leaving a half ring on the rim. She set it down deliberately into a saucer and cleared her throat.

"Scotty, you know both Velma and I love you like you were our own son," she began. Her voice was soft. This wasn't good. Velma had a habit of lowering her voice to command your attention as she whipped you bloody with her words. The depth of her voice when she began to talk was a pretty good indication of just how much trouble you were in. Storm told me once that he'd seen her in court, ripping a CEO to shreds: "The judge told her to talk louder because the court reporter couldn't hear her, and that CEO had just squirmed and got redder in the face as she talked to him," Storm had said. "All I could do was thank God it wasn't *me* she was questioning."

"And we know that you're a grown man of almost thirty and capable of taking care of yourself and making your own decisions, however questionable they might be in our opinion." She went on. "Now, I know you had nothing to do with it, but it's a little worrying to be woken up at five in the morning by the New Orleans police about a murder. Now, we also know that you have little or no control over the actions of other people you may be acquainted with, but that boy who was killed is the one that hangs out around the gate on weekend nights waiting for you, wasn't he?"

I nodded. "Yes, ma'am."

She leaned forward. "And ordinarily, shocking as such a thing is, again, I would be more inclined to dismiss this as another random Quarter tragedy were it not for the fact that when I was letting the police in, I noticed your gym bag sitting in our front hallway right by the door." She pointed to it. "After the police left, I took the liberty of going through your bag." She raised her hand to cut off any comment I might have made. She's very good at this kind of thing. I knew enough not to say anything until she finished, or until she asked me to say something. "Yes, I knew it was an invasion of your privacy; but you did leave it in my house, so I felt I had the right to go through it to try to figure out why you did such a thing. Something you have never done before." She enunciated each syllable as her voice grew even quieter. I glanced over at Velma. She would watch Millie and then her eyes would glance around the room, finding a spot and fixating on it for a few moments. It bothered me. She was avoiding meeting my eyes. This was usually an indication that she was on my side, but Millie was in full charge.

Millie almost always was.

"Well, I—"

Millie's hand came up again, cutting me off. "I found over five hundred dollars in slightly damp cash, some undergarments that were completely soaked, your wallet, and an empty water bottle. Nothing to indicate a reason why you would want to hide it in our apartment. Or why you might want to hide it from the police. Ergo, you must not have been hiding it from the police. So, why?" She pointed a finger at me. "You invited someone home last night that you didn't completely trust not to steal from you, didn't you?"

How to answer that? "Well, it's not that I didn't trust him; I just had to go out again and he was asleep, so I thought it was smarter to not risk it." I was pretty pleased with the answer. It made perfect sense, it sounded like a mature thing to do; surely it would satisfy her.

Wrong. She closed her eyes for a moment and then opened them. "Scotty, I can certainly understand lust and the need to get laid." She gave Velma a quick glance, their eyes met, and they smiled at each other. "But obviously, this man you brought home was someone you had just met and knew nothing about. That's very dangerous. And I'm not talking about safe sex or promiscuity; I am certainly not going to lecture you about that again. Lord knows Velma and I have lectured you about condoms enough to know, or at least think, that it has sunk in. I know you think you're indestructible and nothing is going to happen to you, but most people think that until something bad happens. There are a lot of bad people out there, people who prey on people like you that trust too much and are perfectly willing to bring someone home they know absolutely nothing about. They can steal from you, they could hurt you, they could kill you, and it would be incredibly difficult to trace or catch them."

Now was not the time to tell her he claimed to be a cat burglar.

"Not to mention that by bringing someone in you don't know, you are also putting Velma and me at risk." She sighed, and her voice rose again. "I also am not stupid enough to think you're going to stop picking up strangers, but all I can do is ask you to at least think about what I said, and be a little more cautious." She finally smiled. It was like she became a completely different person. The wrinkled forehead straightened itself out, the eyes warmed, and the other slight wrinkles and lines changed from stern-looking to delighted. "You know we love you, so take your bag and get out of our hair, okay? He's still on the stairs, right?"

"Um, well, yeah, there's someone on the stairs—Jeremy—but he's not the guy from last night."

"You rascal!" She laughed. Velma even grinned. "Got another one already? Is this one a stranger, too?"

Now was not the time to tell either of them that last night's guy was also upstairs. It wasn't a good time to tell them anything else. Let them think what they wanted. The truth, well, the truth was a little hard for even me to swallow. "Um, can I just pick up the bag later?"

Millie rolled her eyes and wagged a finger at me. "Scotty . . ."

I stood up and grinned. "Love ya both." I kissed her cheek quickly, leaned over and gave Velma a quick peck, and headed out of the apartment.

Velma followed me and shut the door behind me. "Everything's okay, isn't it?"

I nodded. "Nothing I can't handle." I hoped.

She gave me a quick hug. "If you need anything, you just let me know, okay?"

I hugged her back. I was so lucky to have the two of them. "Thanks, Aunt Velma."

"Oh, I went ahead and washed your G-strings." She smiled at me and went back inside.

Millie and Velma are really the best.

That over with, I started up the stairs. Jeremy was pacing on the landing outside my apartment, smoking a cigarette. "Can't smoke that in my place, man."

He flicked an ash over the railing. His hands were shaking a little bit. "Mind if I finish it? We're safe out here, right?"

Safe? "Well, no one can get in the gate without a key or unless we buzz them in, and the courtyard is surrounded by eight-foot walls with broken glass embedded in them, so I would say yeah, I guess. Safe from what?"

"I wanted to apologize for acting that way at the gym. I was really glad to see you, but I didn't know who was watching me."

Whoa. Paranoia will destroy ya! "Why would anyone be watching you, Jeremy?"

He pulled on the cigarette. He hadn't shaved in a couple of days, but he was still boyish-looking. I doubted that he could grow a mustache or a beard or a goatee. The stubble was scattered over his cheeks and under his lips like grains of pepper. His hair wasn't combed and looked as if he'd been running his fingers through it a bit too much. He blew the smoke out. "The last year has been really, really hellish, Scotty. You have no idea what's it been like."

I sat down on the top step. "Well, tell me about it, then."

He ground the cigarette out on the railing. Velma had

just painted the railings. I hoped it would wash off. "Can we go inside now?"

I nodded and got up to unlock the door. I opened it. "Colin?"

Jeremy pulled back. "There's someone here? You have a boyfriend?"

"Sort of." How to explain? Why bother? "He's cool; you don't have anything to worry about."

"Okay."

We entered and I shut the door behind us. The television was on in the living room; it sounded like a news program. "Let me make sure he's decent." I gestured to Jeremy to stay by the door. I walked down the hallway.

Colin was sound asleep and stark naked on the couch. His mouth was open and again he was snoring softly.

I walked over to him and touched his shoulder. "Colin. Wake up."

His eyes opened and he smiled at me. He stretched and yawned. Muscles flexed and moved under his skin.

Damn.

"We have company."

He sat up quickly. "The police?"

I sighed. I seemed to be a magnet for people avoiding other people. "No, a former training client of mine; I think he's the one who slipped me the disk last night."

"Did you get the laptop?"

I snapped my fingers. "Piece of cake." I picked up a pair of cotton gym shorts from one of the reclining chairs. *I really need to straighten up more often,* I thought. "Put these on."

He nodded, slipping them on. They were too small and fit him like a glove. The elastic in the waistband was stretched so far, it looked like it was cutting off his circulation. I called back to Jeremy. "Okay, he's decent."

Jeremy walked into the room and did an almost cartoonish double take when he saw Colin. Well, why should he be any different from anyone else? Colin was a double take kind of guy. "Colin, Jeremy; Jeremy, Colin."

They shook hands and then Jeremy sat down in one of my chairs. I joined Colin on the couch, setting the laptop down on my coffee table. Colin reached over and touched my leg. I smiled at him. It was nice to sit there next to him.

"Can I have something to drink?" Jeremy rubbed his eyes.

"Um, I have water, coffee, Coke, orange juice, and milk." Ever the gracious hostess. My grandmothers would be so proud.

"Um, I finished the milk." Colin gave me a nervous grin. "Sorry."

"I'll have a Coke," Jeremy said.

I retrieved the Coke from the kitchen and got myself one, too. A wave of tired swept over me, and I leaned against the refrigerator. The adrenaline was wearing off. My eyes were burning from being tired. I definitely was going to need some sleep soon.

I walked back in and handed Jeremy his can and sat back down. He popped the tab and finished half the can in one drink, then wiped his mouth on his arm and burped.

I started laughing. I couldn't help it. Colin grinned, and Jeremy had the decency to blush a little bit. "Excuse me," he said in a small voice, which only made me laugh harder.

Finally I got a grip. "Okay, Jeremy, tell us what's going on."

He sighed. "I guess I need to start at the beginning."

Chapter Thirteen

SEVEN OF SWORDS

An unwise attempt to take what is not one's own

I already knew something about Jeremy. After all, he'd been a training client of mine for about four months. Being a personal trainer is kind of like being a bartender in many ways. You spend about an hour each session with a person, one on one, taking them through the rigors of a workout, sometimes several times a week. There is a level of trust involved. They are paying you money to help them lose weight, or build muscle, or reshape their body, or just get into better shape and improve their health. In order to give them the best possible workout, you have to find out all kinds of interesting things, like what they do for a living, how much stress is involved in their lives, how and when and what they eat. Do they have any bad habits? Do they smoke cigarettes? Have they ever had heart trouble? Is there a family history of high blood pressure, on and on and on, ad nauseum. That first session is so deadly dull and boring, and then there's always the chance their goals physically are completely ridiculous and unattainable. I had one client who wanted to lose forty pounds for a wedding she was going to in three months. Those people you have to really be gentle with, and explain how unhealthy and unrealistic that goal can be. Once you've discussed all these things and you've trained them a couple of times, the trainer-client completely professional business relationship, in many ways, changes and becomes more of a friend-helping-a-friend thing. It is important for your clients to like and trust you, so you have to be open and honest with them. You ask them about themselves, and frequently, like a bartender or a hairdresser, after a certain period of time you wind up finding out all kinds of information about them that their spouses, partners, and best friends don't even know. It is amazing what people will tell you while they are sweating. And just when you think you've heard almost everything, there's always someone who will surprise you. I'm always afraid I might get called to testify in a divorce suit or something. I mean, I try to maintain strict client confidentiality, but it's not like I'm a lawyer or a doctor or something.

Go figure human nature.

Jeremy had been with me for a little under four months, and I had liked him. He was a cute boy with a very sweet and trusting disposition. He made me laugh. The challenge of training him was putting size on him. He didn't think he could get bigger, but wanted to try. He was a small guy and only weighed about 130 when we met, and it was all in his butt and legs. He didn't have much body fat, maybe a little bit you could pinch around his middle. His butt and legs were strong, big, and muscular from years of playing tennis. Seeing that, I knew that putting him on an intense program of heavy weights and low repetitions, in addition to making him eat properly, would get some muscle on him, and fairly quickly. At the end of the four months, Jeremy had put on fifteen pounds of muscle and had lost that little bit of baby fat.

I am, if I do say so myself, very good at my job.

During the time that I trained Jeremy, I also learned a lot about his personal life. He was born and raised in Biloxi. His parents were divorced and had both remarried. His father and the second wife lived in Pensacola and had very little contact with Jeremy. They had their own kids together, and as far as his father was concerned, his first marriage was just a bad dream that never really happened. Jeremy's mother's second husband was a good ole boy from rural Mississippi, and even though he made good money as an engineer, well, you can take the boy out of rural Mississippi but . . . He thought Jeremy and his brother, who was about the same size as Jeremy, should be football stars and that tennis was a girlie, nonreal sport. It had been rough on them both, but they had each other to help deal with the new dad. Their mom never said anything, being a proper Southern woman raised to never contradict or argue with her husband. Jeremy's brother had escaped to college at Ole Miss and left Jeremy there alone for three years.

That's when things got really hard for him.

Without his older brother to help divert some of the attention away from him, Jeremy got both barrels of stepfatherly disapproval. His stepfather started calling him a "sissy," a "faggot," worthless, and threatened him on a regular basis with military school. He forced Jeremy to go out for the high school football team, and he'd been cut. It wasn't hard to understand why: he was too little. Unfortunately, Jeremy had started becoming aware of his own attraction to other boys, sneaking looks in the locker room and showers, getting crushes, always terrified he would get hard in the showers. His sophomore year in high school, he developed a crush on a senior football player named Ken Delavan. One night, as fate would have it, he and Ken were at a party and started talking. They hit it off, and a couple of six-packs later they were in the backseat of Ken's beat-up old 1973 Impala, sucking each other's dicks on a back road.

That's what they were doing when the county sheriff came across the car.

It was off to military school then for Jeremy. But rather than stomping his homosexuality out of him, making a "man out of him," it was more like a candy store. If Jeremy was to be believed, military school was the stuff of porn films. "I learned things there," he had confided while doing bench presses and trying not to look up my shorts, "that I'd never even dreamed of." Listening to his stories of Alabama Military Academy made me regret not being sent there.

Even so, all he had dreamed of was escaping—escaping the harsh discipline of the school, getting out from under the thumb of his stepfather. After he graduated, he came to New Orleans and started waiting tables. He still kept in close contact with his mother, but he refused to have anything to do with her husband.

When he had started working out with me, he had just ended a two-year relationship with a guy with a serious crack problem. That was part of why he wanted to start working out. "I figured if I had a better body I would attract a better kind of guy." An interesting theory, I thought, given how many guys I knew with worked-out bodies with either serious emotional or drug problems.

Or both.

"I stopped working out with you when I started dating Jamie Winters, remember?" he asked me now. I nodded. I'd forgotten the guy's name. I'd only met him once, when I ran into them at the Pub one night. "Well, Jamie was the perfect guy, I thought. What did I know? I moved in with him, and I thought everything was fine, until I got syphilis from him three months into the relationship. I had caught it from him, and when I confronted him with it, turns out he had been going to the baths, meeting guys off the Internet, the whole time we'd been together!"

Colin's hand tightened on my thigh. "That sucks," I said.

"Yeah, well, I moved out and was all ready to just give up, you know? Being gay had never made me happy, ever. Not once. It was all a lie, being gay and having a good life. I mean, being gay was responsible for everything bad in my life, right? The whole military school thing, all the assholes I'd been involved with? If I'd only been straight, I could have met some nice girl and gotten married."

I chose not to point out there were a lot of unhappy straight people.

"I figured there was no point. And then I came across a flyer for the Church of the Prodigal."

I started. The Church of the Prodigal was Louisiana's leading proponent of the ex-gay ministry. They'd made a lot of noise at first, taking ads out in the *Times-Picayune* and flooding the Quarter and Marigny with flyers about curing homosexuality through prayer. They were regular fixtures outside the gay bars for a while, holding prayer services on the corner of St. Ann and Bourbon, trying to get gay boys to be saved. I always felt sorry for them, not only because they were misguided, but because they were such obvious targets for abuse and ridicule. "Welcoming the prodigals back to God" was their slogan.

"So I started going to services and counseling there." Jeremy took another swig of his Coke. "And you know something? I'm sure you'll think I'm crazy, but it did work. Every time I started thinking about having sex with men, I would just pray to Jesus to give me the strength to resist. I started dating a girl. It seemed to be working. They were very proud of me and started letting me counsel others. *Me.* Can you imagine? The very idea of it all was so strange. But I tell you, it was working."

I couldn't imagine it, any of it. Being gay was such a part of who I was, like my right arm or something. I couldn't imagine giving up having sex with men. I couldn't imagine never setting foot in a gay bar again or feeling a man's arms around me or never kissing another man again. I know that a lot of gay men spent a lot of their lives conflicted about their sexuality, but it hadn't been that way for me. Once again I thanked the Goddess for my parents. It wasn't that I didn't find women attractive; I thought many women were beautiful or sexy, but the idea of having sex with them just didn't work for me.

"Then the Church of the Prodigal got involved with the Willy Perkins campaign."

"Willy Perkins?" The guy who wears a plastic fetus on his lapel for public debates?

"Willy Perkins is for 'family values,' " Jeremy went on. "I started working in his campaign office—running it, actually. I have a gift for organization, it seems. Anyway, a couple of days ago, I needed some information out of the campaign manager's computer, and I came across something that scared the pants off me."

"What was that, Jeremy?" Colin asked. "Is that what's on the disk?"

He nodded. "It was so crazy, I just knew it couldn't be true. It had to be a bad joke of some sort. It was a plan to kill all the gays in New Orleans during Decadence."

My eyes popped open. I was wide awake now. "WHAT?"

Jeremy shook his head. "I know, I know; that was how I reacted. I mean, it had to be some kind of bad joke; it couldn't be true, ya know? But then I started thinking about things I'd heard around the office. Willy hates New Orleans, thinks it's a blot on the face of an otherwise fine Christian state. He refuses to campaign here because he thinks it's a modern-day Sodom. His whole political strategy is based on getting enough votes in the other parishes so that when he loses Orleans by a wide margin he can still win. But it'll be close. Like that other one, where they had to call in the FBI?"

I sighed. Another proud moment in Louisiana political history. A senatorial race was hard-fought and closely contested. The one candidate had been a family values candidate, for God and the family and pro-life. The other had been a liberal. The liberal had lost every parish in the state by a very close margin, but won in a landslide in Orleans Parish. The victory in Orleans Parish swept her into the U.S. Senate. The losing candidate had cried foul, election tampering in New Orleans, and the FBI had been called in. After a six-month investigation, the FBI found the allegations to be unfounded. "So Willy Perkins is afraid the same thing will happen to him?"

"Uh-huh." Jeremy finished the Coke and put the can down. "I heard him say once that he wished God would rain fire and brimstone on Sodom before the election, because if that happened he would win for sure. I thought it was a joke, but then I had to wonder."

"How were they planning on doing it?" Colin asked.

Jeremy swallowed. "Plant bombs in the sewers on St. Ann and Bourbon and detonate them at one in the morning on Saturday night."

"Oh, my Goddess." I glanced over at the altar and sent a quick mental prayer to her.

"I didn't know what to do!" Jeremy sighed. "I called the FBI."

I shook my head. "What?"

"I called the FBI and went in to meet with them. They have an office here, you know." Jeremy looked at me, then at Colin. "They didn't believe me, of course, because I didn't have anything concrete to take with me. It really pissed me off, you know? They acted like I was nuts, like I was absolutely crazy or something. Like I was making it all up.

Like I would make something like that up! So I went back to the office, printed out the first page, and faxed it to them. You bet your ass they called me back yesterday! I told them I could get it all onto a disk, and to send someone to the Pub last night and I would give it to one of their agents."

"Do you know who this agent was?" I finished my own Coke. Crazy, crazy, crazy.

He shook his head. "They wouldn't tell me; said it was safer for both of us that way."

"So why did you slip me the disk?" I had to know.

"I was being followed." He made a gulping noise. "I got the disk yesterday afternoon and was followed. That's why I went to the gym, to try to shake them. I mean, I knew it was goons from the church. Perkins has these paramilitary skinhead freaks that camp out in the swamp, for enforcers, and one of them was following me everywhere. Those guys are crazy, Scotty. They scare the shit out of me, and they do whatever Perkins orders them to do."

Hot Daddy, I remembered. He'd been at the gym, and he'd been at the Pub later as well. "I was scared, so when I saw you up on the bar at the Pub, and the FBI guy was over an hour late, I thought I'd better get rid of the disk so I wouldn't be caught with it. I figured I could just catch up to you later and get it back."

"Why didn't you come back?"

"There were some skinheads across the street." Jeremy shuddered. "Those guys are some scary-ass motherfuckers, Scotty; they really are. I figured I could just catch you at home later. And here we are."

"Well, there's something you should know." I rubbed my eyes. "Kenny Chandler was killed last night."

"Who?"

"A friend of mine." A wave of sadness swept over me.

Poor, innocent Kenny. "His body was found in front of my gate."

"Oh, God." Jeremy paled.

"And we were almost mugged on our way home from the Pub," Colin added. "By a skinhead."

I remembered the swastika on the mugger's chest.

"Oh, my God." Jeremy looked like he was going to be sick. "They must have seen me put the disk in your boot!"

"You couldn't have known." I really didn't know what to think. My head was so tired. It was too much information for me to process. This just doesn't happen. Skinheads. Bombs in the sewers. Kenny dead. Cat burglars.

I stood up. "I need to go lay down."

"Are you okay, honey?" Colin got to his feet, putting his arm around me.

For a brief second I shot a glance at him. *Honey?* But when he touched me, I tripped.

I'm very graceful. I took dance when I was a small child, and, of course, I wrestled in high school. Anyway, because of that kind of training I walk with a kind of grace and dignity that people have noticed and remarked on.

Unfortunately, the comments usually are something like "I can't believe that someone so graceful can be such a klutz!"

I often walk into walls. I trip over anything within a square foot of me when walking. I step off the curb when walking down the sidewalk. It was a wonder I wasn't always in a cast. Of course, that could be because I was so graceful.

This time, the offending object was a house shoe. I never wear my house shoes. When I am in the house I am barefoot. I don't even wear socks in the house. So why on earth my house shoe, a long-ago Christmas gift from Rain, was in the living room in the middle of the floor is beyond me. Near as I could tell, I got up and took a step just as

Colin stood up and put his arm around me. My foot turned over on the shoe and I pitched toward the coffee table. Colin flexed his arm in an attempt to keep me from falling, but all he managed to do was divert the path of my fall away from the coffee table.

And straight into Jeremy's chair.

I put my arms out to catch myself. My knees buckled and hit the floor in another instinctive attempt at self-preservation. My hands landed on Jeremy's knees.

Everything went black.

Chapter Fourteen

NINE OF SWORDS

Suffering, desolation, cruelty, pitilessness, doubt

I had never experienced anything like this before.
I imagined it must be kind of similar to a K-hole. Some
guys I know have gone into those before. You take too
many snorts of ketamine (which is a horse tranquilizer),
and you go into this weird zone where you kind of halluci-
nate. You're slightly aware of your surroundings and
what's going on in reality around you, but it's very much
on the edges. There is a big, black hole in the center of
your vision that changes and rotates around, sometimes
spreading out so far that you can't see anything at all except in your peripheral vision, and even that is kind of
fuzzy and shaky. The hallucinations come inside that black
hole if you've taken enough to get you that far. One guy
described the black hole as a "tunnel you start sliding
through, traveling through space and time and then you're
somewhere else completely, even around different people
maybe than the ones you've gone out with, and you have
conversations with them and even do things . . . and then
it slowly starts to fade away into the black again and then
the hole starts to recede a little bit until you're finally back

to where you started when you went into the hole in the first place, on the dance floor or wherever, just a little shaky."

Apparently, this can last anywhere from five minutes to two hours.

No, thank you. Just one more reason I stay away from that shit.

All I knew was that I had tripped over a shoe in my living room and fallen onto Jeremy. Did I hit my head on my coffee table? I didn't think so, because everything faded to black as I was looking into Jeremy's eyes, and my head hadn't been falling that way.

What the hell happened?

I was floating in a black sky. No clouds, no stars, no moon, no ground apparently. I wasn't falling, but no matter which way I looked, I saw nothing. Nothing but blackness, spreading out in every direction, but it was a benign blackness.

I felt nothing but peace.

Relaxed.

My eyes didn't feel tired anymore.

My feet didn't hurt, either.

Hmmm.

This is nice, I thought as I kept floating. *I like it here. I can get into this.* I closed my eyes and just went with it. There wasn't anything to see anyway except that black. I was perfect. Not too hot, not too cold, not sweating, my muscles all in a total state of relaxation. My hair was probably not messed up. I probably didn't smell bad either. I was just perfect.

This is what they mean when they say bliss, I thought.

I felt a cold wind and shivered, opening my eyes. The blackness was gradually getting a little lighter. I noticed this with a sense of forboding. I didn't want the perfect state to end. I looked around and became aware that my feet were floating downward. It kept getting lighter and then it looked like the blackness was starting to move a bit, curling and moving in little circles, bunches of little circles, some moving one way, others moving the opposite. Then, instead of turning in circles, it began to weave and wave, as though blowing one way by a wind. It was still getting a little colder and lighter.

Fog, I realized with a start. The fucking fog again!

Just like in the dreams or visions or whatever the hell it had been that I'd been having.

And the bliss, the peace, the benevolence, whatever it was I'd been feeling—it was all gone as if I'd never felt it in the first place. Every hair on my body was standing up. My body was becoming tense.

In the distance I heard it. It was hushed, quiet, barely there, so I had to strain to hear it. The screaming. The screams.

The sounds of people dying.

The fog wrapped itself around me, weaving around me, almost pushing me forward, as though it wanted me to see what was happening. It seemed to tug at my right leg, so I gave in to the pressure and let it move forward a step. The fog seemed to sigh, pleased. I took another step.

Good.

I heard it echo in my head, like a sigh. A contented sigh.

This is crazy, I told myself. *It's just fog; fog can't make noises, can't feel emotions.* I was just tired; I was hallucinating all of this.

I wanted to get back to my apartment.

But I couldn't stop moving forward.

The screams seemed to get louder with each step.

I stopped walking.

No, you have to see. The words echoed in my head.

"Well, can't you just take me there?" I asked.

There was a slight hiss, like air leaking from a balloon, and the fog seemed to recoil from me, pull back slightly.

"Okay, okay!" I held up my hands. "Just checking."

I started walking again, wondering about this fog thing. It had come with the visions before. *Yes, I heard, yes, I brought the visions to you.*

It is fated.

"Who are you?"

You know.

"No, I don't."

Yes, you do, but don't worry about who I am.

"How can I not?"

You are safe.

"Whatever," I muttered. No response. Fine. I'm hallucinating, that's what this is; I hit my head on something and I am in some kind of dream world; my mind is worn out from lack of sleep and everything else that's been going on; I am going to wake up and everything's going to be fine. Just go with it and I'll come to at any second.

I kept walking.

It seemed like I walked far enough to get to Baton Rouge. The screams began to fade away again.

Then the fog thickened again and formed a barrier I couldn't penetrate. I tried to take another step but couldn't get through it.

I stopped.

The fog cleared.

I was standing on top of a building looking down on the ruins of the French Quarter.

"Oh my God!" I closed my eyes.

"Are you okay?"

I opened my eyes. Colin and Jeremy were staring down at me, their faces white. Their eyes were wide and round. "Whoa. Did I hit my head?" I let them help me up to a sitting position.

"It was the weirdest thing," Jeremy chattered. "You just

kinda stumbled and started to fall, but your eyes rolled back in your head before you even landed." He grinned weakly. "On me."

Colin knelt down beside me. "Are you sure you're okay?"

"How long was I out?"

"Not long." He glanced over at the VCR clock. "A minute, maybe more."

"That's all?" It felt like I'd been unconscious, in that weird other world, for hours. All that walking. But then, wherever I was, maybe they measure time differently. None of it made any sense to me—none. "I am so tired." Everything hurt. Eyes, feet, calves, even my eyelashes felt like they ached.

"C'mon, let's help him into the bedroom." Colin grabbed me under the arms and lifted me to my feet like I weighed less than a feather. *Damn, he's strong,* I thought. He then proceeded to pick me up in his arms.

"I feel like I'm being carried over the threshold," I said as he carried me into the bedroom.

"I'm not the marrying kind." He laughed.

"Neither am I." He set me down gently on the bed. He turned off the lights and brushed his lips against my cheek. "You get some sleep."

The bed felt so good, like it was sucking me down into its softness. I was asleep before my head hit the pillow.

And I was back on that roof.

The sun was bright, almost blinding in its intensity. The French Quarter was in ruins. Some buildings had been gutted as though by fire. A boat was poling its way down Bourbon Street. The water. It was everywhere, muddy and dark and brown. The waves cast up in the wake of the boat had brown foam, just like the river. That was the truly strange thing. The Quarter looked like Venice, its streets filled with the muddy water. Every so often as a boat passed by, its wake would briefly expose the roof of a submerged car. Every building I could see that still looked intact had shattered windows. I turned to the right and saw fires burning still, flames shooting out of windows, roofs collapsing as I watched. I turned to the left and looked up to the straight end of Bourbon Street. The same. The skyscrapers of the CBD were intact but looked different, lifeless.

And the smell . . .

I smelled death, everywhere the smell of rotting flesh, burning flesh, the sickly-sweet unmistakable odor of death.

The city was dead.

This is what is coming, echoed in my brain.

The horror of it all brought tears to my eyes.

People will die. People will suffer.

"Why?" I shouted, my voice bouncing off the wrecked buildings, coming back at me from several different directions, like I was shouting into a canyon. My voice sounded creepy, eerie in the unnatural silence.

It must be stopped, the voice said again. *It must be stopped.* . . . The voice faded away, echoing away finally into silence.

I sat up, wide awake. Half an hour had passed since I'd gotten into bed. My head was pounding, aching. I got up and walked into the bathroom and took two Extra Strength Tylenols, washing them down with water. I splashed water on my face and looked in the mirror.

I definitely had bed hair. My eyes were bloodshot and puffy from lack of sleep. If I wasn't careful, the bags under my eyes were going to turn into steamer trunks. I had definitely looked better in my life. I couldn't believe I was letting people see me like this. I turned on the hot water spigot and walked back into the living room while the water got hot.

No sign of Colin.

Jeremy was snoring softly on the couch.

I watched him breathe for a few moments. Poor Jeremy. How horrible must it have been to have hated gay life so much that you tried to change your sexual orientation? And through prayer, of all things! Talk about self-loathing. I got myself another cup of coffee and started shuffling the cards, occasionally looking over at him.

What to do with him? Obviously, he was in danger. From everything he'd said, Willy Perkins wanted that disk back, and if what happened to poor, innocent Kenny was any indication, they were more than willing to use any means necessary. I still couldn't figure out why they killed Kenny, and maybe it was all just a big, scary coincidence, but I didn't buy that for a minute. Kenny must have been killed because Jeremy had slipped me the disk, for some reason. It couldn't have just been chance that someone killed him and propped him up against my gate. It was all part of the same thing. They'd seen Jeremy put the disk in my boot, and tried to get it back from me by mugging me on my way home from the bar.

And Kenny had been killed as a result.

As long as we had the disk, we were in danger.

Thank the Goddess nobody had seen me take it over to David's, or there might be another body or two.

I hugged myself to stop the shaking.

I spread the cards out. They told me nothing. Everything was still too unclear.

And where had Colin gone off to?

I reshuffled the cards. What to do with Jeremy?

I turned over the top card. The Empress. I smiled.

Of course.

Mom and Dad.

Mom and Dad always picked up strays. Cats, dogs, people—it didn't matter. Having stoner hippie parents might not seem like the best way to grow up to some people. We definitely did not have traditional family values. Mom and Dad always dragged all three of us to protests when we were growing up and tried very hard to instill their values in us. They certainly failed with Rain. She'd never admit it to anyone in the family, but I suspected Rain had even voted Republican a few times. Rain wanted to be normal, whatever that was, and so she'd married her Uptown doctor. She volunteered for several charities, organized fund-raisers, rode in the Krewe of Iris parade during Mardi Gras. She has someone come and clean her house once a week, do her grocery shopping, all of that typical Uptown society matronly stuff—the very things Mom and Dad had rejected. She had the wing-back chairs and Audubon prints, all the trappings of a conservative, stable Uptown life. Rain, well, Rain was okay, even though she had a weird relationship with Mom and Dad. Mom and Dad still loved her and still tried to raise her political consciousness, but it was more like going through the motions now than anything else.

"Do you think Rain has good sex?" Mom had asked me once casually over dinner, like she was asking me about the weather.

"Mom!" I'd said, horrified.

She shrugged. "She's just so uptight, you know what I mean? I really think if she was getting some really good sex she'd loosen up." Rain's husband, Fred, was relatively attractive and kept himself in pretty good shape jogging and playing tennis. "I just don't think Fred is capable of giving her an orgasm."

"I prefer not to think of them having sex myself," I replied, hoping she'd change the subject.

I think their disappointment with their daughter and Storm's being a lawyer were part of the reason they picked up stray people to nurture. Emily, the cute little lesbian who worked at The Devil's Weed, was their latest project and seemed to be doing well. Emily had gotten a degree from Northwestern and had been teaching high school Spanish in Chicago before she came down for Mardi Gras and fell in love with the city. She chucked her job and moved to New Orleans. Mom and Dad found her an apartment, gave her a job, and encouraged her to sing. She has a beautiful voice, very clear and strong and kind of folksy. Every Saturday night, they had a guitarist come in and play for their patrons. Emily now sang with him. She did have a great voice.

A refugee from the Willy Perkins campaign, a cute young gay boy rejected by his real family, would be perfect for them. He fit all their criteria. Nowhere to turn, nowhere to run to, somewhat in trouble. Mom and Dad would take him in, help him, get him back on his feet again.

He murmured in his sleep and shifted on the couch.

He really is adorable, I thought, feeling very protective of him. *Don't you worry, Jeremy, we'll take care of you.*

I walked out onto the balcony. Damn, it was hot outside. Decatur Street was alive with people now, cars moving at barely five miles an hour when they could move, just another typical Saturday in the Quarter. Clusters of obviously gay men were walking around, checking out the shops, with their shirts off. I watched a group of them standing on the corner. It looked like they were trying to decide on whether to eat at the Louisiana Pizza Kitchen. They were all shirtless, wearing shorts and work boots that had never seen a day's work in their lives, holding the obligatory water bottles. Finally they made a decision and moved down in the direction of the Pizza Kitchen.

Oh, Lord, I gasped. Involuntarily I stepped back into the shade.

Hot Daddy was standing in the shade across the street, on the corner of Barracks and Decatur. He hadn't been visible because of the group that had just moved on. He was talking into a cell phone and he kept looking over at my building. Then he looked up.

Our eyes met.

He closed his cell phone and slipped it into his shorts pocket. He was wearing a white tank top, what the politically incorrect call a wife-beater, and a pair of jean shorts and work boots. To anyone noticing him, he just looked like another one of the gay tourists in town.

He gestured for me to come down.

I shook my head. *Yeah, right,* I thought. *How stupid do you think I am?*

He gestured again.

Obviously pretty stupid, I decided. Okay, it was probably not the smartest thing in the world to do, but I'm kind of impulsive. It's part of my charm; what can I say? And what could he do to me on a crowded street in broad daylight? I shrugged and nodded agreement, pointing down. Might as well get this over with.

Jeremy shifted again as I walked through. I did notice that Colin's laptop was on and sitting on my dining table, and his gym bag was on the floor. So he was planning on coming back, at any rate. Where the hell did he go? I made it to the back door before I remembered the shower and how hellish I looked. I ran into the bathroom and shut the shower off. I pulled a comb through my hair. Well, I looked passable now. As I went down the stairs, I decided to stay inside the gate. It was wrought iron, and I could stand far enough back so that Hot Daddy couldn't grab me or try anything if he was one of the bad guys.

Bad guys. I laughed to myself. This was all so damned insane, I was even thinking in old Western movie terms. *Sheesh.*

I stopped and picked up the phone and dialed Venus Casanova's number. After three rings, her voice mail picked up. I left her a brief message, explaining about the disk. At least, I figured, this way if anything happens to me, someone knows.

Feeling a little better, I went out the back door.

Chapter Fifteen

FIVE OF CUPS, REVERSED

New alliances formed

I stood at the iron grate and looked across the street. Hot Daddy was on his phone again. He was frowning, which made his scar more evident. It was an ugly red gash that ran from just below the right eye in a jagged pattern to his jawline. I leaned against the brick wall, which was damp from precipitation. A couple of Goth kids walked by. Everything about them was black except for their fish-belly white skin. Black T-shirts, black shorts, black boots, hair dyed black. Their exposed arms and legs were covered with vibrant tattoos. One even had a tattoo on her neck. I cringed. That had to have hurt. Their faces were covered with piercings. A trick had once tried to talk me into having my navel pierced.

"You have the cutest, sexiest little belly button," he'd said, leaning over and outlining it with his tongue. I squirmed because it tickled a little bit. "You should get it pierced. No one would be able to resist you then."

"No one can resist me now," I'd replied, putting my hands behind my head and closing my eyes as his tongue slid down lower to the area I'd been wanting him to pay attention to all along rather than my navel. Sometimes tricks just don't get it, which can be more than a little annoying. Now I couldn't remember the guy's name and only vaguely knew what he looked like. Goddess, I was tired.

I looked across the street. Hot Daddy was still talking into his phone. I briefly considered going over there and grabbing the phone away from him and throwing it into the street. How long was I going to wait here? Not much longer. It was too hot and I was too tired. I didn't want to talk to him that badly. Hey, he was the one who wanted to talk to me, and then has the nerve to make me wait. *C'mon, asshole.* Just as I thought that, he turned his head and saw me. He folded the phone quickly and put it into his pocket. He crossed the street.

He didn't really walk. He kind of strutted in a way. *Confidence,* his walk screamed to anyone watching. *I am a hot, attractive man that everyone wants to have sex with.* But it wasn't really arrogance, I decided. It was more of a subconscious thing some terribly sexy guys have. They aren't aware enough of their looks, don't really think about it too much, and the effect they have on other people, but it's there. He also had a powerful masculine energy that I found incredibly attractive. His CD collection probably housed no Streisand, no Judy, and no cast show recordings. It would be a safe bet that he never cranked a Whitney Houston dance remix when alone at home and performed it. There would be no stuffed animals, Scarlett O'Hara collectible plates from the Franklin Mint, no Disney collectible dolls, no black-and-white prints of gorgeous men. His apartment would be extremely masculine with dark wood furniture, possibly an Irish setter, and his bedroom would be a mess, with dirty workout clothes scattered about mixed in with slightly stained white boxer briefs and socks. Definitely not a cat person. There would be no skin or hair care products or colognes in his bathroom—just a shaving kit, a toothbrush, a tube of Crest squeezed from whatever part he happened to pick it up by, and a can of Right Guard. He would never shave the hair on his chest or use Nair on his legs. He'd probably been a jock in high school—football and baseball star, I decided. A guy's guy, the kind the other jocks look up to, the nerds are afraid of, and the girls all wet their panties over.

Yum.

"What do you want?" I asked as he walked up.

"Jeremy Fontaine's in your apartment, isn't he?" His voice was deep, low, almost a growl. The hairs on the back of my neck twitched a little.

"Who wants to know?"

He reached into his back pocket and pulled out a little black leather case. He flipped it open. "Special Agent Frank Sobieski, FBI."

He handed it to me through the fence. Looked official, but what do I know? I handed it back. "What do you want with him?"

A gaggle of laughing teenage girls dressed like Britney Spears in her latest video went by. Tube tops and low-cut hip huggers staying up by some miracle. Tattoos on their lower backs just above the waistline of the pants. Giggling. He wiped sweat off his forehead. "You need to let me in."

"How do I know I can trust you?"

"You can." He folded his arms. Veins leaped out in his forearms, biceps, and shoulders. His tanned forearms were dusted with golden hairs.

I sighed. If he was really a Fed, if I said no, he'd just get some goons and force their way in. Might as well appear to be cooperative. Mom and Dad, of course, would have demanded a warrant, might have actually spit in his face or some such thing. To them, the FBI were just Americanized storm troopers. I unlocked the gate and swung it open. "Come in, Agent Sobieski, but I'm not going to take you upstairs just yet. Jeremy's had a hell of a night, and so have I, and he's asleep."

He bowed his head to me as he stepped past me. I closed the gate and locked it. Be followed me into the courtyard, and I waved him into a seat in the shade. I sat down across the table from him. "You looked better in your workout clothes, Agent Sobieski."

His blue eyes bored into mine. "Mr. Bradley, Jeremy Fontaine is an integral part of a case the FBI is working on."

"Scotty," I said. Nobody ever called me Mr. Bradley. For that matter, no one calls my dad Mr. Bradley either. Mr. Bradley is my grandfather, a rather uptight, mean-spirited old man who spends most of his time puttering with his roses. When he isn't drinking bourbon and yelling at my grandmother, that is. Definitely an old-school control freak.

"In the interests of national security, I can't reveal the details of the case to you—"

"Cut the crap, Agent." I waved my hand. "I know all about it. Jeremy told me. This is about Willy Perkins and his plan to put bombs in the sewers and blow the Quarter to smithereens." For a brief second, my mind flashed back to the devastation I had seen in my dream/vision/whatever-the-hell-it-was. "Although I don't see how it's possible for anyone to get bombs into the sewers, especially in the summertime." One of the most popular urban legends in New Orleans was that in the Quarter, gasses built up in the heat and humidity, creating intense pressure that could only be released by blowing a manhole cover. People have sworn to me that they've seen this happen. Reportedly, the manhole cover will blow about twenty or thirty feet in the air.

Amazing how that can happen without anyone ever getting hurt or a car being damaged, but it is a fun story. I always wanted to see it happen. It was definitely more interesting than the Easter Bunny or Santa Claus. "That's why we need the disk, Mr.—er, Scotty." Agent Sobieski leaned back and crossed his legs. He had beautifully defined calves, which flexed when he did this. Hell, his calves were steers. Like on his forearms, golden hairs glinted. "To make sure this isn't a figment of the imagination of a disgruntled employee."

"Are you people even bothering to check his story?"

He frowned at me and didn't answer.

"Why haven't you evacuated the Quarter?"

"We don't want to create a panic."

Create a panic? I stared at him. "So it would be better to have people get killed?"

Silence.

"Answer me!"

"You live on the third floor, correct?" He stood up.

"Do you have a warrant?" I am not my parents' son for nothing. We stared at each other for a few minutes.

He relented. "We've found nothing, Scotty. And we've searched and searched. Sewer entrances are all covered by agents. As of ten minutes ago, the French Quarter is safe as always."

"I feel so reassured."

"Good." He actually smiled. His stern, gruff-looking face completely changed. Before, he looked as though he belonged in assless leather chaps with a whip in his hand and a harness on. His smiling face looked like something you would want to wake up to every morning. His gray eyes sparkled. I decided not to point out I was being sarcastic. "So, I need that disk. Are you going to help me get it or am I going to have to go get it myself?"

"Why didn't you get it from him last night, like you planned?"

He folded his arms and said nothing.

"Must have been pretty embarrassing to have to go into a gay bar," I said.

"I go where I need to."

"Good for you." He was starting to piss me off. I was beginning to regret letting him in. "What about Kenny?"

"Kenny Chandler?"

"Yes." Before this guy was getting into *my* apartment, he was going to explain to me about Kenny. "Who killed him, and why?"

He shrugged. "We don't know. We didn't have your apartment under surveillance until Jeremy showed up at your gate." It was also obvious he didn't care.

"Good going." I told him about the attempted mugging on my way home. "Their goons obviously saw him talk to me and put the disk in my boot, and then they killed Kenny. So why couldn't the FBI have done something? I'm lucky they didn't break into my house and kill me."

His face whitened. The scar stood out even more. I wondered how he'd gotten it. "*You* have the disk?" His jaw tightened.

I was beginning to understand why my parents had so little faith in our government. I rolled my eyes. "I've had it all along. He slipped it to me last night, while *you* were watching him. I didn't even know I had it until about, oh, hell, some ungodly hour this morning." I laughed. "You mean to tell me Perkins's goons knew I had the disk and you people didn't? Nice work, Sobieski." FBI, obviously, stood for Feeble Bureau of Incompetents.

"Jesus fucking Christ!" He stood up. "Excuse me for a minute." He walked over to the farthest corner of the courtyard away from me and called someone on his cell phone. I couldn't hear what he was saying, but he was very agitated. I grinned to myself. Not so cocksure now, eh, Agent Sobieski? He turned his back to me. His butt looked nice in the shorts. There was a patch of golden hair on his lower back. He did have a nice tan. Muscles flexed and moved in his back as he gestured with his arms as he talked. I watched as he shifted his weight from one leg to the other. It was amazingly erotic. If I weren't so tired . . .

And if he weren't with the FBI, I added.

Voices on the stairs caused me to regretfully stop staring at Agent Sobieski's perfect ass and look up. Velma and Colin were stepping out onto the second-floor landing. Colin hadn't seen me yet, but Velma had. In a brief flicker she glanced from me to Agent Sobieski, back to me and then Colin. Colin started climbing the stairs back up to my apartment. What the hell had he been doing downstairs with my aunts? That didn't bode well for me. What had he told them?

Then I groaned. This was just great. He had wanted to avoid the cops. Surely he'd be thrilled and delighted when I brought an FBI agent up to the apartment. Well, maybe Sobieski wouldn't have any idea that he was a cat burglar. He certainly hadn't proved himself to be all that brilliant so far.

Obviously, this relationship with Colin wasn't going to go anywhere. I mean, how does one date a cat burglar, anyway? It's not like I wouldn't wonder where every gift he ever gave me came from, if he'd actually bought it. Of course, I did have a lawyer for a brother, which could really come in handy. Then again, every time he went out I'd have to wonder if this was the time he got caught or shot or something. Yeah, that wouldn't work. Besides, I didn't want a relationship, anyway. They were more trouble than they were worth. Everyone I knew who was in one spent most of their time bitching about their partners. I also seriously doubted that a professional cat burglar would want one, either. . . .

Goddess, I must have been tired to even be thinking about this!

Velma came down the stairs quietly. She glanced over at Agent Sobieski again and then over to me. I didn't need the gift to read the look on her face. *Another one?* her arched eyebrows asked. *You need to slow down, boy.*

Agent Sobieski closed his phone and shoved it back into his pocket. He turned and saw Velma. He nodded and looked over at me. "Frank Sobieski, my aunt Velma." I waved at both of them.

"Nice to meet you, ma'am." Agent Sobieski walked over and shook her hand.

She just nodded and folded her arms.

An explanation, I need an explanation. I may be a man of easy virtue, but this was a bit much even for Velma. The truth?

Goddess, where would I even start?

Agent Sobieski took care of it by flashing his badge. "I'm with the FBI."

Velma remained expressionless. "Really?"

I smothered a grin. She didn't believe him. Oh, this was going to be priceless. You never have a camcorder with you when you need one.

"Yes."

She looked over at me. "What the hell is going on, young man?" Uh-oh. This tone was "I'm cutting me a switch and we're going out to the woodshed." Mom and Dad didn't believe in spanking, but Aunt Millie and Aunt Velma had. They had warmed our little butts many times when we'd acted up. Velma's students, I am sure, had all had a healthy respect for her before she retired.

"It's about Kenny." In a way, it was, so it wasn't a total lie.

"The FBI is interested in that?" She walked over and lit a Marlboro. She blew the smoke out with a sigh of pleasure. Nobody enjoys their nicotine as much as Aunt Velma.

"Yes, ma'am." Agent Sobieski slid back into his chair. He crossed his legs again. Was it just the denim material bunching correctly for best effect? I looked away.

I really am a sex maniac.

"Scotty, may I speak to you privately?" She pointed over her shoulder with her thumb. Her lips were compressed into a tight line. A vein danced in her throat.

"Sure." I got up. "Excuse us, Frank." I winked at him. He just stared. Asshole.

Aunt Velma didn't say a word until we got up to the second-floor landing. "You better thank your lucky stars Millie had a fund-raiser to go to this morning, or they'd be hell to pay."

"I—"

She cut me off. "Your boy from last night came downstairs and we had a nice chat. Of course, I like to had a heart attack when I opened the door and it wasn't you. And he tells me that other boy you brought upstairs is still there, too, and now I find you in the courtyard with another one." She snorted. "FBI, my ass. Why didn't he just say he was a Jedi knight?"

I tried not to laugh. "Well, it's kind of complicated." I had to make this good. "Jeremy, the guy you saw me with earlier, is his boyfriend, and they had a huge fight and Jeremy came here to get away, and now Frank wants to apologize, and I'm kind of stuck in the middle of it all, and . . ." I shrugged. Better to just leave it hanging and let her draw her own conclusions.

"You boys." Her face lit up with a grin. "Take care of it, boy." She walked into her apartment, and as the door shut behind her she said again, "FBI." She was shaking her head.

I could hear her laughing behind the door.

I'm a pretty good liar.

I leaned over the railing. "Be down in a sec." Sobieski

gave me a thumbs-up. The muscles in his arms flexed. Damn, he had big biceps. He pulled out his phone and punched in some number and started talking. Sheesh, what did they do before cell phones? Walkie-talkies? I climbed up the stairs and walked into the cool of my apartment.

Jeremy was awake. He and Colin were huddled around the laptop. They both looked up when I shut the door behind me.

"You aren't going to believe this shit," Colin said. "He wasn't kidding."

I walked over to the table. "You aren't going to believe who's downstairs." I sat down and put my aching feet up on the table. Not good manners, but oh, well.

"They are going to blow up the Quarter," Colin said. "Dynamite in the sewers, just like Jeremy said."

"Good." I smiled. "We can just turn the disk over to the FBI. An agent is down in the courtyard. And we can all relax. Although this Fed doesn't strike me as the sharpest knife in the drawer."

Colin turned pale. "Downstairs? Now?"

Jeremy looked relieved. "Agent Sobieski?"

I nodded. "I'll have him come up."

"I'm already here," Sobieski said from behind me.

We all turned around.

"Oh, fuck," Colin said.

We were staring down the barrel of a gun.

Chapter Sixteen

TEMPERANCE, REVERSED

Lack of good judgment

There's nothing like having someone hold a gun on you to make you wake up, fast. Adrenaline coursed through my body. My eyes, which had been drooping, opened wide.

The look on Sobieski's face was not pleasant. The scar seemed to be even redder than before. His eyes were narrowed to slits. His jaw was jutting out. His lips were a tight, compressed line. I looked back down to the gun. It looked huge. It also looked like it was aimed at me. Great.

"Now, there's no need for that," Colin said in a reasonable tone. "Nobody here has to be hurt. We'll give you what you want."

"I don't know what the hell you three are up to, but you can just hand over that disk and nobody will get hurt," Sobieski snarled.

My head was spinning. So the FBI ID had been a fake. He was one of Jenkins's skinhead thugs. Damn, damn, damn! Well, how was I supposed to know? I'd never seen an FBI badge before. Jeremy was tugging on me. "What?" I whispered.

"I saw him last night—"

"Shut up!" Sobieski shouted. "Not a word out of the three of you, okay? Put your hands up."

My eyes widened. Aunt Velma was right behind him. Where the hell had she come from? She was moving very silently, and then she raised a frying pan and swung it at the back of his head. There was a loud clang, his eyes rolled up in his head, and he went down in a heap.

I exhaled. I hadn't even known I was holding my breath. "Oh, my God."

Velma bent over and picked up the gun. She looked at me. "Young man, you have some explaining to do." She folded her arms.

"We need to tie him up." Colin got up. He looked at me. "Do you have any handcuffs, rope, anything?"

I shook my head. "No, not my scene."

"They have handcuffs at Gargoyles, right up the street." Jeremy breathed. "I could run down there—"

"There's no time for that," Colin interrupted. "How about an extension cord?"

"That I do have." I ran into the kitchen and grabbed two from the junk drawer.

"Let's carry him into the bedroom," Colin directed, grabbing Sobieski under the arms. Jeremy and I each grabbed a leg and lifted. He weighed a ton. We struggled the whole way down the hall and then swung him up on the bed. Colin grabbed the extension cords from Aunt Velma, who'd followed us in. Quickly he used one to tie Sobieski's arms together above his head and then to the headboard. He followed suit with the legs. He grinned at me. "There."

"You're pretty good at that," I commented.

He shrugged. "You'd be surprised at how much people will pay you to do that to them." He grinned at me.

I didn't want to know. He was rummaging through my chest of drawers and stuffed a pair of underwear in

Sobieski's mouth. "Hey, not the Calvin Kleins." I reached over to pull them out of his mouth. "Use a cheaper pair!"

Colin grabbed my arm. "Scotty, don't worry about it."

He had a point. I dropped my arm.

Aunt Velma had been watching this whole enterprise with her lips pressed together in a prim line. "Shouldn't we be calling the police?"

"Let's go back into the living room," I said. I felt a little dizzy.

Velma sat down in one of the wing-back chairs. "Will someone tell me why we aren't calling the police? And why was that man holding a gun on you three? What the hell is going on around here?" She glared at me. "This is not some lovers' quarrel!"

I opened my mouth, but Jeremy started talking before I could form the words. "It's all my fault." He explained to Velma in more detail, I thought, than was necessary. As he spoke, her jaw dropped. Every once in a while she would look at me through narrowed eye slits.

"How did he get in?" Velma asked when Jeremy finished.

"He showed me an FBI badge," I said. "How was I supposed to know it wasn't real?"

"We need to call the police," Velma said again.

I looked at Colin. "You tell her why we can't."

He shrugged. "We kind of have to now."

"What about you?"

"I'll just get out of here before you call, if that's okay."

"It is most certainly not okay!" Velma's face reddened. Not a good sign. She was inches from blowing a head gasket. "Nobody is going anywhere; do you idiots understand me? I am going to go call the police, and you are all going to sit here like good boys until they get here. Do you all understand me?"

"Wait." I grabbed my wallet and fished out Venus Casanova's card. "We should call Venus." *And right after we do that, I am paging Storm,* I thought. I wanted him here just in case. I had a feeling we were all going to need him.

"Venus?" Velma rolled her eyes.

"She's in charge of the investigation into Kenny's murder," I explained to her.

"The one you lied to?"

"Uh-huh."

"I'm paging Millie."

"Can't we just call Storm?" My voice sounded whiny to me. Storm wouldn't be happy, but I can handle him. Millie would be so pissed off about all of this, she'd probably demand that Venus arrest me on the spot. Which, come to think of it, would probably be better for me than dealing with Millie.

"Why don't I just call the FBI?" Jeremy said. We all looked over at him. He shrugged. "This whole thing is their case, and they want the disk, anyway. Doesn't it make sense to call them?"

Velma rubbed her eyes. "This is all so hard to believe."

"Well," I said, "that's kind of why I didn't want to tell you any of this. Would you have believed me?"

She gave me a dirty look and said to Jeremy, "Call."

Jeremy fished a piece of paper out of his wallet, activated his cell phone, and dialed. I breathed a sigh of relief.

Until I heard the unmistakable sound of a cell phone ringing.

In my bedroom.

We all looked at each other.

"He really is with the FBI," Jeremy whispered, disconnecting the call.

"Way to go, Aunt Velma." I glared at her. Her face had drained of color. "You've assaulted a Fed!"

"Is there anyone else you can call?" Colin asked. He looked tired.

Jeremy shook his head. "That's my contact number."

"Well, what do we do now, Scooby gang?" I stood up. "Let's see if I can tally this up correctly. We have a disk that the skinheads not only want back but are willing to kill for. The FBI wants it as well. We've lied to the police, and our only hope of getting out of this mess is the FBI agent Jeremy's been dealing with, who Aunt Velma brained with a frying pan and is currently tied up with extension cords in my bedroom." I rubbed my forehead and wondered how much a one-way ticket to Rio de Janeiro would cost. I did have that one MasterCard that wasn't maxed out completely. I could just throw a few things in a bag . . .

"Hey, what did you want me to do?" Aunt Velma folded her arms. "I saw him creeping up the stairs with a gun. I was trying to defend you." She looked miserable.

I gave her a quick hug. "Thanks, Aunt Velma."

"How was I supposed to know?"

I patted her hand. "You couldn't have known. You were just looking out for me like you always do."

She smiled at me weakly. "I just hope I haven't made things worse."

I shrugged and walked back to the bedroom. Agent Sobieski's eyes were open, and he was trying to talk through the underwear gag. He struggled with the extension cords. Veins were bulging in his muscles as he strained them. His face was red, and there was a really ugly-looking vein bulging out on his right forehead. "Calm down!" I sighed and took the underwear out of his mouth. "Don't have a stroke!"

"You fucking people are crazy!" he shouted.

I sat down on the edge of the bed. "Look, Agent Sobieski, I'm afraid this has all just been a really big misunderstanding. My aunt Velma saw you coming up the stairs with your gun out, and so she beaned you with a frying pan. Can you blame her? I mean, what did you expect us to do, coming in like that waving your gun around? We thought you were working for Perkins."

"Of all the ridiculous—"

I put my hand over his mouth. "Agent Sobieski, can I call you Frank?" He nodded. "Frank, why did you have your gun out?"

I could tell he was mentally counting to ten before he answered. "The man I saw on the stairs. I recognized him."

"Colin?" Involuntarily I looked over my shoulder. No one was there. "You recognized him? He's not one of Perkins's thugs, is he?" That was all we needed.

"No. He's a jewel thief, wanted for some major heists. I've seen bulletins with his face on them, okay? Now, will you untie me?"

"You do understand that Aunt Velma was only trying to protect me? You're not going to hold it against her, are you?"

"Yes, yes, untie me and get me some aspirin."

With another silent prayer to the Goddess, I untied his legs and arms. I stepped back in case he swung at me. He sat up, moving his arms and legs about. I went into the bathroom to get him his aspirin. He took it from me and drank the full glass of water. He rubbed the back of his head and sighed. "She packs a mean wallop."

"Yeah." She does. Years of tennis and golf had given her a powerful swing. Goddess knows I'd felt it on my butt enough times when I was little. "Maybe we should get you to the hospital or something. You might have a concussion or something."

He pulled out his cell phone. "The call I missed better not have been important." He glared at me as he hit his redial button. A phone started ringing in the living room. He hung up. "What the . . . ?"

"Oh, Jeremy tried to call you after we tied you up. He didn't know you by sight, and we were trying to get ahold of his contact." The ridiculousness of this whole situation swept over me. I really felt tired.

He stood up and swayed a bit. I stood up and slipped my arm around his waist till he regained his balance. "You sure you're okay?"

He nodded. "We don't have much time."

I nodded. "Come on, let's get you that damned disk."

He followed me into the living room. Aunt Velma stood up. "Sir, I need to apologize for whacking you."

Colin was nowhere to be seen.

"It doesn't matter now." He dismissed her with a wave of his hand. "I need that disk, and then I can phone in."

"Get him the disk, Jeremy."

"Where's Colin?" I whispered to Aunt Velma.

"He left via the balcony," she whispered back.

Jeremy walked over to the table. He pressed a button on the computer, and the disk popped out. He handed it over to Frank, who looked at him long and hard. Frank slipped the disk into his shorts pocket. "Okay, now, let's—"

One of the balcony windows exploded. Shards of glass flew everywhere. Velma screamed. Something crashed into the back of the cabinets of my kitchenette and shattered.

I watched as liquid spilled down my cabinets.

I smelled gasoline, the smoke as it ignited.

A sheet of flame enveloped my cabinets.

I watched as flames leaped to the walls.

"Where's the fire extinguisher?" Aunt Velma shouted at me.

"Under the kitchen sink!" I shouted back. The room was starting to fill with smoke. Aunt Velma started to run toward the kitchen just as the flames leaped over to the hallway. That whole side of the apartment was a wall of flame. The heat was intense. I stepped backward away from it.

"Out on the balcony!" Sobieski shouted.

Jeremy was gone in an instant, Velma close behind him. I stood there staring at the flames.

The smoke curled and waved as though trying to tell me something.

"Go!" Sobieski shouted at me. He shoved me toward the balcony, but the backs of my legs hit the coffee table and I tumbled over it. He climbed over the table and pulled me to my feet. "Go!"

I swept up my tarot cards and the blue silk scarf I keep them in and shoved them into my pocket.

"Now!"

I ran over to the balcony windows. I slipped the latch and slid it up. The wood felt hot to the touch. Not good, I thought wildly, and I stepped out just in time to see Aunt Velma go over the railing and slide down one of the balcony poles. I saw Jeremy running in the middle of Decatur Street for the fire station across Esplanade Avenue.

Nothing is more terrifying in the French Quarter than an out-of-control fire. A fire stops everyone in their tracks. "Will this be another bad one?" people ask each other silently as they wait for the fire trucks to come. The city has burned to the ground many times in its long history. The buildings in the Quarter are all old, almost all of them made of wood, and they're too close together. Space is at a premium in the Quarter, so the houses are all built with a minimum of space in between them. The wood they're built of is frequently dry, rotted, termite damaged. That makes it easy for flames to leap from one building to another. The buildings are just so much kindling. Fires spread quickly; buildings are destroyed; people die. Entire blocks can go up in a matter of minutes. I stood there on the balcony and saw flames already on the floor above me. It was hot, getting hotter by the moment. And the smell . . .

The smoke continued to swirl and dance.

Just like in the visions.

I kept staring at it.

Was it trying to tell me something?

"Over the railing!" Sobieski ordered me. He slapped me across the face. "Come on, there isn't much time!"

I came out of it. I rubbed my face. "That hurt." I glared at him.

"Move it, Scotty!" he shouted over the roar of the flames.

I looked over the railing. Heights aren't my favorite thing at the best of times. The pavement looked about a million miles away, and it swam and danced and spun around. I closed my eyes and started taking deep breaths.

"Go, Scotty." He grabbed me and I looked into his eyes. The stern face relaxed a bit.

"I'm afraid of heights." I felt like an idiot.

"I'll help you. Come on. Piece of cake. You can do it."

I took a deep breath and grabbed the railing. It felt warm to the touch. I took a deep breath, closed my eyes, and swung my legs over. My left foot fumbled for the balcony.

The right one slipped.

I screamed and clutched at the railing as my leg fumbled for the balcony. Everything was spinning around. *I'm going to fall,* I thought as I swayed twenty feet above the pavement. As I hung there, flames spurted out onto the roof. Sobieski grabbed me and steadied me. I got my foot back on the side, then held on as I let my legs swing under and around a pole. I slid down, let go of the railing, and quickly grabbed the pole and slid. My feet connected with the railing on Velma and Millie's balcony. I held on to the pole and let my feet swing out. Oh, merciful Goddess, I prayed with my eyes closed as I slid the two feet down to the balcony level. I put my hands on the balcony railing and swung my legs under until they connected with a bottom-level pole. I grabbed it with both hands and slid. I kept my eyes closed until my feet hit the ground with a jarring jolt. I was vaguely aware of Sobieski reaching the ground on another pole. He grabbed my arm and we ran across the street.

A fire siren screamed nearby.

An explosion knocked us all backward as splinters of glass rained down on us.

The fire engine roared to a stop right in front of us.

Vaguely I noticed Jeremy running back toward us.

I saw Aunt Velma with her arms wrapped around herself. There were tears in her eyes.

Colin was nowhere in sight.

I hoped he'd gotten away.

A crowd was slowly gathering.

People were coming out of restaurants and shops up and down Decatur Street and staring, pointing, watching.

The buildings on either side of mine emptied.

A fireman came over and pushed us farther up the street, out of harm's way as another window on the fourth floor exploded outward. "Come on; you're not safe here; move along; you'll just be in the way."

Hoses began spraying water on the roofs of the buildings on either side as well as onto my building.

My home.

The only place I'd ever lived besides over the Devil's Weed and the college dorm.

I felt my cards in the pocket of my sweat pants.

I looked up at the sky, hoping for rain clouds, anything.

The sky, beyond the roiling black smoke, was blue and cloudless.

It was a beautiful day.

I felt the tears coming to my eyes.

I stood there, mesmerized, as my home, my entire life, burned to the ground.

Chapter Seventeen

FIVE OF PENTACLES

Loss of home and possessions

One of the worst things that can ever happen to a person is to watch their home burn down.

The feeling of powerlessness is overwhelming. You just want to do something, anything, but there is nothing. You start to walk toward the building, but the firemen have it all roped off. You think you should call people, let them know you're okay, but my cell phone was in the house—now just a hunk of melted plastic. So was my gym bag, with all of my thongs and jocks and assorted stripper wear, along with all of my tips from the previous night, about four hundred bucks. . . . Come to think of it, Thursday's tips were up there, too. My stereo. My television and VCR. My secondhand furniture from thrift shops all over town. My high school yearbooks. My photo albums. My appointment book and contact numbers for all of my training clients. My receipts for Infernal Revenue. My checkbook. My ATM card. My few paltry, pitiful, maxed-out credit cards. My CD collection. My high school letter jacket. My porn tapes. Anything that had ever meant anything to me in my entire twenty-nine years.

Gone.

People started showing up at some point, besides the weirdo thrill seekers who had no idea that someone's home was going up, and if it even occurred to them, they didn't care one way or the other. They were there to watch and thrill at the sight of a building going up in smoke, not caring or even thinking that years of life and living and loving were going along with the building. At some point David showed up, and he stood there for a while with his arm around me, squeezing me from time to time. He went and got me a Coke from a store at some point.

Millie showed up, her face torn with worry until she saw Velma and me. Then she grabbed Velma and held on for dear life, and they both started to cry. After a bit, Millie pulled me into their hug as well, but I didn't cry. It was worse for them; after all, it was the only home they had ever known, the only place they'd lived in all their years together.

I was just numb.

At some point, Millie must have called my parents, because they showed up. Mom's face was streaked with tears. Her graying hair was pulled back into its traditional ponytail, which I'd never seen her without, wearing a pair of jeans she'd probably bought when Nixon was president, almost see-through in places, they were so worn, and a *LEGALIZE POT* T-shirt with the sleeves torn off. Dad hugged me so tight, I thought he would smother me. He smelled, as always, of pipe tobacco over the slightly sweet smell of marijuana. His graying beard scratched my face. He was wearing cutoff jeans as old as Mom's, if not older, and a T-shirt with the slogan *I'M PROUD OF MY GAY SON* on it.

And still I didn't cry. They stood on either side of me, watching as the building died, their arms around me.

It was nice.

At some point, I lost track of Jeremy and Agent Frank Sobieski. I'd not seen Colin since I'd escaped. Just as well. Cat burglar, whatever the hell he was, it was better that he was gone. As for Agent Sobieski and Jeremy, well, Frank had his precious disk and they could do whatever the hell they wanted. Bombs in the sewers beneath the French Quarter, indeed. It was all a joke someone in the Willy Perkins campaign had played, most likely a stupid computer game that Jeremy stumbled across and overreacted to; that was all.

Kenny had probably been killed in a random act of violence.

I didn't care anymore.

I just wanted to go to sleep.

I said as much to Mom, and she nodded. "Storm and Rain are on their way to the house," Mom said. "I called and told them to meet us there."

"Fine," I think I said. I don't know. I just wanted to lie down somewhere and pretend none of this had happened. I wanted to go to sleep and wake up to find out my house was still intact and everything that had happened since I saw Jeremy at the gym on Friday afternoon had all been a dream, a ridiculous, insane dream.

What else could it have been?

The three of us walked through the lower Quarter in silence. Mom and Dad were holding hands, which they always do when they go anywhere, and Mom had her arm around my waist. It was somewhat comforting. Mom kept murmuring things like "You can just move back in with us for a while; everything will be okay, honey, you'll see; you just don't worry or think about any of that right now; Dad and I will take care of everything; we'll just get you home and put you to bed," and on and on and on. I just didn't care.

We walked past people, groups of gay men, straight

families out doing the tourism thing, people walking their dogs. Some of the gay men looked at me, bedraggled, shirtless, wearing only a pair of cutoff sweatpants. I was dirty, disheveled, and stank of smoke and sweat. Some of them raised their eyebrows as though trying to remember where they knew me from. I thought about screaming at them I was a dancer at the Pub, that they'd probably stroked my ass for a buck or given me a five to look at my dick the night before, but I didn't. Some of them might have been looking at me with lust, but for the first time in my life I didn't care. I was tired. My life was destroyed.

I just wanted to sleep.

The crowds thickened as we got closer to the Devil's Weed. Mom and Dad unlocked the door to the back staircase and we climbed the stone steps in silence. It was quiet and cool. Their back door was open. Rain and Storm were there, in the kitchen, drinking iced tea. They both jumped up and hugged me, their worry and concern on their faces. Rain's pretty hazel eyes welled up with tears and she started to cry, and Storm looked like he wanted to. They didn't know what to say. What was there to say?

"Do you need anything, honey?" Rain asked, her voice quivering. She was wearing a pair of white shorts and a red T-shirt. Her fine brown hair was pulled back into a ponytail. She wasn't wearing any makeup, which was not like her.

"I want to go to sleep," I said.

They all murmured things like "Yes, of course; you get some rest, honey," and other things like that, which didn't really register in my head, and so I walked down the hall to my room. Mom and Dad had kept all three of our bedrooms the way they'd been when we each, in turn, moved out. Storm jokingly referred to them as our shrines, but that day I was glad of it. I was glad my old stuffed animals were still on the same bedspread I'd slept under my whole life. I was glad to see my posters of the Chippendale dancers and Patrick Swayze (what had I been thinking?) and the original Soloflex model and Marky Mark in Calvin Klein underwear grabbing his big dick. I smiled up at Marky. How many times had I beat off to that poster when I was younger?

I walked over to my bookcase and touched the spines of my Hardy Boys books. Not everything was lost, I thought, drawing some comfort from the line of blue spines arranged in order. I picked up a small replica of the Statue of Liberty that I'd gotten on a trip to New York when I was about five. My eyes welled up.

I slipped off my sweatpants and lay down on the bed naked. Facedown. And I finally was able to go to sleep.

The Goddess didn't speak to me in my sleep.

"Scotty." Someone sat down on the bed. "There's someone here to see you."

I rolled over onto my back and opened my eyes. "What time is it?"

"It's almost seven. You've been asleep about five hours," Mom said.

"Who is it?"

She raised one of her eyebrows. "A police detective named Venus Casanova and a Fed." She sniffed. "I can't believe I have a fucking Fed in my house."

I reached for my sweatpants. "Sorry, Mom."

"You don't have to talk to them." She touched my arm softly. "Rain went home, but Storm is still here. He's been talking to them."

"How are Velma and Millie holding up?"

"They're just fine." Mom smiled. "It takes a hell of a lot more than something like a fire to get them down."

"The house?"

The corners of her mouth dropped. "It's a total loss."

I nodded and pulled on my sweatpants. I walked down

the hall with her right behind me. Frank and Venus were in the living room.

I sat down on the sofa and tucked my feet up underneath me. "Well, I was hoping I wouldn't ever have to see either of you again, no offense."

"None taken," Frank replied with a bit of a smile.

"Agent Sobieski told me a very interesting story, Mr. Bradley." Venus stood up, placing one hand on her hip. She was wearing a pair of jeans and a nice white cotton blouse. "Would you mind telling me why you didn't tell me about this disk last night?"

I shrugged. "I didn't think it was important."

Casanova gave an exasperated sigh. "I could arrest you for obstruction of justice."

"I could get that thrown out of court in a second," Storm said. I looked over at my big brother. He was taller than me, about six-three, and was starting to develop a bit of a paunch. He had on khaki shorts and a nice navy blue Polo shirt. His legs and forearms were covered with thick, wiry black hair. His curly black hair was starting to recede a bit at the hairline. Storm loved nothing more than a good fight—verbal, that is. His brownish eyes were snapping with excitement, and he was tapping his foot.

"He lied to the police during the course of a murder investigation." Venus turned away from me and looked at him. "Not once, but twice that I know of."

"And just how did he hinder your investigation?" Storm asked. His tone was very condescending. I hated it when he talked to me like that, and from the expression on her face, Casanova didn't like it, either. "The disk may or may not have been related to Kenny Chandler's death, but certainly at the time Scotty had no reason to believe the two were connected. In fact, as I recall, Agent Sobieski himself, here, said he didn't believe the two were connected."

"He still should have told me," she insisted. "And what about this Bill Palladino person he was hiding in his apartment? I told him very clearly to call me if this man turned up again, so I could speak with him, and he most certainly didn't."

"There wasn't time—" I started to say, but Storm cut me off.

"May I have a moment alone with my client?"

Client? I stared at him. Both of them nodded, and Storm waved me back into the hall. I followed him back to my room.

"You could be in a lot of trouble, my Queen, so talk, and talk fast." He folded his arms.

So, with a sigh of relief, I told him everything that had happened. I didn't leave out anything. When I finished, he whistled.

"All of this is true?"

"Fuck you, Storm." I stood up. "A friend of mine is dead; my apartment burned to the ground; I don't need this shit from you! I don't need your help. I'll just throw myself on the mercy of the court." I started to walk out, but he grabbed me and swung me around. He gave me a great, big hug, almost squeezing the air out of me.

"Listen, my Queen, all you're guilty of is being in the wrong place at the wrong time, is all." He kissed the top of my head. "But Casanova is right—you have hindered her investigation, and that's obstruction of justice. It'd be hard for them to convict, so I doubt that it would ever come to that, but if she wanted to, she could toss your ass in jail, and you'd wind up staying there until the arraignment, which could be dragged out until Tuesday because of the holiday. Come on; let's get back in there, and let me do the talking."

My jaw dropped when I walked back into the living

room. Mom was serving them tea! Mom, who would just as soon spit on a governmental authority figure as look at one; Mom, who had chained herself to the gates of a nuclear power plant; Mom, who circulated petitions for the decriminalization of marijuana. She glanced up at me and our eyes met. In that instant of contact, I realized how worried about me she was, and what she was willing to do to help me out.

What a great fucking mom.

I walked over and gave her a big hug. She clung to me tightly and kissed my cheek. "I love you, son, no matter what," she whispered.

"I love you, too, Mom," and we held on to each other for a few moments.

"All right, people . . ." Storm sat down. "Here's the deal. You aren't going to press charges of any kind against my brother. In return, he will answer any questions you ask, unless I advise him otherwise. He's done nothing wrong and has nothing to hide."

"You're not in a position to make deals, Mr. Bradley." Venus crossed her legs. "And neither am I."

"On the contrary, I am." Storm had that smug look on his face, the one I always hate to see when he's dealing with me. "You see, my brother had no idea that Bill Palladino was wanted on suspicion of theft. He just met him at the bar last night and brought him home. No crime in that, at least not in Louisiana anymore. As for the disk, it was slipped to him at the bar, and he had no idea of what it was or who put it there until this afternoon. He advised Mr. Palladino this afternoon that you wanted to speak with him, Detective, and my brother has no control over when or if Mr. Palladino speaks to you. And Agent Sobieski, I have no idea why the Feds are interested in my brother."

Damn, he was good. Sobieski immediately piped in

with, "I was assaulted in his apartment. It's a felony to assault a government agent."

Storm grinned. "Now, Agent Sobieski, how would your fellow agents—and superiors—react to the information that you were disarmed by a fifty-five-year-old lesbian with a frying pan?"

I almost laughed out loud. Sobieski turned bright red. He said nothing.

"So, our business is finished here." Storm winked at me. I never loved my brother more than I did in that moment.

"Well, no, it's really not," Casanova replied. She turned to me. "You are a target, Scotty, whether you like it or not. Your apartment was firebombed by Molotov cocktails. Who do you think did that?"

I hadn't really thought about it. I didn't answer.

"A young man was murdered and the body left in front of your gate. Your apartment was bombed. Why do you think that is?"

"Perkins's people either followed Jeremy to my place, or they know I have the disk," I said. My stomach dropped to about the level of my feet.

"In either case, you aren't safe," Sobieski continued. "In either case, we'd like your help to flush them out."

"What do you mean?" I had a feeling I knew already.

"We want you to dance tonight, like nothing ever happened. We'll have agents placed for your protection, in case they try anything." Sobieski nodded to me. "We've secured the sewers, so that isn't a problem. But they might try something."

"Too risky," Storm said.

"But they probably won't," I said. "I mean, they probably think the disk was destroyed in the fire, or if not, they think the jig is up. So I'll probably be safe."

"Son." I looked at Mom. "Don't do it. It's too dangerous."

I sighed. "Mom, I need the money." Sad but true. I turned back to Sobieski. "All of my stuff went up in the fire."

He nodded and pulled out a little notebook. "What do you need?"

I thought for a minute. "A pair of white underwear, a pair of black underwear, one brief cut, the other a boxer brief. I need a couple of bikinis, maybe a square-cut suit, and a couple of thongs. I also need a gym bag. They'll probably have everything I need at the Hit Parade—it's across the street from the Pub."

"Size?"

"I have a thirty waist."

He smiled at me. Under any other circumstance I would've thought it was a come-hither lusty glance. Why should an FBI agent be immune to my charms, after all? He'd tried something in the steam room at Riverview Fitness the night before, hadn't he? But I wasn't in the mood for flirtation.

There's a first time for everything, apparently.

"What time do you have to be there?" Casanova asked.

"About nine-thirty. I start at ten."

"I'll be here at nine to make sure everything's okay and to walk you up the street," Sobieski said.

"Terrific." I sighed. Scotty Bradley, undercover stripper. It sounded like a great title for a porn movie.

Chapter Eighteen

THREE OF SWORDS, REVERSED

Disorder, confusion, loss

Mom made me eat something. Tofu lasagna or some-thing like that. Mom and Dad are both avowed veg-etarians, and she always comes up with some bizarre vegetarian twist on regular food. I try not to eat red meat, but not out of a sense of outrage at the slaughter and bru-tal treatment of animals farmed for food. Red meat has a high fat content, no matter how "lean" the label claims it to be. You can't keep a low body-fat percentage and a thirty-inch waist by eating red meat regularly, even with my high metabolism.

And the last thing I need is to get a roll around my stomach. It would be extremely bad for business. My body is my best advertisement for my training.

Storm stuck around for dinner. The three of them made small talk, Storm asking them about how the Devil's Weed was doing businesswise, Mom and Dad asking about the grandkids, stuff like that. I didn't talk much myself. The lasagna, despite Mom's liberal use of spices, was pretty bland and tasteless to me. It was like eating ashes. Bless her heart. Mom tries, but there is only so much you can do with tofu.

Or maybe the smell of smoke on me was altering the taste of everything I put in my mouth.

After dinner, Mom and Dad cleared the plates. It was nine o'clock, and I went down to my old room to shower and get ready for the evening. I pumped up my muscles by doing a hundred push-ups with my feet up on the bed, and then did two hundred crunches. I got in the shower and tried to wash the day off of me. The hot water felt great, invigorating. I scrubbed myself until my skin turned red. I shampooed my hair several times. I couldn't smell like smoke. I seriously doubted that smell would draw dollars into my drawers. I checked my torso for telltale razor stubble and stray hairs. My skin was still fairly smooth, but I used Dad's old electric razor and went over my pecs and stomach. I looked at myself in the mirror.

Looking good, I said to myself.

The bar would be too gloomy for anyone to notice the dark circles under my eyes.

Good thing.

I felt a lot better. I am nothing if not resilient.

Sobieski and Casanova had returned while I was in the shower, and the bag from the Hit Parade was sitting on my bed when I walked back in there with my towel on. I opened it and took everything out. I took the tags off and tried everything on, looking in my three-way mirror. Everything fit nice and snug. Perfect. Some of the colors of the bikinis and thongs weren't quite what I would have picked out for myself, but hey, beggars can't be choosers. I wondered if Sobieski had picked out things he wanted to see me wear. Interesting thought. For a Fed, he'd been pretty sweet out on the balcony.

I owed him my life. If he hadn't helped me, I would have never gotten off the balcony.

I grinned as I flexed my ass cheeks in a neon lime green thong.

My tax dollars at work.

I was starting to feel more like myself. I didn't smell like smoke and sweat anymore, which was a big help. I put on a pair of cutoff sweatpants over the lime green thong. That would be my starter outfit for the evening, I decided. I could tease by pulling the sweatpants down, pulling the thong down with it to give the illusion that I was naked underneath. Cool. That should be good for a few bucks. I picked up the shorts I'd been wearing earlier off the floor. They smelled of smoke, and for a brief moment a wave of nausea swept over me. I felt my cards in the pocket.

I pulled them out and unwrapped them. I knelt by the bed and started shuffling. I spread them out and began to turn the cards over.

Danger.

Destruction.

Upset of plans.

The need for a brave heart.

Slightly unnerved, I swept them all up and folded the silk scarf over them. I stood up and walked over to my old dresser. An old iron candelabra sat on it, with three white candles. I lit them and closed my eyes in order to pray to the Goddess, pray for a brave heart, pray for her protection.

I still was hoping it wasn't necessary, but "better safe than sorry" has always been a theme of mine.

"How are you doing?"

It was Sobieski. He was standing in the doorway. He was still wearing the shorts and tank top from this afternoon.

"A little nervous," I admitted. "Scared."

He came into the room. He shut the door behind him. He looked so damned good. He cleared his throat. "We'll do our best to make sure you're safe."

"I appreciate that."

He reached out with his left hand and pushed a lock of my hair off my forehead. "You're very brave to do this."

"Well, nothing's going to happen, anyway." I shrugged. "I keep telling myself that." Maybe if I could convince myself . . .

He handed me a cell phone. "Keep this in your boot. I've programmed my number into it, speed-dial one. If you see anything suspicious while you're on the bar, pinch your nose and look for me, and point it out. You can do that in an inconspicuous manner, can't you?"

I laughed. "How's this?" I started swiveling my hips, moving my feet to get my hips to sway in a seductive stripper-boy manner. I started moving my arms as well, getting them to move in sync with my legs. I reached over with my right hand and pinched my nose, looked him right in the eyes, and then pointed with the same hand.

"You're a really good dancer." He was breathing a little faster than he had been before.

"Well, thanks." I gave him a lazy grin, the one I think of as my "Give me a dollar, mister" look. "Will that work as a signal?"

"Nobody will think anything of it." He stepped a little closer to me.

I didn't need the gift to know he wanted me.

Yes.

I reached out and touched his scar. "How did this happen?"

"On a case. I got slashed." He reached up and grabbed my hand gently. He leaned his head into my hand. I ran my hand down his cheek. "I don't want to talk about that."

"Do your bosses know you're gay?"

He shook his head. "No."

"That has to suck."

He nodded. "It does. I have to keep it very quiet. I'd be fired. I'd be considered a security risk."

"So what do you do?"

"When I have time off I travel, far from Washington. Nothing as obvious as San Francisco, of course. I usually go up to New York and lose myself in the Village, or Miami to South Beach. Places like that." He sighed. "I get so lonely, Scotty."

I stepped a little closer to him. "You're a very sexy man, Agent Sobieski."

"Frank."

"Frank."

He reached up and touched my chest, making little circles with his index finger on my right pec.

I reached up and touched his chest.

Solid as a rock.

I knew it would be.

I closed my eyes. The candles were lit. Everything was in readiness for the Great Rite.

So why not?

The power of the Great Rite would protect me. I could invoke the Goddess's protection.

I pulled his head to me and we kissed.

He tasted of spearmint gum.

He resisted for a moment, and then his lips relaxed, became softer as his arms went around me and pulled me in tighter to him.

Our crotches grazed each other.

His mouth slid down my face to my neck. His tongue darted out, licking my neck as his lips moved in small circles on my neck.

Oh, Goddess.

It felt incredible.

I focused on the sensations he was raising in me as I formed the words in my head, the incantation, the proper prayer for protection to send to the Goddess.

He picked me up and carried me over to the bed.

He laid me down on the bed and lay down beside me, his mouth never leaving my neck as his hands began to explore my body.

O great Goddess, mother of us all, great protectress of the universe and the earth, Frank and I come together to celebrate the physical beauty that you in your divine graciousness have blessed us both with, and invoke your power and goodness to wrap ourselves in, to protect us from the evil that others would do to us, to ask for your blessing to see us through this evening in safety; through love and the power of white, the power of good, please bless us and protect with your love.

His mouth was on my right nipple, his hand between my legs.

O great Goddess, mother of us all . . .

Sucking, tweaking, pulling on the nipple.

. . . great protectress of the universe and the earth . . .

His hand stroking me.

. . . Frank and I come together to celebrate the physical beauty . . .

He was sliding down my sweatpants.

. . . that you in your divine graciousness have blessed us both with . . .

His tongue darting into my navel.

. . . and invoke your power and goodness to wrap ourselves in . . .

My breath coming quicker and quicker.

. . . to protect us from the evil that others would do to us . . .

My thong sliding down my quads.
. . . to ask for your blessing to see us through . . .
His mouth working again.
. . . this evening in safety . . .
Oh, oh, oh,
. . . through love and the power of white . . .
My body writhing
. . . the power of good . . .
biting my lip
. . . please bless us . . .
ah, uh, ah, uh,
. . . PROTECT US WITH YOUR LOVE!
My entire body shuddered, convulsed, shook.
I closed my eyes.
The fog began to creep in on the outer periphery of my
vision.
Swirling and boiling.
No, not now! Why now?
I leaned my head back.
I could hear Frank saying my name, questioning. "Scotty?
Scotty? Are you okay?"
As my vision began to blur and spin, I saw his face, con-
cerned, blurring at the edges, the scar glowing bright red
through everything as the fog continued to take over my
sight.
It was everywhere.
I resisted.
Not now, oh, please, Goddess, not now . . .
"Scotty?"
O great Goddess, mother of us all . . .
"Scotty?"
. . . we come together . . .
"Scotty?"
Other voices chanting the words with me . . .
"Are you okay?"

. . . invoking her . . .

"Oh my God!"

The fog . . .

"HELP! MRS. BRADLEY!"

And I was gone.

In the far distance I could hear Frank, I could feel my sweatpants being pulled up over my hips, the elastic snapping at my waist.

It was another reality.

I couldn't speak to him.

My old bedroom was a different plane, a different place.

I was back on the rooftop.

Waves were lapping against the buildings.

I heard the voice in my head again.

The river is high, it said, echoing slightly. *Lots of floods this summer in the up-country.*

"I know," I replied. "They've talked about opening the spillway because the river is so high."

The bombs aren't in the sewers.

"The FBI took care of that."

But there are bombs still.

"Where?"

The fog boiled and roiled around me, everything, the desolate, wrecked buildings, getting lost. The sound of the water, the waves lapping against the sides of the buildings the only sound. Silence everywhere.

You have a brave heart, I heard. *Keep your heart brave. You will need it.*

"Scotty?"

My vision swam back into focus.

It was Mom. I looked into her eyes.

Storm. Dad. Venus Casanova. Agent Sobieski.

Frank.

All gathered around my bed.

Staring at me.

I pushed myself up into a sitting position, my back against the headboard. I rubbed my eyes.

You have a brave heart.

"Are you okay?" Storm's face, mapped with concern.

"Yeah." I grinned at all of them.

"What the hell?" Frank's hands were shaking slightly, I noticed.

"A vision?" Mom said softly. "Is that what happened, baby?"

"What?" Frank mopped some sweat off of his forehead. He looked at Mom as though she were crazy.

Mom turned to him. "Agent Sobieski, my son has the gift. Clairvoyance, psychic power, whatever nonbelievers want to call it. He has visions sometimes."

His jaw dropped.

I winked at him.

"What did you see, son?" It was Dad.

"They've changed their plans." I shrugged. I looked into each of their faces. "There are bombs in the Quarter, but not in the sewers." I looked at Frank. "The Quarter has to be evacuated."

"I can't do that." Frank looked at me, then at each of them. "Based on what? A vision? Did you see where they are?"

I shook my head. "No, she chose not to share that information with me."

"She?"

"The Goddess."

He rolled his eyes. "Scotty, please don't take this the wrong way, but you have to understand: I can hardly go to my superiors and tell them we need to evacuate the

Quarter based on a vision that you had. They think every-thing is under control, everything is safe. I need something concrete to take them, some hard evidence."

"It has something to do with the river, because the level is so high; that's all she would tell me."

"The levee?" Mom's eyes widened. "Oh, my Lord . . . the levee!"

I hadn't paid much attention to the news that summer. I never do. But Mom is addicted to the weather channel. She won't watch anything else on television. This is be-cause she and Dad both believe that television is con-trolled by the government to turn Americans into mindless zombies. Of course, Mom gets sucked into watching the weather channel for hours. Talk about mindless zombie! The house could burn down around her and she wouldn't notice.

Maybe she has a point.

"There's been a lot of rain and flooding in the Missouri and Ohio River Valleys these last months," she explained. "The river is dangerously high now, high enough to threaten the stability of the levees. The city council is currently de-bating with the levee board on whether to open the Bonne Carre Spillway to divert the excess water into Lake Pontchartrain. The levee board is insisting it needs to be done, but the fishermen filed an injunction to stop them."

"Why?" Frank stared at her. "If the levee is threat-ened—"

"The fishermen claim that the river pollution wrecks the lake, and that affects their ability to make a living. Kills the fish and the crawfish, and since that's how they make money . . ." Mom shrugged.

"So it would be better for the city to flood." Storm laughed. "Welcome to Louisiana."

"It happens every time the river gets high and the spill-way has to be opened," Mom explained. "The fishermen sue to stop it, they fight in court for a while, and the judge always ends up ruling against them. The fishermen are just the little people, you know, and their opinions don't matter."

"Mom, you don't think they should win, do you?" Storm stared at her.

She laughed. "Well, on principle I'm on their side. The little people always get the shaft, you know."

"If the levee was blown up . . ." Dad started.

"The devastation would be mind-numbing," Mom finished.

"You've got to do something, Frank." I stared at him. "Have the levee searched?"

"Scotty." He stared back into my eyes. His eyes were so beautiful. "I can*not* go to my superiors and ask them to pull teams of agents from watching the sewers to search the levee, all based on a vision. I need something more concrete, some hard physical evidence that they changed their plans."

"Can't you get a warrant and search their campaign headquarters or something?" I asked. "Wasn't the disk enough evidence to get something started?"

"Since when have the Feds needed warrants?" Mom folded her arms and glared at him.

"Mrs. Bradley." Frank looked at her. "I know you have a low opinion of the FBI, but we are bound by laws just the same as the police."

"Even in an emergency?"

This could go on forever. Knowing Mom, it probably would. And it would be completely pointless. It was frustrating. I *knew* the levee was the target. But Frank was right. Even if he went to his superiors, they wouldn't do anything based on a psychic vision by some stripper. All that would happen was that Frank's reputation would be damaged, even if it turned out to be true, but by that time it would be too late. New Orleans would be gone. I swallowed deeply.

I swung my legs over to the side of the bed. "And I need to get to work."

"Scotty . . ."

"Yes, Mom?"

She hugged me. "Please, please be careful."

"*Careful* is my middle name."

"We'll have agents stationed all over the bar, Mrs. Bradley," Frank replied.

"See that you do." Mom pointed her finger at him, her eyes flashing. "Because if anything happens to my son, it doesn't matter how far you run. I will find you. I will find you if it takes the rest of my life, and I will—"

"Mom," Storm said warningly.

"Hunt you down like a dog," she finished. She smiled. It sent chills down my spine. "Do I make myself clear?"

"Crystal clear, Mrs. Bradley." Frank looked at me. "But you don't have to worry, ma'am. I am taking charge of this personally."

"Somehow that doesn't make me feel any better."

"Mom." I kissed her on the cheek and gave her a big hug. "Nothing's going to happen to me. I promise."

At least I hoped not.

Chapter Nineteen

TWO OF SWORDS

Possible trouble ahead

I figured the safest way to walk to the Pub from Mom and Dad's would be to head up a block to Dumaine and Bourbon, turn left there, and head down a block. Cafe Lafitte in Exile was on the corner of Dumaine and Bourbon, which guaranteed that there would be a crowd of guys out in the street. Bourbon Street between Dumaine and St. Ann would also be clogged with people. I figured as long as there were crowds of people around, I'd be safe.

I walked out by myself. The air felt funny, and I looked up. Sure enough, the evening sky was filled with clouds. It was still hot, but the air was even damper than usual. What that meant was a thunderstorm, and a big one. *Terrific,* I thought to myself as I shifted my bag on my shoulder. Even the elements were conspiring to help out Willy Perkins.

New Orleans is below sea level, and sinks a fraction of an inch every year farther into the swamp on which it was built. When the rain comes in fast and hard, there isn't anywhere for the water to go. It can't soak into the ground, because the water table is so high that the very dirt is already fairly saturated. The runoff from the roofs can drench you in a half second. The sewers and drains back up with water immediately, and the streets fill with water before the pumps can get started going. I wasn't sure where the pumps actually put the water they removed—drainage canals or the river or the lake—but with the river so high already, and the possibility of the levee being blown . . .

I shivered in spite of the heat.

I kept my eyes moving, scanning the faces of the people on the street. Anyone with a shaved head, I stared at for a moment, unless I spotted the telltale markings of the gay tribe. Tattoos around the biceps, jeans hanging low off hips with no underwear underneath, showing off the whiteness of the upper buttocks and the start of the crack, the dilated pupils of the party drug, piercings of the nipple or navel.

I stopped at the corner of Dumaine and Bourbon and surveyed the crowd. It looked normal, or as normal as a Decadence crowd can look. The balcony at Lafitte's was crowded with guys with camcorders and cameras. Some guys were leaning over the railing with beads in their hands. Every once in a while, all attention on the balcony would turn to a spot, the guys up there would applaud or cheer, and a string of beads would be tossed down into the crowd. That usually meant someone had succumbed to the pressure or the liquor or the drugs or a combination of the three and pulled his dick out for beads.

Little did the fool know that he was being videotaped, and for months, maybe years, in the future his dick would flash across the television screens in any or all of the Quarter gay bars. Occasionally, the guy filming would be really considerate and not include a face shot of the guy waving his dick at the world, but not always.

I learned this lesson the hard way. When I was twenty-one or two, I got really drunk at Decadence and was convinced to show my dick for beads. Like I needed more beads anyway—the last thing natives need is more of those. But it seemed like fun, and at the time it sounded like a good idea. It was a nice set of red beads that I wore proudly as my prize all night long.

A week later I walked into Lafitte's with some friends and looked up at the video screen, and there I was: no shirt, unbuttoning my jeans, and waving my dick at the camera.

I was mortified.

Everyone looked like they were having a good time, enjoying their weekend. I was happy for them. Good for them. I would probably never be able to look at Decadence the same way again.

Was it just last night I had made this same trip, whistling, my bag over my shoulder with Kenny walking along beside me, hoping that he would meet the man of his dreams?

I closed my eyes and took a deep breath.

The image of Kenny's body propped up against my gate came to me.

I forced it out. No time for that now. I turned and looked back down Dumaine Street. Dad was standing on the corner at Royal, smoking a cigar. Mom and Storm were standing there as well, watching me. I gave them a little halfhearted wave and turned to walk up Bourbon Street.

"Scotty!"

I stopped. David was walking up to me. He was wearing black leather shorts, a black leather cap, boots, and not much of anything else. He had a vodka and tonic in a go cup in his hand.

"Hey, man!" He hugged me. "You doing okay?"

"All things considered, yeah." I shrugged. "Just on my way to work. Meeting up with Ramón tonight?"

"Maybe." He shrugged. "We'll see if he shows up, ya know? If not, I had a good time." David used to want a boyfriend so bad he could taste it. Hanging out with me had changed all that. I'm still not sure if that was a good thing. "I heard about Kenny on the news."

"Yeah, it's been a hell of a day."

"You know I used to date him?"

I stared at him. "No, I didn't know that. When?"

"Before you and I met. He was my last boyfriend." He laughed. "You look so surprised."

"Why didn't you ever tell me about that?"

He took a swig of his drink. "Never really thought about it, to tell you the truth. I mean, he was harmless, right? I mean, I knew you knew him and all—you slept with him once, right? I just never saw any need to say anything. What a shame."

I should have known. New Orleans is a small town, and in the gay community we're all one degree of separation from everyone else. David and I had undoubtedly shared, unknowingly, numerous tricks over the years. "Yeah, I can't think why anyone would want to kill him."

"Said on the news it was probably a mugging gone wrong." David shrugged. "His dad is probably jumping for joy right now as we speak."

"Why?"

"His dad disowned him years ago when he came out. Chandler wasn't his real last name, you know. He changed it. He didn't want anyone to know he was related to his dad. His dad was a Southern Baptist minister."

Poor Kenny, I thought, thanking the Goddess again for my parents. I started walking up Bourbon. David fell into step beside me. "What was his real name?"

"I don't remember." He scratched his crotch. "Damn, these shorts are hot. I'm gonna go home and change into jeans." We weaved through the crowds of revelers. Some of them stared at me; some of them stared at David. An occasional hand reached out and stroked my chest or grabbed my ass as we walked. I smiled at them and kept walking.

When we reached the Pub, I impulsively gave David a hug. "You have fun tonight, okay? And be careful."

"Yeah." He kissed me on the cheek. "You, too." He faded away into the crowd.

I stood there for a moment and reached into my boot for the cell phone Frank gave me. I turned it on and hit speed-dial 1.

It beeped. *Signal lost,* the readout screen said. "Shit." I looked around. There were shaved heads scattered throughout the crowd. I didn't see Frank anywhere. I turned the phone off and slid it back into my boot just as lightning flashed, followed by the loud rumble of thunder. Everyone looked up at the sky just as the rain started. I ducked underneath the Parade's balcony as the streets cleared. The areas under the balcony were wall-to-wall people. Great. How the hell was I going to fight through these people to get inside?

I stepped out into the street and put my bag over my head, hoping Frank had gotten me a waterproof one. It would totally suck to have all my new stripper wear get soaked on my way. The gutter was filling with water. I walked around the corner. Still the same scene. Crowds of people under the balcony, talking, laughing, dancing, flirting. I ran down to the entrance to the bar on St. Ann. It wasn't protected by the balcony, so I shot right in out of the rain. I nodded to the guy behind the cash register. Dane, I think, was his name, but I wasn't completely sure.

I reached for the phone again and punched the key for speed-dial 1. It rang this time.

"Sobieski."

"Frank, it's Scotty. I've arrived at the bar."

"I have you in sight."

"Where are you?"

"Right now on the balcony of the Bourbon Orleans. I was watching you." The Bourbon Orleans hotel was kitty-corner from the Pub on the other side of Bourbon. I let out a sigh of relief. "Don't worry. I have agents in the crowd. As soon as you start dancing, I'll be there."

I looked across the street at the balcony of the hotel. It was crowded. I thought I saw him. "Good." I disconnected the phone and headed back to the office. I pounded on the door.

Cody Dallas opened it. "Little dude!" He grinned and threw his arms around me, lifting me up in the air. He was wearing nothing but a leopard-print thong. He planted a wet kiss on my cheek.

"Put me down, Cody." I grinned down at him. When he did, I asked, "Is Colin here yet?"

He shook his head. "Little dude, I haven't seen him all day."

"Have you slept yet?"

"Nope." He gave me his lopsided grin again. We shut the door behind us. I put my bag down and peeled off my sweatpants. "Nice." He whistled.

"Thanks." I sat down on the couch. Where the hell was he? Had he left town? Why did I care? He was just a trick. A really hot one, but a trick nevertheless. Did a couple of hours in bed mean I owed him anything? No, not really, but at the same time, he'd seemed like a nice guy.

For a cat burglar.

I laughed out loud. Cody turned to me with his eyebrows up. I just grinned at him.

The office door opened and Colin walked in. He smiled at me. "Hey, babe."

"I'm getting a drink. You boys want anything?" Cody asked. We both shook our heads. The door shut behind him.

Colin sat down on the couch beside me. "Are you okay?"

"I could ask you the same thing. Where did you go?"

"Here and there, nothing important." He shrugged. "I would have tried to find you but had no idea where to look."

Well, that did make sense, and besides, I wasn't mad at him. "It's cool, Colin, but you've got to get out of here. The police and the FBI are crawling all over this place. If they see you..." I let my voice trail off. Somehow, I couldn't see either the Feds or the cops fighting through the crowd and dragging him off the bar.

"I can't think of anywhere I'm safer." He put his hand on my leg. "Can you?"

Much as I hated to do it, I had to agree with him. "Yeah." Safe from being arrested by the FBI, maybe, but not from being shot at.

"Are you okay?"

"No, I'm really not." I sighed. "I'm scared and I'm tired and I'm pretty well stressed out. And I have to dance tonight and put a fake smile on my face and flirt with people and I'm just not really in the mood."

"Who can blame you? Why are you even here?"

I opened my mouth and then changed my mind. No need to tell him I was Scotty Bradley, undercover stripper. "I need the money. All my tips from the last two days went up in smoke."

"Do you need money?" His voice seemed sincere. The look on his face was so caring and tender, I felt tears coming. I quickly blinked them away. What a sweetheart.

"No, I'll be fine. I'm sure Velma and Millie were insured."

There was a knock on the door, and Dane or whoever he was stuck his head in. "You guys are up."

We looked at each other and hugged, and headed out into the bar.

It was still raining, and thus the bar was even more crowded. Everyone was crowding in off the street. I excused myself to about a thousand people and made my way to the bar and hoisted myself up. The song playing was a remix of Stevie Nicks's "Planets of the Universe," a great song to dance to. I started moving my hips and scanning the crowd, looking for shaved heads, looking for anyone that looked like a Fed, looking for Frank. Of course, I had no clue what a Fed would look like. Frank was the only one I knew. Cody was at the other end of the bar, and Colin was up dancing, too. I knelt down and took a dollar or two, slipping them into my boot. Someone stroked my calf and I turned to him, wiggled my dick a little to make it bounce, and got a five. Cool. I straightened back up and started dancing again, turning my back to the crowd and flexing my beautiful butt cheeks at them, making them bounce and jiggle a bit. That almost always got a few dollar bills out. I turned around and, sure enough, saw bills in hands. I knelt down, took them, and gave out a couple of light kisses. Still no sign of Frank. Damn it, where the hell was he? Someone stroked my ass, and I scooted down the bar a few inches to give the guy my full attention.

He was tall and completely hairless on his head. Thick black eyebrows, a strong nose, a tightly clenched jaw. He was wearing a gray tank top—a little lean for my tastes, but still kind of attractive in his own way. He had a couple of zits spread out over his forehead and chin.

I smiled at him. "Hi, Happy Decadence!"

He raised an eyebrow at me. He reached up and touched my chest. I kept my smile in place. There was something about this one I didn't like. I stood back up and walked

down the bar to an older guy who had a dollar out. I knelt
down and let him touch my abs. He put the dollar in my
G-string. I looked back at the other guy. He was gone.

Where the hell was Frank?

That's it. I was going to call him and tell him to get his
ass over here, or I was going home. Fuck this.

I jumped down off the bar and headed for the office.
The hairless guy stepped in front of me.

"What do you want?" I raised one of my eyebrows.

"You know what I want." He smirked at me.

I started to back up a little bit. This wasn't cool. Maybe
he was just an asshole, but I had a bad feeling.

"ASSHOLE MOTHERFUCKER!" someone shouted.

I turned my head just in time to see someone smash a
beer bottle over someone's head. The guy who'd been hit
fell backward toward me into a crowd of other guys, who
shoved him back. Someone else jumped on the back of the
guy who'd hit him and they went down in a tumble.
Suddenly, cups and fists were flying everywhere in a melee.
Oh, my God, I thought, and tried to head for the side exit.

I've never seen a fight like this break out in a gay bar.
I've seen bitch fights before, where a couple of drunk
queens get their backs up and start screaming at each
other. They might even go so far as to start slapping each
other, but not this. Punches were flying and bottles were
being broken. It was like something you'd see in one of
those corny old Western movies, with bodies flying and tables and chairs being knocked over.

I just stared in horror, taking steps backward. The exits
were clogging with people trying to get out, people trying
to get in.

Someone grabbed me from behind and clamped my arms
down to my sides, and started dragging me outside into
the rain.

"Hey!" I leaned backward and then moved my weight

forward quickly to throw whoever it was off balance. I managed to break his hold—I *did* use to be a wrestler—and spun around.

It was the hairless guy. He held up his hands. "Hey, man, just trying to help you out."

His tank top had slipped to one side, and I could see the edge of a swastika tattoo on his left pec.

Oh, sweet Goddess!

I bent down to reach for my boot, but he grabbed me into a headlock and twisted my other arm behind my back.

It hurt.

"HELP!" I screamed, but no one could hear me over the music, the violence going on as the bar brawl grew even bigger. And then one of the bartenders jumped up on the bar with a gun in his hand and he fired it into the air, but nothing changed; no one stopped, and I tried to kick the guy holding me as he dragged me to one of the side exit doors and out into the rain.

"FRANK!" I screamed.

And I smelled it, too late.

Chloroform.

And everything went dark.

Chapter Twenty

SIX OF SWORDS

Journey by water

I woke up with a headache to the sound of Guns N' Roses being played very, very loud. "Welcome to the Jungle." I never liked that song very much.

A guy who'd lived on my dorm floor in college had loved—no, worshipped—Axl Rose. He blared every Guns N' Roses CD nonstop on his stereo, but his particular favorite was *Welcome to the Jungle*. You'd walk past his room and the door would be open. You could see him very plainly doing Axl Rose, with a hairbrush as his microphone, mimicking that weird snakelike dance Axl used to do in his videos. It drove everyone insane. We finally were able to get the RA to get him to keep it down to a reasonable level, but you could still hear it on your way to the showers or the bathroom or class. Nobody ever really talked to the guy. His roommate moved out after a week, and no one moved in to take his place. He had long, stringy black hair, a bad complexion, and was about six feet tall. He maybe weighed 130 pounds on a good day. His skin was pasty white, like he never went out into the sun. His name was Kevin Beasley and he was from Bethesda, Maryland. I tried once to engage him in a conversation in the bathroom while I was washing my face and he was shaving. All of his answers were monosyllabic. I gave up after a while. I figured he was either a genius of some sort or one of those people who would end up shooting up a McDonald's in some small town in the Southwest somewhere with a Spanish name. Everyone was relieved when he didn't come back the next semester.

Right now, though, someone else who was a big fan was singing along at a high volume, which I could hear quite easily over Axl's amplified screeching. He was off key and flat, a deadly combination. I opened my eyes. I was staring at the roof of a van. I turned my head to one side and then the other. It looked like some kind of worker's van. No carpet, no decor, nothing. The grooves in the floor I could feel through my bare back. I tried to move my hands, but they were tied together. My mouth was taped shut. My legs, I found, were likewise bound up.

I thought about the cell phone in my boot. Like I could reach it, and even if I could, how would I dial? How would I speak? Maybe it was a gadget that emitted a sound wave no one could hear, like a homing beacon, and even as I bumped along in the back, the FBI was hot on my trail. . . .

And any minute Arnold Schwarzenegger was going to kick open the back doors and rescue me.

Keep dreaming. The FBI couldn't even stop them from grabbing me out of a fucking public place.

We hit a pothole deep enough to send me into the air. I landed on my side with a painful thud. *"Ooof"* was all the sound that could penetrate the tape. I tried to catch my breath again, which is not easy when you are trying to take in gulps through your nose.

I pulled my knees up to my chest and swung them up in the air. I then put my feet down. So far, so good. I contracted my ab muscles and started trying to raise my shoulders up. I wished, for a moment, they'd had the decency to tie my hands behind my back, so I could use my arms for leverage. I got my shoulders up and then started moving back and forth slowly, trying to build up enough momentum to sit up. My lower back started to hurt. I was almost there when we hit another pothole.

Again I rose up into the air. I shoved my head forward as I started my descent, and tried to pull my legs back. It was so fast, I didn't have much time. I wound up with too much momentum and landed flat on my stomach. Actually, my stomach landed on my tied hands.

That hurt.

I lay there trying to catch enough breath through my nose, my eyes watering from the pain in my abs, which were apparently not in as good a shape as I had thought. I realized that I could now actually get up. All I'd really had to do before was just roll over onto my stomach. I pulled my knees up and pushed with my hands and I rose up into a doggie-style stance. I looked forward at the two seats in the front of the van. I could see through the windshield that we were on I-10, heading toward Baton Rouge. On the left was the guy who was the Axl Rose fan. His head was moving in time with the music, and every once in a while he played an imaginary drum on the dashboard with his right hand. He had long hair that flew around as he moved his head. On the right was another guy. He had a shaved head. Swastika tattoo, no doubt.

Okay, take stock of the situation, I told myself. *Tied up and gagged in the back of a moving van. Two guys. I am wearing nothing but a lime green thong. There is a strong possibility nobody has the slightest idea where I am. I am heading out of New Orleans, in the general direction of Baton Rouge. Of course, we have to pass through the Atchafalaya Swamp to get there.*

The swamp.

They were going to kill me and dump me in the swamp. I'd never be found. An alligator would have me for dinner. Fuck, fuck, fuck.

Think, Scotty, think. You've got to get out of this somehow.

The guy on the right looked around his seat. It *was* the guy from the bar. He had barbed wire tattooed around his left biceps. I thought only gay men did that. So much for gay tribal markings.

"Hey, look, the fag's awake." He grinned. His teeth were kind of yellowed. I started moving to the back of the van. Great. Gay-hating skinheads. Being an alligator's dinner would be easy compared to what they could do to me. He climbed around the seat and stooped over, balancing against the weaving of the van. He walked back to me until I was cornered. His jeans were ripped in places, and I could see extremely white skin and some coarse reddish-brown hairs.

"Fag." His foot shot out. I had just enough time to tighten my abs. They still hurt from landing on my hands, and his kick knocked all the breath out of me. I grunted. Have you ever had all of your breath expelled out through your nose because your mouth is taped shut? It *hurts.* My eyes swam, tears of pain forming. I blinked as fast as I could to keep them from spilling out.

He had taken off his tank top. His right nipple was pierced. So now even the skinheads were appropriating gay stuff? Was nothing indeed sacred? Next thing you knew, they'd be buying Liza records and old Joan Crawford videos, and quoting lines from *What Ever Happened to Baby Jane?*

He was grinning. His hands went to his fly. He started to unbutton it.

Oh, no.

"You fags like to suck dick, don't you?"

Not that.

He finished, and his loose jeans dropped to his knees. He had on a ratty pair of white underwear that looked like they could use a good bleaching. There were piss stains in the front. They hung loosely from his bony hips.

He reached down and ripped the tape off my mouth, taking what felt like a good share of my lips with it. I took some deep breaths to try to absorb the pain. My abs hurt.

He shoved his crotch at me. It stank of must and sweat and sour piss.

I turned my head.

He slapped me.

Hard.

My head exploded. I saw stars through the water in my eyes. My left cheek stung. My jaw popped when he hit me, and I moved it to make sure it worked. There was a weird inner noise on that side.

I looked up at him.

He was grinning, the bastard.

I started to get mad.

Okay, motherfucker, I said to myself. *You're gonna pay for this.*

He grabbed my hair and pulled my head into his crotch. His erection smacked against my face. I looked up at him. Yeah, still grinning. Still grinning about getting the free blow job from the fag cocksucker.

I bit him.

There was a roaring in my ears as he pummeled my head. Above it all I could hear him screaming. I kept my jaw clenched until it started to ache. *How's this feel, asshole?* I shouted in my head. *Feeling pretty good? Gonna come soon? Huh? Hope you're enjoying this as much as I am!*

I let go.

He collapsed in a heap. He was moaning and holding on to his crotch.

"I hope you bleed to death, asshole." I kept moving my jaw. It didn't seem to be broken, but it was still making funny noises.

The van was no longer moving.

The driver was gone.

The back of the van opened.

This guy was huge. He was wearing a sleeveless red-and-black flannel shirt that had seen better days. His arms hung at his sides, heavy and meaty. His jeans hung low because he couldn't pull them up over that sagging belly. He was wearing a baseball cap with the logo of a major tractor company on it. He was holding a gun in his right hand. He had to weigh about three hundred pounds, easy. He moved gracefully for such a big guy, kind of like a professional wrestler.

"Hospital," the bar guy was gasping. He was holding his crotch with both hands. Blood was flowing freely over them.

"And tell them what, fuck-head? That you got bit by a fag? The same one we got tied up in the back of the van?" He shook his head. He didn't have a neck. He climbed up into the van, which sagged under his weight. He hunched over the bar guy. His back was to me. I looked out the open doors. We weren't on the highway anymore. I saw trees, Spanish moss hanging from the branches. Frogs croaking. Water splashed every once in a while. Birds. Rustling in the branches. I thought about throwing myself out the doors, but then what? If we weren't on the highway I didn't have a chance. He had a gun. I couldn't run. *Well, maybe after what I did to the bar guy they'll just shoot me.*

I sent a quick prayer to the Goddess.

The big dude turned to me. He was holding electrical tape in his hand.

"No, don't tape my mouth again, please?"

The pleading did me no good. The tape gum stung my raw lips. My eyes swam again. It fucking hurt. He stepped down out of the van and slid his big hands under me and lifted me up into the air. He didn't strain at all. I saw night sky above me. Stars, clear skies. He carried me down a ramp and then put me gently down into the back of a pirogue. It rose in the water as he stepped back ashore. I watched him go up the ramp.

I heard a shot.

He came back down carrying something wrapped in a tarp. It had to be the bar guy. I closed my eyes.

Oh, please, Goddess, watch out for me; I am in the hands of dangerous people; please watch for me. I called on her warlike incarnations. Athena. Kali. Please help me. Athena, give me the strength to be a warrior in your name. Kali, give me the spirit to fight for my life; Athena, Kali, please help me.

He put the tarp down in the front and untied the pirogue. He used a pole to push away from the dock. The pirogue slid out onto the open water. He lit a lantern and set it in the front. He started poling the pirogue.

In the distance I could hear the sound of cars on the highway. Even if I could scream, they'd never hear me.

The sky gave way to tree branches as we made our way through the swamp. I kept listening for anything that sounded like human civilization: music, TV, anything. There was nothing but the sounds of the swamp.

Mosquitoes buzzed around me, landing on me. I tossed my head around, trying to shoo them away. They just came back, the wretched things. He slapped at a few, then stopped poling. He put the pole down and sprayed himself liberally with insect repellent. He looked back at me and then came back to where I was sprawled in the bottom. He started spraying my legs, my back, my chest and arms. He rubbed it into the skin. His big, clumsy-looking hands were surprisingly gentle. "Close your eyes," he said. I did and he rubbed the repellent on my face. When he was finished I opened my eyes. He was looking down at me.

"There ya go." He walked back to the front.

That had to be a good sign. If the plan was just to kill me and dump my body in the swamp, surely he wouldn't have put insect repellent on me. What difference would a few mosquito bites make to anything? No, he was trying to make me as comfortable as possible. That had to be a good sign.

Hope is a truly wonderful thing. *I can get out of this,* I thought, and began to believe it. *I still have the cell phone in my boot, if I can only get it out and use it.* Of course, I had no idea where we were, just somewhere in the swamp, but couldn't they trace the location of my cell phone through a satellite or something? Mom and Dad always railed against cell phones for that very reason. "The satellites are all under the government's control." I could hear her voice in my head. "It's the start of Big Brother; you mark my words. And aren't those kinds of calls a lot easier to intercept? And they don't have the same privacy laws for cell phones that they do for land lines."

She also thought they caused brain cancer.

I closed my eyes and started praying again to the Goddess.

"I'm gonna go pole the pirogue down the bayou. Pick guitar, fill fruit jar, and be gay-o . . ."

He was singing "Jambalaya."

He had a pleasant baritone voice, which was quite a difference from his shrieking imitation of Axl Rose. I allowed myself to relax a bit. No sense in remaining all tense, anyway. I stared at the pleasant Louisiana night sky and sang along with him in my mind.

After he finished singing that, he started in on "Your Cheatin' Heart." Quite a renaissance man, my kidnapper. Axl Rose and Hank Williams. I sang along with him again in my head. I know all of Hank Williams's songs by heart. My mom considered him the greatest white blues singer of all time. I thought he had a high, whiny, extremely nasal voice myself, but Mom would go into rhapsodies over Hank's musical genius. My mom might be a hippie, but she has very eclectic taste in music.

He had just finished the second chorus when he stopped poling again. I looked over at him. He set the pole down and picked up the tarp with the bar guy in it. He shoved it over the side. It hit the water with a loud splash. Some of the spray hit my legs. We just drifted in silence for a moment, and then I heard the splashing sound of something moving through the water. He was standing, watching, with his arms crossed.

"Good-bye, jackass," he called out, and it echoed in the swamp. Some birds called back. He looked back at me, and his face softened in the moonlight. He stepped back over to me and gently peeled the tape off of my mouth. "Don't worry, son, I'm not gonna feed ya to the gators."

"Could I have something to drink?" I was dehydrated. The warm, thick, heavy air of the swamp had me covered in sweat.

"Sure, boy." He got a bottle of water out of a cooler I hadn't noticed, and got himself a Dixie beer. He flipped the cap into the water. He held the bottle up to my mouth and I drank from it gratefully. "I'd untie ya, boy, but I can't trust ya enough to do that."

"Why did you guys grab me?"

He shrugged. "Boss wanted us to. We don't ask no questions."

"Where are you taking me?"

"To see the boss. He wants to see you for some reason." He downed the Dixie in one gulp and tossed the bottle overboard. He gave me another drink of the water and then recapped it. "You want more water, just ask, okay? And don't bother to scream, cuz ain't no one out to hear and if they was, they wouldn't be helpin' ya, okay?"

I nodded. "Who's the boss?" Couldn't hurt to ask.

"You'll find out soon enough."

He stood up and picked up the pole. "Oh, mister?"

"Yeah?" He pushed the pole into the water.

"You have a nice singing voice."

He laughed, long and loud. "Well, thank ya, boy. And call me Virgil, okay? You want me to sing some more?"

"Yeah, that would be great." I closed my eyes and leaned back.

And he launched into "Welcome to the Jungle."

Chapter Twenty-one

KING OF WANDS, REVERSED

A severe, unyielding man who is intolerant and prejudiced

I didn't think it was in my best interests to request a return to Hank Williams, so I listened to the extent of Virgil's Guns N' Roses repertoire. Fortunately for me, he only knew the words to two other songs, "Sweet Child O' Mine" and "I Used to Love Her." The latter didn't do much for my mood, since it was a love song about a man who killed his girlfriend and buried her in the backyard. You haven't lived until you've been serenaded in a swamp with that song.

After that, though, he switched to Billy Joel. He really did have a pleasant voice, with a nice range, when he wasn't being a head-banger. He did a very sweet-sounding rendition of "Piano Man," which he followed up with "Just The Way You Are." Once finished with Billy Joel, he lapsed into silence again. The only sound was the gentle slapping of water against the side of the boat and the occasional small splash of the pole entering the water again. He was very good at moving the boat silently.

"Virgil?"

"Yeah, boy?"

"Could I have some more water?"

"We're almost there now; can you wait a bit, boy?"

"Yes."

There. Where I was being taken to meet the boss. Virgil said he wasn't going to feed me to the gators, but he did what the boss told him to. That wasn't on my agenda for the evening.

Yet.

"I'm sorry about your friend," I was. If I'd known what was going to happen, I wouldn't have bit him. Granted, having your mouth raped isn't a pleasant experience, but I still didn't want him to end up dead.

Virgil threw his head back and laughed up at the sky. "Boy, you did me a favor. Rusty Bindle was nothin' but trouble, and he wasn't no friend of mine. He was nothin' but trouble, every time we tried to do anything. He's the one that killed that friend of yours last night."

"Kenny?"

"Was that his name?" Virgil shrugged. "Don't matter now, nohow. Now, I ask you, boy, did that boy look anything like Jeremy Fontaine?"

"No, although they were about the same size, I guess."

Virgil snorted. "Exactly. I told that jackass it wasn't Jeremy; I knows Jeremy like I knows the back of my hand. But no, he kept insisting that it was—wasn't he waiting for you at your gate? And who else would be there at that hour of the night? So he jumps out of the van all cocked up like he's Clint Eastwood and goes after him, and sure enough, it ain't Jeremy. And then he just shoots him." He pointed his index finger at me and cocked his thumb. "Wuddn't no reason for that boy to die, none at all. You know, boy, we ain't all bad people, ya know. Ain't nothing bad gonna happen to you here, boy. Boss just wants to talk to ya, is all. We ain't into killin' people."

"Who are you, anyway?"

"Ain't for me to say." He shrugged. "Now shut up; we're almost there." With a speed that seemed impossible for his size, he retaped my mouth and poled the boat into a brightly lit clearing.

It was an island of sorts in the middle of the swamp. A long, low building stretched almost its entire length. Every ten feet or so was a window. Some of them were lit up. There were about five long piers extending out like fingers, with plenty of boats tied to them. I didn't see any signs of life. Virgil poled the boat over to one of the piers and tied up to it. He picked me up and threw me over his shoulder and climbed out. The pier groaned just a bit. Virgil started whistling "Crazy" by Patsy Kline.

How appropriate.

He carried me up a low rise. I could hear his boots squishing in the mud. Then we reached a concrete walkway. We went up a couple of steps that groaned under our weight.

He opened the door and we entered into an air-conditioned room. He set me down. He wasn't even breathing hard. "Hey, guys, I got him."

Four guys were playing cards at a makeshift card table. Empty bags of chips were scattered around the floor around them. Empty beer bottles and overflowing ashtrays were scattered over the top of the table. They were all shirtless and young, about the late unlamented Rusty Bindle's age. They, too, were tattooed, but not in gay tribal designs. One had a swastika on his pale chest, just like Rusty Bindle. Our eyes met. His were pale green and cold. They narrowed. He . . .

He was the mugger from last night.

I looked away. Watch for that one, I thought. The others didn't seem too interested in our arrival. I turned my eyes back. He was still watching me. I shivered. His eyes—his eyes were so cold . . .

Pray for a brave heart.

He'd just as soon kill me as look at me, I thought.

"Boss here yet?" Virgil helped himself to a beer.

"Not yet. Put him in the back," Swastika Tattoo said without looking up from his cards.

Virgil shrugged. He bent down and lifted me onto his shoulder without spilling his beer. He walked over to a far corner of the room, opened a door, and switched on a light. The room was bare; just a wooden floor, a steel bed, and a steel pole in the direct center of the room. The only light was provided by a single bare bulb hanging from the ceiling. It swung back and forth, throwing light in a weird swaying movement, the shadows dancing and moving. There was a small cardboard dresser in a corner. He set me down by the pole, which I leaned against, and got a pair of handcuffs out of the dresser. He cuffed my left wrist to the pole, removed the tape from my mouth again just as gently as before, and then cut my hands and legs free. My feet were numb. I shook them to get circulation going again and to loosen them up. "You still thirsty, boy?"

"Uh-huh."

He handed me the beer. I drank from it. I don't generally like beer, but its liquid coldness felt great.

"Shouldn't be too much longer. The boss doesn't like to keep people waiting." Virgil winked at me. He then walked out and closed the door. I heard the key turn in the lock.

Oh, thank you, Goddess! I slid my arm down the pole and reached into my right boot. Yes, the precious phone was still there. I managed to flip it open and activate it.

I let out a huge sign of relief as the little screen glowed green. I hit speed-dial 1.

I cradled it between my head and my shoulder. "Come on, come on, come on, Frank, answer the fucking phone!"

"You have reached the voice mail messaging service for

Frank Sobieski. Press 'one' to leave a message, or wait for the beep."

I counted to ten while I waited for the beep. I couldn't believe it. Oh, you'll be safe, Scotty; we'll have you covered from every angle; there will be agents all over the place; they can't get to you, and I'll have my phone with me; speed-dial one; you can reach me anytime you need me; make sure you keep this phone with you at all times.

Worthless piece-of-crap FBI agent.

Beep. "Look, Frank, you fuck, thanks for nothing, you asshole; I'm in the middle of the swamp who knows the fuck where; they don't know I have the phone so don't fucking call me back; thanks for nothing and thanks for not having your fucking phone on, you amazing asshole—" *Beep.* End of message.

Fucking asshole didn't even have the decency to have a long enough voice mail so that I could tell his ass off!

I was completely on my own.

Okay, Scotty, think.

I sighed and turned the phone off. I slid it back into my boot. "Feeble Bureau of Incompetents" was right, I thought as I slid down and sat down on the wood floor. I tugged at the handcuffs, but the pole didn't even slightly budge the least little bit. Great. Even if I could escape, though, where would I go? I could possibly slip past them and get a boat, but I had no idea where I was. We had traveled so deep into the swamp, too far for me to use the noise of cars on the highway for direction.

I could pole around in the swamp forever and never find my way out.

And nobody would be looking for me there.

The door opened.

I looked up as a man walked in. He was wearing a three-piece suit and a tie, and looked absolutely perspiration-free. How the hell had he gotten here? My hair was hanging in a limp and sodden mass. I had dried in the air-conditioning, but I could also smell the dried sweat mixed in with the insect repellant. He had light-brown hair that can best be described as televangelist hair. You know, the kind that doesn't look quite real? Immaculately groomed, every well-behaved hair in place, that doesn't move no matter what? Gale-force winds? No problem, the hair doesn't go anywhere. I often wondered what kind of hairspray they used, or if it was even real hair. His eyebrows were the same color, and he had narrow, beady gray eyes too closely set on either side of his hawklike nose. His lips were thin and mean-looking. He was carrying more weight than he should, with the start of jowls forming at the sides of his face. His skin was kind of mottled-looking, like he'd had serious acne problems when he was a teenager. Reddish in places, little holes in others. Maybe he'd just had chicken pox really bad. Virgil came in behind him and shut the door.

"For Jesus's sake, give him something to wear! Cover him up!" His voice was nasal, twangy, and perhaps an octave too high. He looked away from me as though my nakedness was offensive to his eyes. Maybe looking at my bare skin was a sin. Who knew? Virgil obligingly grabbed a blanket off the bed and tucked it around me.

"He's covered, boss." Virgil leaned against the wall, folding his arms in front.

The boss knelt down beside me. "First of all, Mr. Bradley, I want to apologize for the necessity of arranging a meeting this way. We aren't bad people."

"You know my name; what's yours?" Not exactly dialogue by Noel Coward, but it was the best I could come up with on such short notice.

He laughed. It sounded like a horse neighing. "My campaign must be in trouble, boy, if you don't recognize me."

It had to be Willy Perkins himself. I shrugged. "I don't watch the news or read the paper."

"I am Willy Perkins, the next governor of Louisiana." He hooked his thumbs inside the lapels of his jacket proudly. "And I have to tell you, boy, that you have given us quite a run for our money."

"Glad to be of service."

He slapped me. "Don't get smart with me, boy. In case you haven't noticed, you're in no position to be a smart aleck with me."

Did he really say 'smart aleck'? I shook my head. My ears were ringing again. "So sorry, Mr. Perkins."

"It's quite all right, Scotty. Jesus forgives all, after all." He smiled at me. His face glowed. "All I want to know is this: does the FBI have the disk?"

"It didn't go up in the fire." Why not tell him? "They know all about your plans to blow up the sewers."

He closed his eyes for a minute. "And Jeremy Fontaine, that Judas?"

"He's with them."

He stood up, taking deep breaths. He turned his back to me. He clenched and unclenched his fists. He knelt down right in front of me and I looked directly into his eyes. They were empty, devoid of anything. If eyes are the windows to the soul, then either he didn't have one or his was so dark it couldn't be seen through his eyes. Involuntarily I shivered. I wanted to look away and couldn't. It was like staring at a cobra. They say that a cobra hypnotizes its prey, immobilizing it so it can kill and eat it. This was kind of the same thing. He smiled at me. His teeth were perfectly straight, perfectly spaced, and very white. "It doesn't matter. It doesn't matter at all. You see, Scott—I can call you Scott, can't I?—it was all just a joke, a sad, ridiculous joke. I have this reputation, thanks to the media in this state, of being this man who hates others, can you believe that? A man who goes to church three times per week and reads the Bible every day? It's just not possible for a Christian to hate."

"That's true." What else was there to say?

"And I have called New Orleans a city of sin. Well, son, it is a city of sin, but it's not for me to pass judgment; that's God's job, and I don't presume to speak for the Lord." His voice was soft, soothing, convincing. "So, someone on my campaign staff thought I'd find it amusing to put together a video game of God taking his wrath out on New Orleans, much as He did with Sodom and Gomorrah in the Good Book. Was it in poor taste? Certainly. And definitely something unfortunate for a young Christian like Jeremy to come across. Imagine if that tasteless but harmless information fell into the hands of a newspaper or television station. You saw the effect it had on a good young man like Jeremy. It caused him to turn his back on God and revert back to his un-Christian behavior patterns."

"But one of your people killed Kenny Chandler last night." Maybe it wasn't the smartest thing to bring up, but I am nothing if not the child of my parents. Mom and Dad would have asked.

He sighed and clasped his hands together as though to pray. "An extremely misguided young man, overzealous in his devotion to his God, and to my campaign's success, crossed a line that I would never condone or counsel. Poor young Rusty had such a terrible life, so many burdens for his young soul to carry. We're trying to help him, and were making progress . . ."

He was very good. It was very easy to buy into everything he was saying. This was why he was running for governor of Louisiana with a fifty-fifty shot at winning and taking up residence in Baton Rouge. He would be able to convince enough people of his sincerity that he still had a shot at winning. He was certainly not stupid enough to leave his fingerprints on anything. "Plausible deniability," Storm called it. *An overzealous follower committed a crime without my knowledge. I certainly did not order him to kill anyone. I certainly do not condone his actions.*

"And kidnapping me?"

"Again, overzealous followers misinterpreted my desire to meet with you in person." He sighed. "A terrible misunderstanding. You are, of course, free to go anytime you wish."

"And just where would I go? Someone would have to take me."

"Virgil will take you at any time you wish to return to New Orleans."

Of course Virgil would. He was smiling at me behind Perkins's back. Giving me a thumbs-up. Apparently, they thought I had been born very recently.

"Well, I kind of would like to get back."

"Virgil, take him." Perkins stood up.

Virgil reached for my handcuffs. "See, I told you we weren't bad people. We don't kill people."

"You killed Rusty."

Perkins stopped at the door. "What did you say?" His head whipped around. His eyes had narrowed.

Oh, fuck. Way to go, Scotty, perfect timing to bring *that* up.

"That was your fault, son." Virgil helped me up to my feet. "You'd better wear that blanket after all. The boss doesn't want you running around bare-assed."

"How was what happened to Rusty my fault?" I pulled the blanket around me.

"You hurt him so bad he needed to go to the hospital."

Virgil looked at me as though I were insane. "I couldn't take him to no hospital. So I had to shoot him. If you hadn't hurt him so bad I wouldn't have had to."

They could justify anything, switch blame with the blink of an eye.

Perkins stepped back into the room and shut the door. "Virgil, am I to understand that Rusty is dead?"

Virgil swallowed and went pale. Perkins's tone didn't sound good. For either one of us. "Yes, boss." He was terrified. I could hear it. Oh, Goddess, protect me.

"This wisp of a boy hurt him so bad you had to kill him; is that what you said?" Perkins clasped his hands together and walked toward us.

"Yes, boss." Virgil was looking down.

"And this boy witnessed the entire thing?"

"Yes, boss."

I winced as Perkins slapped Virgil across the face. And back across. Again and again and again until Virgil's face was reddened and blood was dripping out of his nose. "AND YOU WERE GOING TO LET HIM GO FREE? WITHOUT TELLING ME ANY OF THIS? YOU STUPID FUCKING MORON, DON'T YOU HAVE ANY BRAINS IN THAT FAT MOUNTAIN?" Spit was flying out of his mouth. He stopped slapping Virgil. He was breathing hard.

He looked at me. "Kill him."

The door slammed behind him.

Virgil wiped the blood off his nose. He looked sad.

Everything went black.

Chapter Twenty-two

NINE OF PENTACLES, REVERSED

Move with caution

I woke up with a raging headache, a dry mouth, and staring at a tin roof. I tried to move but couldn't. I was restrained to the bed. I turned my head in each direction. It was the same room where I'd had my little chat with Perkins. They were going to kill me.

They were going to blow up the levee.

New Orleans was going to be destroyed.

I was wearing a T-shirt and a pair of camouflage pants. Somebody had covered my nakedness. Thank goodness I was being held hostage by good, decent people. At least they hadn't gagged me again. I was beginning to think my lips were never going to recover from the tape abuse they'd received. Then again, they might not ever have the chance to heal. *Like hell*, I thought; *I'm getting out of here.*

The door opened and Virgil came in. His shoulders were slumped, his head bowed slightly forward. His whole bulk seemed to be sagging a bit. "Boy, I sure am sorry about all this."

"You're not the only one."

He sat down on the edge of the bed. It tipped and tilted dangerously for a few seconds, then settled. "I was gonna take you back to the city—I swear I was, boy—but then, you heard the boss."

"Why don't you just kill me?" I would have shrugged, but I couldn't move anything.

"That wouldn't be right." Virgil shook his head. "It wasn't your fault. It was mine. This ain't right."

Oh, that was it. The fault transference hadn't really started working yet. Soon, it would be "Sorry I have to kill you, but it's your fault for seeing something you weren't supposed to see." And that was when he would put me in the pirogue, paddle me away from the island, put a bullet in my skull, and feed my body to the alligators.

"Okay, thanks." I smiled at him.

"You seem like such a good boy." Virgil looked at me and patted my hand. "I don't understand why you aren't a Christian, why you aren't saved. Why do you choose to be a homosexual and turn your back on God's love?"

"Virgil, I really didn't have a choice."

"We always have a choice, boy. That was God's gift to us, the ability to choose between good and evil. The Bible tells us what He expects of us, and it's up to us to choose to live as He wants. I just don't understand why people don't always choose good."

Great. Tied to a bed and now I have to have the choice/ biological debate with a simpleminded Christian.

"Jeremy'll eventually choose good, you know." Virgil was rocking back and forth. The bedsprings squealed with each movement. "He was on the path to evil, and he returned to God. He's had a minor lapse, but he will soon see the error of his ways and God will welcome him back into the Church like the prodigal son."

"I'm really happy for him." I held my head. "Virgil, my

head really hurts. Is there any aspirin or anything that I can have?"

"I'm sorry about that, too." His head dropped lower. "I hit you in the head. I didn't know what else to do. I only wish I had thought to knock you out before you said anything. If I only had, we'd be on our way to New Orleans right now."

"Aspirin?"

"Yes, boy, I believe I do have some. I bet you're thirsty, too." He rose up off the bed and walked over to the door. He was feeling much better than he had when he came in. He was practically skipping, if someone that size could be said to skip.

Okay, Virgil was on my side, at least so far. As long as he kept thinking there was no reason to kill me, he wouldn't. Even though it was what the boss wanted. Of course, any of the other skinheads could kill me at any time—Swastika Pecs seemed a very likely candidate—but as long as Virgil was around, I somehow had the feeling that I was okay.

Until he decided it was my fault.

Then I was a dead man.

I closed my eyes. My stomach still hurt from being kicked by Rusty. My shoulders and hips were getting stiff. My jaw ached. Maybe going to sleep wouldn't be such a bad thing. And hey, if Virgil changed his mind, wouldn't it be better to go in your sleep instead of being conscious and waiting for the gun to go off? Granted, I probably wouldn't sleep well or deeply, not being able to move and all, but it couldn't hurt to try.

Virgil came back in. "Open your mouth." I did and he popped two aspirins in and then poured some water into it. I swallowed but not fast enough and ended up gagging on the water.

"Can't you drink?" Virgil smacked me hard in the stomach. I gasped and tried to catch my breath. "Sweet Jesus, boy, look at the mess you made."

"I'm sorry," I gasped out.

He shook his head. "You're such a good boy, but sometimes you could try the patience of a saint!"

"Sorry, Virgil, sorry." I could breathe easily again, but my abs were undoubtedly black and blue. They ached every time I breathed in. "Would it be okay if I took a little nap?"

He grinned. "Want me to sing you to sleep?"

"Sure." I hazarded a smile at him. "That would be nice."

I closed my eyes as he started to sing "Welcome to the Jungle" again. But this time it wasn't being screeched at top volume. This time, he sang it in his gentle baritone, as though singing a lullaby.

It was oddly beautiful.

Behind my eyes, the fog began to roll into my inner vision. Curling and beckoning me to walk, to follow it. I rose up out of my bed, freed from my shackles, and followed the fog out of the room and outside into the night. It had cooled down a bit, but the air was still heavy. The storm from New Orleans must be drawing near. I followed the fog out onto a pier and into a motorboat. I started the motor and followed the fog as it sped away from me across the water, through trees. The sky was starting to lighten a bit in the far east, but the cloud cover kept the swamp dark. The wind began to blow as I maneuvered the boat on a path I didn't know. I just knew that I had to follow the wisps of fog, and they would see me through. After what seemed like an eternity, my boat came upon the spot where the van was parked. I pulled the boat up to the ramp and tied it off. It was one of those off-ramps into the swamp. I got into the van and the keys were in the ignition. I started it up and looked back through the mirrors to back up.

I saw Rusty's blood smeared and spattered all over the walls in the back.

I gagged and took a brief moment to stop myself from throwing up.

Come on, the fog beckoned. *There isn't time.*

I took the on-ramp back onto the highway and headed back into New Orleans. There was little or no traffic, so I made excellent time. It didn't seem to take too long before I was passing into Kenner and past the airport. The sun continued to brighten the sky, much quicker than it should have been. I was maybe fifteen minutes away from downtown, but the sun had risen. It seemed like noon by the time I reached the Vieux Carre exit. Just as I started to take it, there was a loud explosion from down by the river.

I stopped the van and shut off the engine.

Other cars on the highway were stopping.

I could hear the roar of water, the screams.

The screams of the dying.

Plumes of smoke were rising from the Quarter.

"Oh dear God," a woman standing near me said, and began to cry.

I could see a wall of water heading for where we were.

This is what can come to pass, I heard inside my head.

I opened my eyes.

Virgil was hovering almost directly over me. "Are you okay, boy?"

"Virgil, what is the boss's plan?"

He shook his head. "I can't tell you that."

"He's going to blow up the levee, right?"

His eyes opened wide. "How did you know that?" and then he clamped his hand over his mouth.

"God spoke to me in a dream just now, Virgil." I hated myself for lying to him, but I didn't really see another choice. After all, Christians could interpret my gift as being from God, right? "He showed me what is going to happen. All those innocent people are going to die, Virgil, and for what? They didn't do anything wrong."

"New Orleans is the modern-day Sodom."

"But not everyone there is a sinner, Virgil. There's lots of good Christian tourists who come to New Orleans to see the sites and eat the food, Virgil. It's not all about sex and alcohol and homosexuality. Families, Virgil—have you ever seen the families in Jackson Square? The innocent children? The babies? They will all die with New Orleans, Virgil—even the babies."

"It's not my decision to make. It's God's will."

"God spoke to me, Virgil. This isn't what He wants. He wants you to stop it." I tried to keep my voice calm and cool. It was hard. "And didn't the boss say he didn't want anything bad to happen to me? Didn't he say I was free to go back to New Orleans whenever I wanted and you would take me?"

"That was before he knew about Rusty."

"But you know what Rusty was trying to do to me, don't you? That was a sin; it was wrong, and I was just trying to save myself from it. And it wasn't your fault you had to kill him. He was a bad man, a sinner. So it has to be okay, right, Virgil?" I really wished I were Storm. Storm could talk a nun out of her underwear.

"I don't know! You're confusing me!" I saw the blow coming but couldn't do anything to avoid it. My head swam, and everything went dark again.

I was back on the Vieux Carre off-ramp. The screams and sounds of destruction as the wall of muddy water headed for where I was standing. The highway was raised high enough for the water to pass under, but I could see bodies floating in the mud. Chairs, tables, articles of clothing, a baby carriage. I sank down to the pavement because I didn't want to see anything else, witness any more of the horror. Everyone I loved was probably dead: Mom, Dad, Storm, Millie, Velma, Mark, Emily—everyone I knew or cared about. My neighborhood was destroyed, gone, eradicated.

It doesn't have to be—that voice in my head again.

It can be altered; the future is fluid. It can always be changed. You must act.

"But how?" I shouted to the voice. "I'm trapped in the middle of the swamp with a crazy guard who could snap and kill me at any minute—tied down, I might add, with no way to get back into the city, no way to get in touch with anyone who could help me, and no one seems to be busting down the door to rescue me at any time soon.

There's always a way. You know what to do.

I opened my eyes as Virgil cut my legs free. "Virgil?"

"I'm taking you back home, boy. It's what the boss wanted. Rusty was a bad man, a sinner. The boss knew that." He shook his head. "He couldn't have meant it when he told me to kill you. You're innocent. And the innocent can't be killed."

I could have kissed him. Probably not a wise idea, I amended, and waited as he cut my hands free. I sat up on the bed, rubbing my wrists. Virgil had a way with knots. He could probably teach Colin a few things. "Thanks, Virgil."

He smiled at me. Our eyes met. His soul was there, simple and loving and trusting. *Who are you, Virgil?* I wanted to ask. *What made you this way? What happened to you? You're a good person, a simple soul. Why has your life taken this path?*

He opened the door and peered out. "They're still out

loading the boats with the dynamite. We'll go out the back way."

His poor simple mind. It hadn't occurred to him that in saving me he was taking me back to a city about to be destroyed. I wanted to scream at him, but stopped myself. He was on my side now, and I had to keep him there. I needed him to get me out of the swamp. If I could just get back to New Orleans, I could use the damned phone.

If Frank could be bothered to answer his, the jackass.

I'd even request the screeching version of "Welcome to the Jungle" if it made Virgil happy. Keep him happy; keep him on my side.

He unlocked the back door and we walked out there. There was another pier in the back, with a single pirogue tied to it. I climbed into it and sat in the back. He untied it and pushed off, going into the swamp directly behind so as not to be seen by Swastika Pecs and the others.

"Virgil—"

"Shhhhh! Sound carries over the water!" He held a finger up to his lips.

I closed my mouth and looked up at the sky. The air was damp, heavier and cooler than usual. The stars had vanished behind clouds. Dark clouds. The storm was coming. Virgil directed us silently through trees, turning right then left. I was hopelessly confused and turned around. It seemed like we were just going in circles sometimes. Eventually, the bright light from the island began to fade into the distance. He apparently knew what he was doing. *Who are you, Virgil?* I asked myself again.

Virgil stopped poling. "I think we got away."

"Thanks, Virgil."

"Sure thing, boy. It's what the boss wanted." He shoved the pole into the water. "And now to get you back to the city."

"Thanks, Virgil."

"It's what's right, boy."

We slid through the swamp in silence. The entire swamp seemed silent. Then the entire swamp lit up with blue light that made all of my hair stand on end, and then my ears rang with the sound of thunder.

The sky opened.

It was much worse than in the city. The rain came down in sheets: hard, heavy, cold, wet drops that stung. It had already been dark in the swamp, but now it was impossible to see anything. I couldn't even make out the trees anymore through the rain. The only time I could catch a glimpse of Virgil was in the brief seconds when the lightning illuminated everything. He was still in the front of the boat with his pole, piloting the boat on a path that he seemed to know. I was soaked and shivering. Rainwater was starting to accumulate in the bottom of the boat. I felt around and found a rusty Folger's coffee can and started trying to bail water over the side. It was a losing battle. I only hoped we didn't take on too much water and sink.

The phone! I pressed my leg against it in my boot. I reached down with one hand and held the top of my boot closed.

And then, miraculously, somehow we came into a clearing. I could see the van sitting there in the parking lot. He poled the boat over to the pier and tied it off, holding it steady while I climbed out; then he followed.

He grinned at me in the rain. "I told you."

I wanted to fall down and kiss the pavement.

"Let's go!" He gestured toward the van.

I ran behind him through the water. He ran around to one side of the van and I went to the passenger side. I opened the door.

Swastika Pecs sat there, with a gun aimed at me. "Surprise."

There was a shot, and Virgil went down on the other side of the van.

"Put your hands up," Swastika Pecs directed.

I did.

"Now, walk around to the back of the van." I started walking and could feel the gun against my back as he shoved me forward. I opened the back doors of the van and climbed in.

"Take off that shirt and those pants."

I unbuttoned the shirt slowly and put it down.

"Throw it out here."

I picked it up and threw it out the back.

"Now the pants."

I untied the ankles and the waist and slid them down over my boots. I tossed them out and sat there in my lime green thong.

Swastika Pecs smiled. "There, now you look like the cocksucking faggot you are. Jesse, tie him up."

Jesse, who'd been one of the card players, had a pierced nipple and a lightning bolt tattoo on his right shoulder. He tied my ankles together with electric cord, and then my wrists.

And good little skinhead that he was, he didn't forget the electrical tape for my poor lips.

After he was finished, he climbed back into the driver's seat.

Swastika Pecs climbed into the back with me and shut the doors. "I should just shoot you here, but I have a better idea."

He swung the gun at my head.

Just before it hit me, it occurred to me that I was getting knocked out a lot.

Chapter Twenty-three

SEVEN OF WANDS

Victory depends on courage

The van was moving.

I became aware of the sound of tires moving over pavement first, feeling the vibrations through the floor of the van. I opened my eyes yet again. I had a really nasty headache. I was staring at the ceiling of the van. It was still dark out. I tried to sit up. It only took a couple of tries. I was getting good at moving around with my hands and feet tied up. Hopefully, it was a skill I would never have call to use ever again.

Jesse and Swastika Pecs, unlike Virgil, weren't playing any music.

I'd gotten Virgil killed.

I closed my eyes. Kenny. Rusty. Virgil. So far, I was partly responsible for three murders. I might not have done the actual killing, but if it weren't for me, all three would still be alive. Well, okay, maybe Rusty was a wretched, vile, trigger-happy murderer that no one would miss, and Virgil wasn't much better. He'd shot Rusty without hesitation, without a second thought. He'd have killed me in an instant if he'd been able to justify doing it. Kenny, on the other hand, had been a complete innocent. I was carrying an awful karmic debt there. I closed my eyes and prayed to the Goddess again, for strength, for a brave heart, and for Kenny.

Oh, who was I fooling? Virgil had been a sweet soul; I'd seen it in his eyes, and I had used and manipulated him just as much as these other bastards had. And now he was dead because I had convinced him to help me.

I was as bad as they were.

The van turned and I slid forward. We were exiting the highway, obviously. I opened my eyes. It was the Vieux Carre exit; I was almost positive of it. I could see the old Civic Auditorium and Armstrong Park. We got stopped by the light on Rampart. I leaned back against some of the crates. The dynamite. That's what they were going to use. They were going to blow the levee somewhere in the Quarter.

I had to do something.

But what? I was bound and gagged. If only I were telepathic. If only I were telekinetic. Oh, no, my gift had to be the occasional vision and the ability to read the cards— nothing that would be of any use to me now. I didn't even have the damned cards with me.

Okay, think, Scotty. If you were going to blow up the levee, where would it cause the most damage?

Jackson Square.

The river twists and turns its way through New Orleans, kind of snakelike. It's why one of the nicknames of the city is the Crescent City. New Orleans spreads out along both sides of the river, following its bends and twists. The levee runs along the river on either side, but the closest the river ever gets to the actual city itself is at Jackson Square. Decatur Street, where I used to live, runs in front of the Square. If you walk across Decatur in the direction of the river, there's a walkway up to the top of the levee. Built directly into the walkway is a little magazine/

newsstand. On that side of the street there's also a little miniamphitheater, where on sunny days mimes, dancers, jugglers, and magicians perform for tips for tourists who fill the stone benches. On one side is Café du Monde, which is always packed with tourists drinking café au lait and eating beignets. On the other side is Jax Brewery, which has been turned into a shopping mall.

And across Decatur Street from there are Jackson Square and St. Louis Cathedral, the two most famous landmarks of the city.

The river is less than twenty yards from Decatur Street there.

The perfect place to blow it up.

Surely Venus Casanova and Frank had been able to figure that out. But Frank had wanted concrete evidence, proof of what they were going to do. I hadn't been able to give them anything but a vision, and he couldn't very well go to his superiors with that. They'd think he was nuts and take him in for psychiatric counseling. And even if, somehow, he'd been able to convince them, they would have found nothing, I realized. The dynamite was in this van with me. That was why the plan was so clever. There was nothing to look for. They'd probably set the timer for long enough time for them to get back onto the highway and out of the city.

And nobody had the slightest idea. The FBI was watching the goddamned sewers!

And Frank wouldn't have risked his entire career, his credibility, just because he had slept with me. Hell, I didn't even know if he believed me or not.

Not bloody likely.

What was the point of having a gift when no one believed you?

Like Cassandra.

The van came to a stop. Swastika Pecs came into the back with me and threw a tarp over me. I heard the back doors of the van open, and then I was lifted. It was silent, very quiet. I could smell horse manure. I tried to wiggle, make some kind of noise, something someone would notice, that would call attention to us. They were holding me too tight. I let my entire body go limp, dead weight. They slowed a bit but kept moving. *Damn it, are all these goons strong as oxen?* I heard a car driving past. *Please, oh please, let a cop stop us.* I heard someone fumbling with keys and I was set down on pavement.

"Get the alarm," Swastika Pecs hissed. The sound of movement, and then the faint sound of buttons being pressed, emitting electronic tones. Then I was lifted again and carried into air-conditioning.

Another door opened, and I was set down on carpeting. Swastika Pecs took the tarp off of me. He was smiling at me. His front teeth were yellowish and chipped. His green eyes were cold as ever. I shivered. "Well, cocksucker, this is where we have to say good-bye to you."

I strained against the ropes he had tied me with.

He laughed. "Congratulations, cocksucker. You better make your peace with Jesus while you're in here, because yours is going to be the first soul sent to heaven when these babies go off." He patted a crate of dynamite. A couple of skinheads brought another in and set it down next to the others.

"Come on, Pete, set the damned charge and let's get the fuck out of here," one of the others said.

He looked at me with a big grin and then turned his attention to a device sitting on top of one of the crates. He fiddled with it a bit and then put his hands on his hips. He knelt down in front of me and whispered, "Two hours, cocksucker, and then its good-bye to New Orleans. 'And the Lord rained down fire and brimstone on the cities of the plain.' " He stood up and kicked me in the ribs. "And that's for Rusty, you worthless piece of shit."

I rolled over onto my side. I felt a stabbing pain where he'd kicked me. He probably broke one of my ribs. I started taking shallower breaths. If it was broken, I didn't want it to puncture my lung.

As long as I was alive, I had a chance.

The door shut behind him.

I could hear the timer running.

I looked around the room. Stacks of magazines wrapped in plastic were piled high. *Vanity Fair. Time. Newsweek. Better Homes and Gardens. Good Housekeeping.* I shook myself free of the tarp.

The magazines were all bound. I'd worked in a bookstore once when I was in high school, for about three weeks. Mom and Dad decided that I shouldn't live a life of privilege and should learn what it's like to work. We always had box cutters at the bookstore to cut open the bundles. There had to be a couple of box cutters in here somewhere. Of course, the skinheads might have thought of that and removed them all, but I was willing to bet the farm they hadn't. They weren't expecting to have to leave someone back here. They also didn't strike me as being all that smart.

No, they wouldn't have thought of it. They thought I was completely helpless. Besides, I was a fag cocksucker, and everyone knew fag cocksuckers were wimps, sissies. No, they probably figured I would just lie here crying until the bomb went off, and my life would end.

Fuck you, bastards. I gritted my teeth. I was going to get out of this.

I leaned back against the dynamite box and pushed with my legs. The box was wedged against the wall, and my butt rose a couple of inches off the floor. I started wiggling my shoulders, still pushing, and moving my feet in closer. Slowly but surely I got to my feet and looked around. Naturally, there wasn't one lying around in plain sight. I was going to have to hop around and find one.

The timer kept ticking.

The easiest place to start was the stacks nearby. If the newsstand employees were anything like my co-workers and I had been, they would have left a box cutter sitting on the last stack of magazines they'd used it on. So it stood to reason that the shortest stack of magazines was the one most likely to have a box cutter sitting on it.

And of course, the shortest stack was the farthest one away.

Okay, then, just look for one that's open.

Ah, there we go. *Conde Nast Traveler.* Just a few feet away. I leaned back against the dynamite boxes again that were right behind me, and started inching my way over there. It seemed to take me forever. I had to make sure I didn't fall. My ribs were still aching. A fall—well, I didn't want to even think about that, so I kept taking it slow. Patience has never been one of my virtues. I wanted to scream in frustration, but I took some shallow breaths and rested for a minute. Getting frustrated wouldn't do any good. I'd get in a hurry and fall over; the rib could be broken and would puncture my lung; then I really wouldn't be able to breathe, and then the pain would be so intense I could pass out. And if I passed out I was a goner.

I prayed to the Goddess for the patience to do this. I chanted the prayer over and over again.

Sweat began rolling down my face, and my armpits were getting wet.

Tick . . . tick . . . tick.

I finished the prayer and opened my eyes.

It didn't look that far, after all. Just a few more minutes. Sweat rolled into my left eye.

I started inching to my right again. Slowly. Carefully, making sure to maintain my balance.

After several lifetimes had passed, I was there. And sure enough, inside the plastic, sitting on top of the magazines, was a box cutter.

Thank you, Goddess!

I pushed against the short stack of magazines with my shoulder. It started to rock just a little bit. Again I pushed against it, and it rocked a little farther. Third push, and bingo! It toppled over. I almost screamed with joy. The box cutter hit the carpet and skidded a few feet. I got down on my knees and hopped over to it. Sweat was running into my eyes.

Tick . . . tick . . . tick . . .

I turned around and leaned backward. Thank you, Mom and Dad, for putting me in gymnastics when I was a child so I was flexible enough to bend backward. Thank you, Goddess, for giving me the interest in yoga as an adult so I maintained the flexibility. I got my hands on the box cutter and straightened back up. Okay, I wasn't that flexible. It was starting to hurt.

Okay, now how the hell was I going to get my hands free?

Start with the feet, worry about that later.

I leaned backward, holding the box cutter in my right hand until I felt my feet. I moved my hands up to my ankles. There they were, the knotted electric cords. I dragged the box cutter along the cord. I applied a little more pressure. My back was starting to ache a bit. I straightened back up again. I was breathing hard. My entire body was damp with sweat. I took some deep breaths. I was running out of time.

Go, Scotty, go.

Back down I went. Sawing and working the box cutter. A couple of times I slipped and cut myself. I wasn't sure if it was blood or sweat running down my calves, but it stung.

And finally, I felt the cords give.

I dropped the box cutter and lay down on my stomach. I pulled my legs apart as hard and as fast as I could, and they broke free. I rolled over onto my back and sat up. I was breathing hard. It was stuffy in the little storage room. Now for my hands. How the hell was I going to be able to get my hands free?

The logical answer was to wedge the box cutter somewhere and then saw them free.

I rolled over to where the box cutter was lying on the carpet and picked it up with my hands. I smiled. I was getting pretty good at maneuvering while tied up. I rolled over to a stack of magazines and wedged it in pretty tight. I turned my back to it, estimating where, exactly, it was located by feeling the magazine stacks with my shoulder blades, and brought my hands down where I hoped the cutter was.

It was there, all right. I just missed my estimate by about an inch.

I screamed into the electrical tape. I'd sliced my arm.

I gritted my teeth and brought it down again. This time, I could feel the razor blade cutting into the cords. Again. Sweat ran into my eyes. I kept my eyes on the timing device as I worked. As soon as I got the cords off my hands . . .

They gave.

I pulled my arms apart and rotated my shoulders. They were stiff and sore. I stood up and peeled the tape off my mouth. Whatever was left of my lips was now gone. I blinked back tears and reached down into my boot.

The phone was still fucking there!

Skinheads, I decided, were idiots.

I flipped the phone open and hit speed-dial 1. The little clock on the face of the screen said 7:32 A.M. Answer the fucking phone, Frank; answer the fucking phone.

"Scotty! Where are you?"

I sank back down to the floor in relief. "Right now, I'm locked in the storage room of the magazine stand in front of Jackson Square with about enough dynamite to blow the levee to kingdom come."

"I'll get someone there immediately!"

"The dynamite is on a timer."

"How much time?"

I got up and walked over to the timer. My heart sank. "Oh my God, Frank, less than five minutes!"

I stared at the digital display as the seconds continued to run off: *4:37 . . . 4:36 . . . 4:35 . . .*

"Scotty, you're going to have to disarm the bomb."

I closed my eyes.

Pray for a brave heart.

It can still be changed, the future is fluid.

She had been trying to tell me all along.

It was going to come down to me, Scotty Bradley, personal trainer and part-time go-go boy, to save the city.

"Tell me what to do, Frank."

"Hang on for a second."

"WHAT?" I stared at the phone. "Are you insane?"

"I hate to say this, but I am going to have to patch you through to a bomb expert, okay?"

I sat there, my eyes on the timer.

4:12 . . . 4:11 . . . 4:10 . . .

The silence on the phone was deafening.

I closed my eyes and prayed.

3:56 . . . 3:55 . . . 3:54 . . .

Come on, Frank!

3:40 . . . 3:39 . . . 3:38 . . .

A strange voice spoke into the phone. "Describe the timer to me."

"There's a digital clock. There are a couple of wires running from it into the crate of dynamite it is sitting on."

3:20 . . . 3:19 . . . 3:18 . . .

"Okay, this should be pretty simple. It's a very simple bomb. There are just the two wires?"

"Three."

3:05 . . . 3:04 . . . 3:03 . . .

"Okay. One of them is a trip wire. You can't disconnect that one."

"All right."

2:52 . . . 2:51 . . . 2:50 . . .

"Do you have anything you can cut the wires with?"

The box cutter. I walked back to where I had left it.

"Yes."

2:34 . . . 2:33 . . . 2:32 . . .

The phone beeped and went dead.

I stared at it in horror.

Which two wires?

2:19 . . . 2:18 . . . 2:17 . . .

You have no choice, I said to myself. *You have to try. It'll go off anyway if you don't try.*

2:01 . . . 2:00 . . . 1:59 . . .

Please, Goddess, help me make the right choice!

My hands trembled. I looked at the wires. Which one looked like a trip wire?

1:55 . . . 1:54 . . . 1:53 . . .

I picked up a wire.

I sawed at it.

It split.

1:47 . . . 1:46 . . . 1:45 . . .

Which one of these two wires is the right one?

1:32 . . . 1:31 . . . 1:30 . . .
One of the wires felt really loose in my hand.
It went into the back of the clock.
1:24 . . . 1:23 . . . 1:22 . . .
The other one didn't feel loose at all.
The loose one.
I took hold of it.
1:17 . . . 1:16 . . . 1:15 . . .
I started sawing at it with the box cutter.
1:14 . . .
So far, so good.
1:13 . . .
Help me, Goddess . . .
1:12 . . .
It separated in my hand.
1:11 . . .
1:11 . . .
1:11 . . .
I slid to the floor.
I started taking deep breaths.
There was a crash outside.
The storage room door kicked open.
Two Feds stormed into the room with their guns pulled.
"About fucking time," I said, and then must have passed
out.

Chapter Twenty-four

THE CHARIOT

Triumph over enemies

I am sure the last thing the tourists milling about Jackson Square expected to see on a Sunday afternoon was FBI agents storming a magazine stand and then, a few moments later, carrying out a guy wearing only a lime green thong.

It certainly gave them something to talk about when they got home.

And isn't that why people really come to New Orleans in the first place?

It's not the heat. . . .

I don't remember any of that. I was unconscious. Fortunately, a local camera crew had been down at Jackson Square taping a "local color" segment when the trucks with the FBI agents and bomb squads came screeching up. They caught it all on tape, and it was on the news. David taped it for me. Yes, there I was, for all New Orleans to see, strapped to a gurney in all my glory, being carried out on a stretcher.

I had no idea lime green picked up so well on television. It made my package look *huge*.

That should have done wonders for my reputation. Might even get me some more clients. Or dancing gigs. Unfortunately, I missed out on the marketing opportunity because the newscasters didn't know my name and I, alas, was unconscious. Just an unidentified young man in a lime green thong who was found in the storage room of a magazine shop near Jackson Square. He'd been kidnapped from the gay bar where he'd been dancing the night before. More news as it develops. No mention of the dynamite or my heroics.

Ah, well. It was probably best that no one know how close New Orleans came to destruction. One minute and eleven seconds, to be exact. Just thinking about it makes me shudder, so it made sense to try to keep it all quiet. Why create a panic after the fact?

I came to in the ambulance. It's kind of hard to remain unconscious with that horrible screeching siren going. If you think it's loud when one goes past your house, try riding in one. I think they should soundproof the interiors of ambulances. How do heart attack patients live through an ambulance ride? It's beyond me. Someone should really look into that.

The first face I saw was Frank's. "Hey," he said. "You look terrible."

"Stop flirting with me. That kind of talk will turn my head."

He touched my face. "You've got some really bad bruises."

"Are you telling me I'm not pretty anymore?"

He smiled down at me. "You will always be pretty, Scotty."

Aw, what a sweetheart.

Then the paramedics started asking me questions. Was I dizzy? Did I have double vision? On and on and on. Then we got to the hospital. I won't bore you with the details of the endless tests they did. They checked me for skull damage and possible concussion. Constant poking with needles until I am sure I looked like a muscular pincushion. Finally they finished, and decided to keep me overnight for observation. They wrapped my ribs, which were only bruised. They hooked me up to an IV because I was suffering from severe dehydration. They put some kind of healing balm on my poor, battered lips.

At least I wasn't going to need a lip graft.

I had assorted other bruises and abrasions. They tested me for HIV because I'd bitten the bar guy, and made me take some pills. I had several lumps on my head but no concussion, but they wanted to keep me for observation.

Then it was time for my debriefing. Frank, Venus, and a stenographer came into my room, and I had to tell my story. "Before I do that"—I glared at Frank—"where the hell were the FBI agents who were supposed to be protecting me?"

Frank had the decency to flush. "The bar fight distracted them. So much was happening so fast, and when they realized what was happening, they were on the wrong side of the fight. They couldn't get to you; they couldn't get outside."

"We think Perkins's men started the fight," Venus went on. "They created a distraction, one we weren't prepared for. Bar fights in gay bars are pretty rare."

"That's because gay people are more civilized than straight people," I pointed out.

They didn't answer that. I grinned. How could they? "All right," I sighed. I took a drink from a glass of water. The IV just wasn't hydrating me fast enough. I was thirsty all the time. The inside of my mouth felt like a great, big ball of cotton was in it. "I came to in the back of a van. I was bound and gagged with electrical tape." I pointed at my lips. "That's how these got all fucked up." I explained about the drive out to the swamp, and what Rusty Bindle had tried to do to me in the back of the van.

"Good going," Venus said, her eyes stormy when I told them what I'd done to him. "If you are being sexually assaulted, you should fight back."

"Well, I wasn't about to just let him have his way with me," I went on. I detailed Virgil's shooting of Rusty. They kept interrupting me with questions. And they both got real excited when I told them that the man himself, Willy Perkins, showed up at the house in the swamp. That he knew about Rusty Bindle's murder. That he had ordered mine.

"You heard him tell Virgil to kill you?" Venus's eyes glittered.

"His exact words were 'Kill him.' " I rolled my eyes at her. "What else could he have meant?" I told them about how Virgil tried to save me. "And you know the rest." I shrugged. "They brought me back into the city to go up with the dynamite."

"How did you get loose?" This from Venus.

I explained about the box cutter. She whistled.

The stenographer told me she'd type it up for my signature, and left the room.

"Scotty, I don't know what to say." Venus stood up. "Thank you from everyone in the city. You did an amazing thing. You showed a lot of courage and resourcefulness. I've heard the mayor himself is planning on coming down to see you and thank you personally." She walked over to the door. "If you ever want to pursue a career in law enforcement, you let me know." The door shut behind her.

I started laughing.

"What's so funny, Scotty?" Frank asked.

"A career in law enforcement. Could you imagine my

mother's reaction to that?" I shrugged. But I would look good in the uniform.

"Your mother is a pretty remarkable lady." He walked over and sat on the edge of the bed. He grinned. "I'm really glad you turned up. I wasn't sure I could run far or fast enough from her."

"Mom's cool." I grinned back at him. "She would have hunted you down."

"I had no doubt."

He kept staring at me. Finally, after a few minutes, I said, "*What?*"

"Venus is right, you know. You have great instincts. If it weren't for you . . ." His voice trailed off. "I'm sorry I didn't believe you about the levee."

"It's okay, Frank." I waved my hand. "It would sound crazy to me, too."

"How long have you had this 'gift'?"

"As long as I can remember."

"How does it work?"

"Most of the time it doesn't." I shrugged. "I have no control over it at all. Sometimes I have visions, go off into a trance. Sometimes it comes to me in dreams. The easiest thing for me is to read the cards. The cards tell me what I want to know—but sometimes it's very cloudy, and I can't understand what the cards are trying to tell me." I thought for a minute. "But they really do have messages for me; it's just that sometimes when I am reading them, the message isn't clear enough for me, or I don't know enough at that time to understand. But later, it makes sense." Some of those weird readings I'd been having lately made sense now.

"So you can't tell the future?"

"Don't make fun of me."

"I'm not." He took my hand. "I was just going to

ask"—he hesitated for just a beat—"if you were able to see a future for us."

"For us?" I was startled. I looked at his face. I remembered him helping me off the balcony when I would surely have fallen. I remembered the look on his face when we performed the Great Rite. "Well, anything's possible," I blustered. A relationship? With a Fed?

"I'm tired of the Bureau." He reached down and kissed my forehead. "I'm tired of hiding who I am. I have enough time in to put in for early retirement. It'll take a few months, but I could be here in New Orleans by March."

Oh, boy. "Don't move here for me, Frank." I hoped this didn't sound as harsh to him as it did to me. "Move here because you want to live here, not for me. Don't give up your life because of me."

"I'd been thinking about it." He shrugged. "There's nothing to hold me in Washington except my job, and I like New Orleans."

Once it gets in your blood, New Orleans never lets go.

"Frank . . ." I fumbled for the words. "Please don't take this the wrong way, okay?"

He frowned. That vein popped out in his forehead again. "This doesn't sound promising."

"I'm a tramp." There, I'd said it. "I've never had a boyfriend before. I don't know if I can do it."

"A tramp?"

"I sleep around." I blushed. That was a surprise. I didn't think I could anymore. "A lot. I like having sex. I like having sex with a lot of different people." Well, that certainly sounded attractive. Who would pass up on someone like that? Sounded like every gay man's ideal.

"So why have you never had a boyfriend? No one ever interested?" He was smiling now.

"Lots of people have been interested!" I took a deep

breath. "I guess I've never found anyone I ever wanted to be around all the time."

"And you don't think I am that person?"

I looked into his eyes. I saw him again on the balcony. I saw him walking across the street toward me, watching him through the gate. I saw him working out at the gym. I saw his body stretched out naked in the steam room. "Well, I won't deny that I have an overpowering physical attraction to you."

"That's a start." He laughed. "Christ, Scotty, I'm not asking you to marry me. I like you a lot—more than any other man I've ever met before. I don't know if we're compatible, or if we could even stand the sight of each other after a couple of weeks. I'm just saying that we should give this a chance."

"You're not madly in love with me?"

"I'm in love with your body." He traced a finger down my chest. "And what I've seen of your personality I like a lot. I'd like to get to know you better."

"Okay." This would have been a good moment for him to reach down and kiss me, but he didn't.

We sat there looking at each other for a while. "So if you retire from the FBI, what will you do for a living in New Orleans?"

He shrugged. "I've always wanted to go into business for myself."

"Doing what?"

"Private eye."

"Really? How cool!"

I pictured him in a trench coat and a fedora. It looked good on him, sexy. But then, there really wasn't anything I could imagine Frank wearing that wouldn't look sexy on him.

"Maybe we could be partners in business, too." Frank grinned at me.

"*Me?* A private eye?" I pictured myself in a trench coat and a fedora. It looked pretty hot on me, if I did say so myself.

"You don't have to make up your mind right now." Now he leaned down and brushed his lips against mine. "Now, you need to get some rest." He paused at the door. "I'll see you in the morning." I slid back down in the bed. Me, a private eye? Silly, I thought. Sobieski and Bradley, private eyes. Bradley and Sobieski.

Finally, I fell into a deep, blissful sleep.

I didn't dream.

What a blessed relief.

The next day, I was released from the hospital. Mom came and picked me up. They took me back to their place. It dawned on me as we climbed the back steps that I had no clothes, nothing to change into. Sigh. Back to reality. What was I going to do for money now?

I sat down in the living room while Mom made tea in the kitchen. I heard her and Dad talking, then the back door shut.

"Are you going to keep seeing that agent?" Mom said, bringing the tea in.

"He wants to move here. Take early retirement from the FBI and go into business for himself." I smiled at her.

"Well, if he's not working for those fascists anymore, I guess it would be okay." She looked at me. "You are going to keep seeing him, aren't you?"

"He wants to." I shrugged.

She sighed. "So then I'm going to have to be nice to him, huh?"

"Afraid so."

She lit a joint and inhaled deeply. "First, Storm marries some empty-headed debutante and becomes a lawyer. Then Rain marries a doctor and becomes an empty-headed

Uptown wife. And now you're going to marry an FBI agent. Where did your father and I go wrong?"

"Who said anything about getting married?" I put up both hands. "Whoa, there, Mom! We're just going to see how it goes."

"Oh, you'll wind up married to him, I have no doubts on that score." She sighed and looked over at her altar. "Aphrodite, where did I go wrong with these kids?"

"By raising us to have our own minds." I shrugged. "And who said I was going to marry him, anyway? We like each other, and we're just going to see where it goes."

She just sighed. "Famous last words. That's what I said about your father."

When Frank showed up later, she was polite. Give her credit for that. I led him back to my bedroom so we could have some privacy.

We kissed once the door was shut behind us.

"We haven't picked up Perkins yet," he said as we sat down on the bed. "But we will."

"You always get your man, Agent Sobieski?"

"Without fail." He kissed me again.

"What about Colin?"

"Who?" He was kissing my neck.

"Colin. Bill. Whatever his real name was."

Frank stopped kissing me. "You slept with him, didn't you?"

Uh-oh. "I didn't even know you existed then."

He smiled at me. "It doesn't matter if you did or not. We didn't get him. He wasn't our priority. Finding you was." He shrugged. "But we will get him eventually."

"You always get your man."

"I certainly try."

I hoped not. I sent a prayer to the Goddess to keep Colin safe from arrest. I liked him, and I had a feeling he was going to be giving up the cat burglar business fairly soon.

I lay back on the bed and pulled him down to me. "Well, you can get me anytime you want."

"Woof." He grinned at me as I pulled my shirt up over my head. "Such a sexy boy."

"Flattery will get you everywhere."

"Everywhere?" He took off his own shirt.

I tweaked his nipples—"Pretty much"—and pulled him down on top of me.

EPILOGUE

They did catch Perkins. Frank was nothing if not a man of his word. They caught him at a fund-raising party for his campaign in Lafayette. Arrogant to the end and protesting his innocence, he was caught by a camera crew blaming it all on a conspiracy hatched by "faggots, baby-killers, feminists, and blacks." Only he used the *N* word. He refused to withdraw from the governor's race even after he was indicted.

The election was a lot closer than you would think, which is kind of scary. He was convicted on several charges of conspiracy—conspiracy to commit murder, ordering a murder (mine)—and he was shipped off to Angola. He is appealing his convictions, of course. Both Storm and Millie don't think he has a chance in hell of getting the convictions overturned.

I hope to hell not. He is one scary motherfucker.

I had to testify at Swastika Pecs' trial. His name turned out to be Peter Valentine, but I will always think of him as Swastika Pecs. He was convicted and sent to Angola

Prison. He'll be a very old man if he ever gets out. If he lives that long. I had a feeling a white supremacist wouldn't last very long in that environment.

Millie and Velma are rebuilding the house. There was quite a bit of insurance on the building, and I'm going to move back in once it's finished. Until then, I'm living with Mom and Dad. Millie and Velma come by almost every day with new plans. My apartment is going to be even cooler than it was before.

I'm taking a course in becoming a private eye. Mom and Dad don't think it's a great idea, but Storm has promised that once I get licensed, he'll throw lots of work my way from his firm. Millie has said the same thing. So, who knows? I might actually start making some real money for a change.

I've decided to use Dick Dansoir as my private eye name. After all, a private eye is called a dick, right? The name served me well when I danced under it, and so I hope it'll do okay for a private eye.

After the trials were over, Frank returned to Washington. He called me every other day at first, but then he took on another case and doesn't get to call as frequently. We're taking it pretty slow for now, and we decided not to commit to monogamy for now. When he retires and gets to New Orleans, then it'll be a different story. I don't see myself as the monogamous type, but we'll see how it goes. I do like him an awful lot.

About a week after Decadence, I got a letter in care of the Devil's Weed. It was postmarked in Puerto Vallarta, with no return address. I opened it.

> *Dear Scotty,*
> *I saw on the news that you are okay. I was really happy to find that out. After what happened*

on Saturday night, I decided it was probably in my best interests to get out of the country for a while. I am going to travel for a few months and lay low.

I really enjoyed our time together, and felt like we connected on a level other than just sexually. Maybe I was wrong, but you struck me as the kind of guy that I would like to get to know better and spend more time with.

I'm not always going to be a cat burglar. I'm kind of tired of being on the run all the time, and some of the thrill of it is gone now. I know we can't possibly have a future together until I get my act together and go straight (well, not sexually, but you know what I mean).

I'd like to give it a try. I think about you every day, and someday I'd like to come back into your life. I don't expect you to wait for me, but it's a chance I'm willing to take.

Think of me every once in a while. I only wish I'd had the chance to say good-bye properly.

> *Thinking of you,*
> *Colin*

I folded the letter and put it back in its envelope.

I lit a candle for him and prayed to the Goddess for his safety.

I do think of him every once in a while.

I'm sure he's okay wherever he is.

And if he should show up one day, well, I'll cross that bridge when I come to it.

Why worry about something that may never even happen?

So, that's my story. Things seem kind of quiet now, but

then again, you never know what's going to happen, what's just around the corner. That's the great thing about life. You just never know.

Somehow, I just don't think I am destined for a quiet life.

Please turn the page for an exciting sneak peek
of Greg Herren's next
Scotty Bradley mystery
JACKSON SQUARE JAZZ
coming in April 2004
wherever hardcover mysteries are sold!

Chapter One

PAGE OF WANDS

A young man with blond hair

I woke up with what was easily the worst hangover of my life.

It was horrible. My teeth felt like they'd grown hair while I slept. My eyelids felt like they were glued shut. My head was pounding, like the seven dwarves were in there, thinking my head was a diamond mine and cheerfully digging their pickaxes into the sides. My stomach was churning. My skin felt hot. I was sweating under the blankets. My tongue had somehow managed to swell up to twice its usual size, and sometime during the night it had apparently become as absorbent as cotton. I was so dehydrated it felt like I'd been wandering in the desert for several days. I fought to get my eyes open. After what seemed like an eternity, the left came open, then the right. The light streaming through the bedroom window blinds pierced my corneas like a laser, cutting right through into my brain. I quickly threw one of my arms across my eyes to block it, but the movement made the sulfuric acid eating through my stomach lining splash around. My head swam; my vision briefly blurred. My stomach clenched, and I fought down the urge to throw up. It's one of my rules to never throw up anywhere other than the toilet. Throwing up is unpleasant enough in and of itself, but then to have to clean up the rancid mess on top of that? Just the thought brought the nausea back in a swelling wave. Yuck.

I closed my eyes and opened them again. I swallowed and took several deep, cleansing breaths. There, that was better. What the hell had I been drinking the night before? Oh yeah, tequila shots. Never a smart thing to do. The ever-popular mentality of "oh gee, I'm not getting drunk fast enough, so I'll do some shots. Yeah, that's the thing to do." Ugh.

Jose Cuervo, you are NOT a friend of mine.

That's when I became aware of the arm around my waist.

Oh, boy. I thought for a minute. Okay, who the hell is this? But I still felt like someone had lobbed a hand grenade into my head. Nothing was clear. The memory banks had been neatly erased by the alcohol. He wasn't lying next to me— his arm was just kind of loosely thrown over my waist. His skin felt deliciously cool, but I needed to get out of the bed. I wasn't in the right frame of mind to deal with him just yet, so I gently lifted the arm up and slid out from under it. Just as gently I set it back down and slid slowly out of the bed, not wanting the bed to bounce and wake him up. Mission accomplished, I realized with a start that I was completely naked. Well, that really shouldn't have come as a surprise. Had we had sex?

I stared down at his face. He had sandy reddish blond hair, and a sprinkle of freckles across his face. The hair was standing out in all directions from his head. His mouth was open and he was breathing through it. He looked completely at peace with the world. Damn, he was a little cutie, I thought as I stared at him. He also looked really young. Who the hell was he? And where had I found him?

I padded into the kitchen and started coffee. I popped a couple of aspirin and washed them down with water. My stomach was still churning, so I got out a couple of pieces of bread. The bread just dried my mouth out again. My tongue felt like it was sticking to the roof of my mouth, which had apparently grown some fur during the night. I washed the bread down with water. Maybe that would help absorb the alcohol in my stomach and stop the churning, keep the nausea down. What I really needed was a greasy bacon cheeseburger, fat grams be damned. I walked back into the bedroom. The bread was helping a little bit. Each step didn't make me think my head was going to fall off.

He hadn't moved. I stared at him for a few minutes, but still nothing came to mind.

Okay, what did I do last night? I asked myself as I walked into the bathroom and scraped the fur out of my mouth with my toothbrush. Even after brushing, my teeth felt weird to my tongue. I started the shower. I got back from Washington around five and David picked me up at the airport.

Oh, yeah, the fucking trip. I gulped down several handfuls of cold water from the tap while the shower got hot. I was starting to come out of it.

The trip had been a disaster, almost completely. I'd flown into Reagan Airport the previous Saturday. (Mom and Dad would have thought the name of the airport was a bad omen.) Frank was waiting for me at the security checkpoint. He looked so damned good I wanted to jump his bones right there. He was wearing a black turtleneck sweater and a pair of tightly pressed khaki pants, with a black leather jacket. The outfit showed off his heavily muscled body to perfection. Of course, we couldn't hug or kiss or anything like that at the airport. Some of Frank's coworkers or someone else who knew him might see him. Ah, the joys of being a homo working for the Federal government. I could tell, even though we didn't do anything more than shake hands, that he was glad to see me. All I had to do was look at the bulge in the zipper area.

We got my suitcases and headed back into the city to his apartment. He drove me past monuments and statues, showed me the FBI Building where he worked, all the normal tourist crap. I was in a pretty good mood. It was a beautiful autumn day, though a little chilly. The streets were packed with cars, the sidewalks jammed with pedestrians. The city fairly hummed with life.

The whole time he drove my hand was in his crotch. Yeah, he was definitely glad to see me all right. Every once in a while he would look over at me and smile, or just put his hand on my inner thigh.

His apartment was in the city's gay ghetto, DuPont Circle, which I thought was odd for a closeted Fed. There were a lot of pretty boys walking along the sidewalks as he headed up Sixteenth Street. Some were walking dogs, others were holding hands, others were obviously just with friends. Occasionally, I spotted some straight people too, pushing baby carriages, carrying bags or briefcases, or walking alone jabbering away on cell phones. They were all dressed extremely well, in nice slacks and overcoats. I tried to imagine what it would be like in the summer when everyone would be in shorts and tank tops.

It would be a gay man's candy store was what it would be, I thought as Frank found a place to park his little blue Miata on S Street. We got my bags out of the trunk and started walking up to Seventeenth Street. His apartment was on Seventeenth, between S and T Streets. Someone put a lot of thought into naming the streets here, I thought. Okay, I'm a little spoiled, coming from New Orleans, with our great street names. The area kind of reminded me a little of the Quarter—the number of people walking around, the old-looking houses and buildings, and the trees. I smiled at a hot-looking guy as we passed each other and our eyes met. He immediately looked away.

Huh? Did I suddenly grow two heads? I looked back after him. He was walking even faster than he had been before. Definitely strange.

Frank's place was in an extremely sterile-looking yellow brick apartment building on the corner of Seventeenth and New Hampshire. He let us in through the glass door with his key. A couple of people were waiting for the elevator. One of them was wearing a sweaty white T-shirt and black bike shorts with blue stripes up the sides. He was holding a bicycle and breathing a little hard. I took in his smooth legs and noted a little razor cut just below his muscular calf. Definitely family, I thought, as he pointedly watched the lighted numbers above the elevator door change. The other person was a woman in a gray overcoat. She was holding a plastic bag of groceries. She was wearing sunglasses, and her graying black hair was pulled back into a severe bun at the nape of her neck. I glanced into her bag. Fettucini, a jar of spaghetti sauce, a loaf of garlic bread. The elevator door slid silently open and we all got inside, various people hitting numbered buttons, which lit up. I kept looking back and forth at the strangers. No one spoke as the elevator moved up. No one said hello; no greetings, no smiles of recognition. I looked at Frank and he winked at me, but didn't say anything. The elevator smelled vaguely of body odor—like a pair of sweat socks I'd taught aerobics in and then left in my gym bag for a few days.

The guy with the bike got out on three. The woman with the bag got off on four. Again, total silence.

It was creepy.

We got off on five and I breathed a sigh of relief. I'd been getting claustrophobic in that stale air. Frank led me along a dingy hallway with the drabbest brown carpet I'd ever seen. He stopped at a door with the numbers 522 on the frame. The door was forest green. He pushed the door open and held it for me.

"Welcome." He smiled at me.

I walked into the smallest apartment I had ever seen an adult out of college living in. It couldn't have been more than four hundred square feet, tops. The whole place would have fit into my living room with some square footage left over. There was a tiny kitchen directly to my right, complete with a refrigerator, sink, and stove that looked about the same size as the ones in Barbie's dream house. There was also a walk-in closet right beside the kitchen, and I could see the bathroom opened off of it. There was a simple table with a computer and a printer sitting on it. There was another small table with a television sitting on it, with a VCR on top of that. The clock on the VCR was flashing 12:00. There was a double bed pushed up against the wall with the lone window. The window had yellowed blinds but no curtains. There was nothing on the beige walls: no posters, no artwork, nothing. Everything was neatly put away. There was no dust anywhere. Everything gleamed and looked brand new.

There was a small wooden bookcase with three shelves sitting in the corner by the computer desk. I set my bag down and said, "Wow." Not exactly dialogue by Noel Coward, but I didn't know what else to say. I wandered over to the bookcase and looked at the names on the spines. The books were all hardcover, and apparently each was a nonfiction study of a specific serial killer. I swallowed.

How romantic.

Frank took off his jacket and held out his hands for mine. I shrugged it off and handed it to him, watching him as he walked into the closet to hang them up. He switched on the closet light, and I glimpsed clothes hanging, sorted by style and color. Everything in its place, a place for everything.

He walked out of the closet with a big grin on his face, and took me into his arms, kissing my neck. "God, how I've missed you."

Finally, I was being greeted the way I wanted to be.

The rest of the week was spent going to movies, and museums, and drives in the country. There isn't a battlefield in Northern Virginia I didn't see. We ate every meal out. Frank's kitchen was much too small to cook in. Besides, if I wasn't sleeping or having sex I wanted out of that horribly sterile little apartment. I didn't meet any of Frank's friends or coworkers. His phone never rang. Frank had told me he was pretty much married to his job, but I thought he was exaggerating. It's just a phrase, right? But the week I spent up there, despite the fact that I had a great time and we got along great, had me doubting if Frank and I had a future.

How can we ever have a relationship if Frank has no friends? I like people. I like being around people. Frank didn't want to go dancing or go to any of the bars. Maybe it was an in-the-closet-at-work thing, but I wasn't about to give up going out. I like dancing. I like seeing people I know at bars, and chatting and gossiping about nothing. Okay, maybe it was just a Washington thing for him, and he'd be different in New Orleans, but Goddess help me! I couldn't be the only person in his life. There were even times during the trip I felt claustrophobic with him. Maybe it was the tiny apartment. Maybe it was that dreadful elevator and all those people who wouldn't even nod, let alone smile at me.

I brooded on the plane all the way back to New Orleans. Frank had dropped me off at the passenger drop-off place, and as I climbed out of the car he smiled at me. "I'll be down for Mardi Gras," he said, before I shut the car door, "if not sooner."

Mardi Gras?

The first thing I did when the drink cart came around

was beg for a Bloody Mary. I envisioned spending the rest of my life with Frank, 24/7, never escaping from him, having no privacy, no private time for myself, not being able to talk to people because Frank was always around. I was no saint, and Frank seemed not to care, but maybe that was because he'd never been with me in a bar in New Orleans, surrounded by lots of guys I'd had sex with. Frank was a Fed. If he came down for Mardi Gras I certainly wouldn't feel comfortable doing Ecstasy and going out dancing with him in tow. He might even arrest me on the spot!

By the time I saw David's silver Accord drive up at the passenger pickup in New Orleans, I had worked myself into a fine state.

"How was the trip?" he asked as I threw my bags into his back seat.

"I need to get drunk."

"That bad?" He shook his head as we drove out of the airport. David's a great guy, one of the best friends I've ever had. We'd been friends for three years, and workout partners for the last year or so. He had grayish eyes and graying reddish blond hair he kept cut very short, and a reddish mustache with some stray white hairs starting to creep into it. He doesn't tan very easily. I often teased him about being the "whitest queen this side of Elizabeth II." He glanced at his watch as we headed up the on-ramp to I-10. "Kinda early, isn't it?"

"Yeah, well."

He opened the ashtray and pulled out a freshly rolled joint. "Here."

I took it from him and hesitated. I was already feeling really paranoid about this whole thing with Frank; this might make it worse. Then I thought, "Fuck it," and lit it.

By the time we reached Causeway Boulevard ten minutes later, I was pleasantly stoned. Everything would work out with Frank if it was meant to, and if it didn't, oh well.

It wasn't my idea for him to move to New Orleans in the first place. David and I agreed to meet a little later for dinner before we went out, and I headed into my apartment to unpack.

I was still feeling a little shaky, but at least I was able to remember yesterday. I stepped into the hot spray of shower water. Okay, good. I held my head under the spray. As I massaged shampoo into my hair, I remembered unpacking, showering, and getting dressed. I met David at La Peniche, on Royal Street in the Marigny. After we ate, we went back over to his place. We smoked another joint and had a couple of drinks. We made it down to the corner of Bourbon and St. Ann around eleven o'clock, prime party time. We had a couple of shots the minute we walked into the Pub, and then . . .

Blank. Completely blank.

I finished rinsing the soap off my body and climbed out of the shower. I toweled dry my hair, vigorously rubbing the water off my body. I looked at myself in the fogged mirror. I still didn't feel great, but it was better. I walked into the kitchen and poured myself a cup of coffee before wandering back into the bedroom. I put on underwear and cutoff sweatpants and stood there staring at the kid. Who the hell are you? Where did I meet you?

His eyes opened. They were liquid brown, but slightly bloodshot. He smiled at me. "Morning." He yawned and stretched as he sat up in bed.

"Morning." His chest was completely hairless. His entire torso was free of hair, and free of body fat. He was fair skinned, and there were freckles spreading across the top of his chest and shoulders.

He smiled at me. "Scotty, right?"

Okay, so he was one up on me. "Yeah."

"Bryce." He kept smiling. "You kept calling me Brian last night."

I sat down on the edge of the bed. "Sorry about that."
" 's okay." He yawned again. "You were pretty drunk."
"Yeah, I was. You want some coffee?"

He shook his head. "Don't drink it. Do you have any
green tea?"

My parents being who they are, of course I did. "I'll
make you some. Do you want to shower?"

He nodded at me sleepily. He climbed out from under
the covers. He was also naked. But where the muscles of his
upper body were wiry and lean, his legs were thickly and
heavily muscled, completely and perfectly defined. There
was reddish blond hair on his calves, but very little above
the knee. And his butt was round and hard and looked
solid as a rock.

It was very impressive.

He picked up his underwear and walked into the bathroom. "Towels are under the sink," I called after him.
Who the hell were you, Brian? Where did I meet you?

I sat the green tea down on the coffee table in the living
room. I heard the water stop running, and I quickly shuffled my tarot cards and spread them out in a reading. I have
a gift for reading tarot cards—I'm a little psychic. I can't
predict lottery numbers or earthquakes, but I was pretty
good at the cards. Not many people know about it—it's
not something you make public knowledge. Not even David
knows.

He's a troubled soul, the cards told me, *in need of guid-
ance. Be careful of what you do or say. He's vulnerable.*

Terrific.

He came into the living room with one of my green towels wrapped around his waist. His wet hair hung into his
face. He grinned at me. Damn, but he was a cutie. He sat
down and he sipped his tea. "You read the cards?"

"A little." I shrugged. "It's a hobby." I smiled at him.
"Want me to read them for you?"

He shuddered and looked away. "No thanks. I don't want to know what the future is."

Hmmm. Interesting. I picked up the cards and started shuffling them. "Brian, I was pretty drunk last night . . ."

"Oh, don't worry," he said quickly. "I'm not looking for a boyfriend or anything, and as soon as I finish my tea I'll be on my way."

His face was so earnest I had to laugh. "That's not what I meant. I mean, I don't remember meeting you, or even where we met."

"You were pretty bombed." He laughed with me. "We met at the Brass Rail at about three in the morning."

It came back to me in a flash. I had been pretty drunk. At two thirty I'd staggered out of the Pub determined to go home. I'd flirted with a couple of cute guys but changed my mind at the last minute. I'd walked home down St. Philip Street, weaving, actually, and stopped in at the Brass Rail to get a bottled water. He'd been sitting there on a barstool, completely out of place amongst the older men. The Brass Rail was more of a tavern than a bar, and they had a strip show every Friday and Saturday night. Their stage even had a pole on it. I'd never danced there, although in my drunken stupor I thought swinging on that pole in a thong might be fun. I walked up to the bar and ordered my water right next to where he was sitting. He said hello, and half an hour later we were heading back to my place.

"You remember now, don't you?"

"Yeah." I smiled at him. "Did you have a good time?"

He grinned back at me. "The best." He set his teacup down. "I'd better get dressed. They'll be wondering where I am." His face clouded for a moment, and he scowled. "Good."

"They?"

"Never mind." He got up and walked back to the bedroom. I stared after him, then reshuffled the cards. Before

I even had the chance to lay out another reading, he came back out fully dressed. He kissed my cheek. "Thanks, Scotty. That was great."

I walked him to the door. "Sure, man."

He waved as he walked down the stairs.

I shut the door and walked back into the living room. I picked up the cards and started shuffling them again. I laid them out. This time there was no questioning their meaning.

He needed help.

I debated going after him, but I still felt woozy from the hangover. And by the time I could throw on some clothes and go after him, he'd be long gone. I didn't even know his last name. Great going, Scotty. Ah, well, I thought, picking up the phone to order a bacon cheeseburger from Verdi Marte, it's not like I'll ever see him again.

Boy, was I wrong. So much for being psychic.